The International Love Story

By: Jonas Noelting

Jonas Noelting

For Molly, Vidhi, and Toni.

Thank you for being.

Breakfast-Bench For Life!

Jonas Noelting

The International Love Story

By Jonas Noelting

Jonas Noelting

CHAPTER 1

Liam

Life hasn't always dealt me the best cards, not even close. It started with my whole life being ripped away from me, everything I knew and grew comfortable with. Everyone I knew was suddenly only a screen, except for my parents, but I don't know how much that helped at all. Ever since then, life has been going downhill for me. Growing up in an unknown environment was *interesting*, to say the least. Though, I never really liked it here. People at school were never really fond of me. I don't know why, I tried being nice and helpful to everyone around me and people didn't respond, so I drew back until I barely even talked to teachers. That's what it's like now, on average talking to one person every three days.

At first, I thought it was because I was the new kid, but I'm going to an international school where kids drop in every few weeks, so that wasn't the problem. It bothered me of course, that no one seemed to stand me enough to talk to me but I kind of just grew immune to it. It unlocked, and greatly developed, a lot of insecurities in me. Since second grade I wondered what was wrong with me. I tried changing my attitude, my style, and my appearance, and tried searching up every variation of '*What's wrong with me?*' and '*How do I make people like me?*'. After all of that, nothing changed and I came to the conclusion, in about sixth grade, that I must just be a terrible person overall.

That is probably true which made my mental image decay to whatever rotten version of it is left now. But if I were to tell someone, other than Tess, about my issues, they simply wouldn't care. I'm not going to lie, I can't blame them. I grew up with so much privilege— learning about so many new cultures all around me and getting to explore the world so much at my young age— which I am really grateful for, but sometimes I catch myself thinking what it would be like if I didn't have this much privilege, if I had just stayed at home. *Would I be very different from who I am now? Would I still be as unlikeable? Would I be as selfish as I am today?*

Would I be so tough on myself?

On the other hand, I wouldn't have grown so close to Tess. We met in primary school back in Germany, and have been close friends since then. That sounds cliché, but I swear, we are inseparable. They were the only one who bothered enough to keep up after I moved. Others, like Camilla and Mia, ghosted me at the first chance they got.

My phone vibrates in the back pocket of my jeans when I reach the bottom of the staircase of the place it took me so long to call home. A

9

message pops up on the top of my screen, from Tess, of course. I make a mental note to reply later because I can see both of my parents staring at me from the kitchen.

"Oh no!", I say, half joking, "Both parents at the same time? What happened? Who died? Oh! Are you pregnant?" They both stare at me without saying a word, their expressions unreadable.

Oh shit! It doesn't take long for me to realize what was happening. It's not the first time and I'm afraid it won't be the last. Sweat gathers in my palm, my skin suddenly burns and my mouth falls wide open, without a sound. I pull down the sleeves of my hoodie, just enough to dry my palm.

My dad stays at home and does all the housekeeping, including taking care of me. He dropped his own handyman business when I was born so that Mom could pursue her career while he would be at home, with me. *Way to not make me feel responsible for him having to drop his dream of helping people, by fixing their homes for them.* I used to tell myself that it was not my fault, but that is simply not true. Mom got promoted again and again over the years. *Which is great! Really great! Great, great!* And at some point, when I was younger, she got a job offer in Singapore. At first, both of them were considerate and asked about my view on it. But I was nine. So I told them to go for it, but what was I supposed to say?

You can't move us to the end of the world, just for a job. We all have friends and a life right here. We have family here! You have a perfectly fine job already. I don't want your career to grow because of my selfishness. I want us to stay.

When they told me about moving, all I could think about was my one and only friend. The most important person in my life. Tess. They were the only person who would talk to me at school.

"Where?" I ask, anticipating an answer.

Anything but China or the USA.

"Georgia." My mom was the one who answered, as always.

"The State?!" My voice is angrier than I expected.

"Mhm." My dad nods.

Shit.

I really don't want to move to the US because of all the political shit going on. Most of the assaults and shootings I hear about on the news are happening in the US. It's supposed to be all about freedom, but what about safety? No, it is not one of the most dangerous countries in the world, but I would still rather move somewhere to Denmark or maybe France, to at least feel safe. I'm probably overreacting, but what else am I supposed to do? All I hear about the USA are tragedies through the news or social media.

At this exact moment though, I'm not sure whether that is a good thing or not. The only thing I know about Georgia is, it's in the South-East region of the United States, and it is famous for its peaches. I guess I'm also glad about moving again. Just a little bit. I haven't made any friends in the eight years I've been here. The only thing I've gained is cultural experience, and the ability to speak fluent Mandarin. Growing up in my household, a German dad and a French mom in a country where English and Mandarin are dominant languages. Mandarin was the fourth language that I started learning in fifth grade, and am somehow more fluent in it than French. My mom never had much time to teach me herself and my dad doesn't speak it well enough to teach me much more, so it's kind of just stuck on a weird level.

I'm fluent in English, German, and Mandarin now, but not without the typical Singaporean accent mixed with my German one, so when I speak it's pretty weird to most people. Another thing that's wrong with me.

"Okay," I say. Finally, turn around and slowly step back up the stairs. Tears push in my eyes, waiting to drop. Choosing to make that decision later, I make sure I turn the lock before I let go.

That was kind of pathetic. My parents just told me some news that isn't extremely horrible, and the first thing I do is cry? *Pathetic as ever!* I get up from my bed, walk to the bathroom, and wash all my tears away. I'm only hoping the move doesn't have the same effects on me as the first time. Last time, my heart got shattered in pieces, because I knew I wouldn't get to see Tess any time soon. In the past 8 years, we met twice in real life, both times because my mom brought me along on a work trip back to Germany. She didn't change much, probably because we had FaceTimed every day. Sure, the time difference made it difficult, but we made it work.

My parents are still downstairs. I hear them talk, trying to whisper when I go back to my room.

That's how things work in this house, my parents and I get angry at each other, I go to my room, cry, go to the bathroom, and when I go back I hear them argue. The next morning we act like nothing happened.

But that won't be happening this time. How long do I even have left here? In my home? I have to say goodbye to my friends. *Never mind, that won't be a problem.* I have to help my parents to pack our belongings, which probably includes sorting out trash.

Theirs and mine. The imagination sends chills down my spine.

I grab my jacket from my chair, put on my sneakers, and run down the stairs, two steps at a time. I enter the kitchen, where Mom and Dad now stand opposite of each other, and snatch my keys from the counter. I leave as fast as I can, and don't look back, not even when Mom asks me where I'm going. I step outside and throw the door close behind me.

The streets are almost empty, except for a small car parked by the sidewalk. I begin to walk out of our area, Farm Hill, past a few stores, past a gas station, until I finally enter the real city. Where the buildings are almost as high as the majority of people. I follow my usual route, past Chuántǒng De Wǎncān, a Singaporean restaurant with the best dumplings in the country.

My parents would take me there every time there was something to celebrate, no matter how big or small. Whether it was a promotion, birthday, or just a good grade, we would be there. I would always eat vegetarian dumplings, even though we were always sharing whatever my parents had. We stopped after eighth grade because there was barely anything to celebrate.

The restaurant now is shortly before bankruptcy. Not because the people don't like the food, because they surely do, but because not many

13

people know the restaurant even exists. If you are new here and would see the building for the first time, you could assume it's a closed-down bar.

The street seems to be endless under the hot afternoon sun. You would think that after multiple years of living here, you would get used to the heat. Wrong. The high humidity balances it out for the most part, but not around this time.

With my jacket bound around my waist, I walk up the stairs of a park house, all the way up to the roof. I used to hang around here with some classmates, who I thought could be my friends. When I cut them out of my life as much as possible, I didn't think I would ever find myself up here again. But here I am, at the only place I can remember to ever think clearly. I walk slowly toward the edge of the roof. Getting in more and more of the view of the streets. I lean against the moldy railing, letting my arms hang over the edge.

Flashes enter my mind, the night my mom told me we were moving, my first day of school — *Ew! Why can't I just forget it and not cringe every time thinking about it* — my first birthday here, first Christmas, New Year, and lots of other firsts. Maybe the US won't be so bad after all. Another set of firsts just waiting to be explored.

I sit on the railing now, letting my legs dangle, my eyes closed.

CHAPTER 2

Liam

My dad's house shoes at the front door indicate that he left, probably buying himself a beer at the closest Seven-Eleven. Wouldn't surprise me. The house is silent. No mom nagging on about chores to be done, no dad running after me, telling me how much better the neighbors' kids are doing. Just silence. It's weird to enter the house with no one there. I'm seventeen and my parents haven't left me alone in the house for more than an hour. Not even once. They probably don't trust me enough to survive. Though, there isn't much I can do about that.

What do people do when they move? People my age… Say goodbye to their friends? That should be rather easy. My bed is inviting me to lie down and never stand back up. It takes all of my willpower to resist. Instead, I open every closet door, every drawer, and every box in my room, trying to decide what to throw away. The most painful part will be choosing books to come with me and books to give away.

That's when it hits me. I have a sudden urge to go upstairs and start packing everything into boxes, as fast as I can. I want to get it over with. Right now. I walk upstairs with a goal. Form two piles, a getting-rid pile, and a keeping pile.

I know damn well that I can't finish everything today, but I have to start anyway. I open the closet doors in my room. Taking out each piece of clothing, one after another. A final glance deciding whether I will keep it or not. Throwing clothes around hasn't been this fun in forever, probably because I had to clean them up after.

When I'm done with the closet, I look at the two piles and notice that I didn't even know I had this many things to wear. Though I admit most of the stuff I'll throw away because it looks hideous on me or I've grown out of them. I turn my head slightly, glancing at my bookshelf. My most precious possession in my room. So many universes, characters, and stories. I sometimes wish I could just jump into one of these books. Live in a castle or another planet, with nothing to worry about, except getting my powers back or deciding who to sleep with. Some might consider that crazy, but I think a life in books is always easier than in real life. More exciting for sure.

I'm sure as hell not ready to get rid of some of these. They are my childhood, my happiness, my life. I can't just leave all that behind.

It is fully dark outside now. I've been in my room for longer than I thought. Neither Mom or Dad tried to speak to me. Which I appreciate, but at the same time I kind of wish they did. That doesn't even make sense to me, so I couldn't explain it to them if I wanted to.

Once the closet is fully emptied I'm exhausted. I stumble through the mess that is my room, falling on the bed. I take my phone and click the call button. The dialing sound makes my heart race in my chest. I don't know why I'm this nervous to tell them, but I have to anyway. Any other normal person would be asleep at four in the morning, but I know Tess. They are probably still wide awake in their bed, lowkey stalking some new crush they're obsessed with.

"Hiiiiiiiii," I say as convincingly as I can.

"Li, what's wrong? You're using that voice again, where everything is bad, but you pretend like it's fine."

They know me really well, huh? That is kind of concerning, but what can you do?

"I got news," I tell them, which isn't a lie, "and I want you to not freak out about it, because I already got that part covered." Silence fills the atmosphere and it takes me a minute to realize that Tess is expecting me to go on.

"We are moving… surprise?!"

Their voice is more exciting than I thought it would be. Switching from English to German, they literally scream their reply.

"Oh my god, back to Germany? *Pleeeeeasssse* come back to Germany, we haven't seen each other in years!!!"

"I know and I would if I could, because trust me, I do not want to go to Georgia!" My tone is angry and harsh, but I know Tess doesn't mind.

They let out a laugh, "You're going to the US? You're joking right?"

"I wish I was." And I mean it. The only advantage I can see is that geographically I'll be closer to my all-time dream. The one and only actual goal I have. Stanford University. It's been my dream for years now. I fell in love with the architecture the first time I saw it in a TV show. I kept searching it up the following days to find out more about the university buildings themselves because they were the most beautiful thing to me. I was about 12 so I didn't really care for much else. Nowadays I already looked into its programs, especially in English and Creative Writing. With that, a few years ago I figured that Stanford is my destiny.

It has one of the best creative writing programs in the United States and is a dream school worldwide. But that's all it is, a dream. I don't have the grades to even consider applying right now.

"Oh come on, you are going to be fine. OH! I just realized, you can see for yourself if the American education system is as bad as they make it seem on the internet," Tess teases.

I let out a small sound, something between a giggle and a snort. Which makes both of us laugh uncontrollably. With that, the conversation continues flawlessly. The jokes practically wrote themselves.

Our conversation continues well into the night until eventually Tess passes out and I have to be responsible for ending the call. Then passing out myself.

Weeks passed, and the house got emptier and emptier. The first victim of our move was the living room- the couch, the TV, even the chairs. Everything is now somewhere in a container. Then the kitchen, all the glasses, plates, cups, bowls, forks, spoons, knives, and all other items are stored away. The rooms feel hollow and we have to eat on carton boxes and plastic containers, which is more comfortable than I would have guessed.

Then came the hallways, every piece of furniture and decor gone. Then my parents' office. Then our bed and bathrooms. It surprises me that our whole house can fit in a container, no matter how big they are. What would happen if the ship with our container sank? Everything would be gone! Do we have insurance on that?

Mental note to myself: Ask Mom about furniture insurance.

Seeing all of this happen again brings back too many memories. Sure, I was young, but I still remember the feeling, the same one that's hovering in my chest now, of being completely unable to do anything about the situation. The feeling of being defenseless and scared of the uncertainty of what comes next.

Now there are only the most important items left in the house: my phone, laptop, four books, and a week's worth of clothing. All the things that can fit in a normal suitcase.

The day has come. The day I was afraid of for the past few months. The day I knew I couldn't avoid, even though I wanted to. My mom is sitting next to me, my dad behind her. On our final flight out of Singapore. I will miss the city. *Wow, never thought I was going to hear*

19

myself think that. But here we are. When I look out the window, I see the plane speed over the runway and take off not soon after. A single tear rolls out of my eye, down my cheek, and into my lap.

CHAPTER 3

Liam

The sun is too high up for a January evening. I thought I would be used to high temperatures after nine years in Singapore, though I would probably choose death over this. If I didn't know any better, I would think it is because of the different locations. Which is only half true. Singapore had a way higher humidity than anywhere in the US, at least from what I've experienced. It's horrible.

On top of that, my parents made it their personal mission to buy a house within a month. It's smaller than back in Singapore but feels way cozier, even if we don't have all of our furniture yet. I spent most of the day laying on a mattress in an otherwise empty room.

What will school be like tomorrow? What will I wear? Are there uniforms like in Singapore? What if there is? I haven't gotten any! What if people won't understand my English because of my accent? What if school will be too hard for me to jump into?

21

I'm going to be the outcast again, but this time it'll be worse. I'm jumping into the school, in the middle of the first semester, instead of the beginning. I have emailed the counselor, who I have met only once, with all my questions, but she hasn't replied yet. I might just have a panic attack tomorrow morning and then not go. *How am I supposed to find my classes? Never mind, I don't need to worry about that, I will just follow someone from my class. That worked back in Singapore so it has to work here as well.*

Now it's 6:45 am, on a random Monday, and I'm standing outside the counselor's office, as she had instructed me to at our previous meeting. If I understood correctly, they will provide me my schedule, and a guy who will show me where my classes are. I'm nervous, not about my classes, at least not right now, but because I will have to talk to that person. *Will they even understand me?*

I walk through the only familiar door and talk to the lady at the front desk. I tell her my name and she hands me my schedule and tells me to sit and wait in one of three black cushioned chairs. I sit on the chairs closest to the wall, impatiently waiting for something to happen. My mind wanders off in an attempt to distract myself.

Unfortunately, it wanders to my choice of clothing today. I went with a mostly neutral color scheme, Black T-shirt, black jeans, black socks, and black sneakers. However, I did want to look gay enough, so people would know without having to do the whole coming out thing. That's why I'm wearing all of my eight rings, silver colored, duh. My silver chain necklaces, stainless steel rings

My hair is a whole different story, now a light brown-ish color mixed with the faint red I had before, and messy as never before. *I should have at least combed through that!*

I check my phone again, 6:59 am. Something should happen soon, it better does. The bell rings, a new and strangely comfortable tone in my ear. I turn my head, left and right, looking for something or someone to do something. And finally, after at least 20 seconds of unnecessary suspense, two guys my age stand up, and one of them gestures for me to stand up as well. The two of them are around my age. Maybe even the same class. One takes my schedule from my hands, without saying a word. While the other leaves the office in an instant. This might be even more uncomfortable than I thought it would be. Again he says nothing as he steps out of the office as well, but he holds the door open waiting for me to follow him. Rereading the countless emails I had gotten the last week, was pretty much the only thing keeping me from going insane. It's unbelievable how little there is to prepare for a situation like this.

I read my schedule multiple times while sitting in that stupid office, over and over. First, at fucking 7:10 in the morning, I have Calculus. *Fun!* Just thinking about math gives me a headache. As expected, my guide brings me to meet my teacher for that class first, which is also the first time he opens his mouth. I introduce myself, trying my best to speak with an American accent. My guide leads me to the classrooms of the rest of my classes, where I repeat the same sentence again and again.

23

"Hi, I'm Liam. My family just moved here so today is my first day."

Two of them, my Psychology and History teacher, asked follow-up questions like where I moved from and where I was originally from.

During our walks, my guide made awkward small talk after stopping by my third period, Psychology. He, Jackson, is a senior and tells me how he is there for any questions I might have. It takes everything in me to not just roll my eyes because of how wrong that statement is. Eventually, he asks me if I'm familiar with the school system, to which I just shake my head.

Jackson talks about everyone having a different schedule and different classes most of the time. So I will have different people in different classes. *Great! Ruined is my plan of following people!* If this continues to go downhill all day, I'll have no choice but to retreat into a lonely corner somewhere and sob the frustration out of me.

The end of the tour was also the first stop. Calculus. I don't remember the name of my teacher. I step inside and just sit in the only free space available. I don't listen to the last few minutes of class, being too distracted from the doom of what today will bring.

Luckily, fourth period, English, rolls by without any more disturbances. After the bell releases us, I walk straight to the big hall that I came through this morning, which now has been transformed into the cafeteria. Six rows of tables spreading through the entire thing. Seeing how packed it is, I decide that I don't want to sit next to anyone, so I turn right around and wander through the clearing halls until I find a spot far enough from any people. I slump myself against the wall on the floor and open my unread messages on my phone. All from Tess. They must want to know how school is so far, which is fair enough because I haven't bothered to report anything on my own.

I scan through all of the messages, which all lead toward one question as I expected. So I reply with simple and short messages because that's what people do, right?!

School is fine, but soooo weird.

Nobody tried talking to me yet, so yay!!

Three dots appear at the bottom of the screen until they dissolve into nothing. I can only imagine how much they want to say to me right now, probably complaining about how little info I'm providing. It wouldn't surprise me if they were to call me right now and make me walk them through the entire campus. To my delight that doesn't happen, instead, a new message reads:

lol any hot guys around at least?

And no not really, or at least I haven't seen any yet. It would be kind of a shame if the whole models-in-high-school thing was *only* in the movies. I mean, at a school as large as this one, there must be some attractive people somewhere. One just has to find them.

My *no* message gets nothing but an emoji back. And not even a nice one. The emoji has three straight lines across its face, two resembling the eyes, and one the mouth.

Of course, they are mad. As if hot guys were the most important thing in the world right now... There is so much I want to tell them, but I

25

won't have time, nor do I have the energy. First days are draining. However, I promise them to call after school, whenever that may be, and spend the rest of my lunchtime thinking about the US, like all the weird things that only exist here. I've been here for less than half a year and there are already so many.

For example Target. What is that place? It has everything. It is a fucking mall but disguised as a store. They have groceries, furniture, clothing, cosmetics, a pharmacy, and even a coffee shop!!! Why don't Americans just go to a mall? It is so extra fancy. And all the employees are gay. I've been to Target twice and my gay-dar went off for around 90% of the employees.

Or small talk. When you just walk by someone, they ask how you are, and you say "Good", knowing damn well they don't care, and then you ask the same. I even had a guy come up to me, while I was reading in a park, asking what I was doing. After I told him that I'm just reading, he left. *Huh? May I know what the purpose of that, so-called, conversation was?*

The rest of my day was decent compared to my previous experiences. I did my best to look as unapproachable as possible. I can tell it worked, because nobody approached me, not even the teachers after our little conversations this morning.

The thing that still confuses me, though, is why I didn't have to introduce myself to the rest of the class. In all my other schools I had to at least stand up and talk to the class about who I am and where I am from. I've seen it happen in American High School movies as well and have been anxious about that for almost two weeks before school even started. But now I don't even have to do it? And I've been anxious for nothing?!

I shrug, letting go of the thought for now. I don't have any homework, though I have to figure out how I can contact my teachers and, especially, my counselor.

I do exactly that every day after school in my bedroom. Well, when I'm not stuck in a book. I finished three books in the last five days, just because I have so much free time. Besides reading, I use my free time to go through the school's website, social media accounts, and everything else I could find online to figure out how these schools work. For example, I found out what a 'GPA' is but I still don't know what the hell it's there for, and I looked into pathways for classes this and next year. It's much more complicated than it was in Singapore.

The first week goes by smoothly. I talk to all teachers at some point in the week. Some are more helpful and welcoming than others. My APUSH teacher, Mr. Lungthorn, even told me how good my English is. Not sure how to feel about that.

On the other hand, my counselor had nothing useful to offer whatsoever. Though I didn't actually think there was going to be more.

So far, my school experience has been borderline horrific. But, as for now, it is still better than Singaporean schools. They may teach more advanced materials, but the way they do teach could be improved a lot.

On the weekend I do everything I ever dreamed of doing in a weekend. Sleep, eat, read, and sleep again. Which means I shouldn't

27

have been surprised when it's suddenly over within a heartbeat. If it continues like this, the last year and a half of high school will go by just as fast. Easy classes, almost no homework, stress-free and so much available free time to enjoy. Still a little surprising though, I purposefully chose to do four AP classes and two honors classes. I didn't want to be bored, yet I still am most of the day.

I should enjoy it while I can because I know classes at Stanford will be so much more challenging and time-consuming.

Stanford has been my dream school since eighth grade when I found out what a beautiful library they had. At first, that was the only real reason why I wanted to go there, but the list has been growing ever since. Stanford has a beautiful overall campus, a great overall feeling, and something very exciting to it. Plus it's an ivy league, so when I get in I can actually brag about it. Sure, other ivys also exist but either the campus doesn't live up to Stanford, or the vibe just doesn't sit right with me. *Some might call those opinions rather unreasonable but that won't stop me from thinking about it. Just because it makes more sense this way.*

Before it never seemed like an actual possibility since I never wanted to move to the USA just for school. But I'm already here now, so might as well follow my dreams and all of that.

Monday, it's the last class of the day. I walk into French and sit in my assigned seat, noticing only two of my classmates. The classroom is empty, except for us three. I do the most logical thing and the only thing I can think of. I reach into my bag and pull out a notebook and a pen. I start writing. I don't want people to be able to read what I write—

because it sometimes does get way too intimate— so I write in Mandarin. I would write in German, but the school offers Germans as one of the foreign language choices, so the risk is too high for someone to be able to understand something.

Every time someone enters the classroom, I look up out of instinct, expecting Madame, whatever her name is, *Veilleux? Peilleux? Peignoir?*, to walk through the doors and finally start the class.

And that's when I saw him.

CHAPTER 4

Liam

He walks into our classroom, to the front row. He puts his bag on the floor and settles in his chair. The same chair he sat in last week, but somehow I didn't see him then.

But I do now.

The boy turns backward, chatting with his friend until the teacher walks in and starts the class. I do my best to concentrate on the lesson but my eyes keep finding the back of the boy's head.

Weeks went by with nothing happening except a few times, when we made eye contact, but one of us always looked away after two seconds. I regretted looking away most of the time, though I can't bring myself to keep looking. My nerves always get in the way of that.

Why do I care whether I look away or not? What do I care about eye contact with him? I don't even know that guy! The only thing I do know is his name, Matthew. EVEN IF I were interested, which I am obviously not, I don't even know if he is into guys. *Gosh, that is pathetic! Thinking about some guy who I met almost a month ago?* Actually, I never officially met him, but I'm thinking it's better that way. I would totally freak him out. He would run faster than Tess when I ask them for an opinion on a story I'd written. And that means something!

"Guys, look on the screen and find your group. *Quietly!*" Madame Veilleux, *yes I finally learned her name*, takes her time pronouncing the last word, making sure everyone gets it.

I freeze on the spot. My eyes are fixed on the big screen in between two whiteboards.

Group 4:

Patricia

Matthew

Liam

Oh shit! I have to be smart about this. My hands are shaking. Unsure what the right thing to do is, I clear my things from the empty desk next to mine. In case either of them wants to sit here and have a "group discussion".

The thought makes me want to dig a hole so deep until I would melt right into the earth's core itself. If things were only that easy… I look around the classroom, trying to figure out who Patricia is. I give the search up quickly when Matthew looks at me. I wave a shaking hand, trying to be cool. Instant regret hits me like a wrecking ball.

My whole strategy in this new school was to only let people see what I want them to see. The same pens, the same rings, the same shoes, the same flannel, every day. The less they know about me, the less they

31

can judge me for. But from now on, when Matthew thinks back on this project or about who I am, he will always have me doing the most awkward hand gesture in all of history in mind. Not that I think he will even remember me, but if he does, it will be for THIS.

A short girl, with shoulder-length brown hair, makes her way over and sits next to me.

"Hey," she says.

"Hi," I reply, "Patricia, right?" She nods.

Luckily, she isn't much of a talker. We could be friends. I'm surprised she even knows who I am. After all, I've only been here for a month. Sure, Madame Veilleux has called my name here and there, but to be fair, I didn't know who Patricia was either.

Two years ago, Austin, a former classmate, and I were supposed to do a presentation about history's most important invention. We didn't know each other at first but got to know one another while creating the project. We ended up hating each other and actively avoiding the other until I left. Glad that's done.

That is a thing I hope not to do with Matthew and possibly even Patricia.

Some might even consider group projects to be fun. I have yet to meet someone like that though. There always is a problem. Either you are doing all the work, including trying to motivate your group members to contribute. Which, as we all know, doesn't always work out great. Or you are the unmotivated one, the one who doesn't care about anything. Not about the project, losing respect from the teachers, least of all grades. Nothing and no one can make you participate.

The key to the perfect collaboration is doing a bit of both.

When Matthew is finally over here, my breathing feels heavier than before. Uncontrollable even. I try to slow my heart down by taking long and deep breaths. He leans forward looking right at me. "Hey," I say. *God. Why am I so stupid? 'Hey'? Really? I thought I could do better than that. Apparently not.*

He nods before opening his mouth to say something. He closes it again, as if not sure what to say. And all of it is my fault. I said one word and already made it awkward. *Great job! Really great job!*

"So how do we do this?" I ask, hoping to distract from the awkwardness in the air.

"I think we should meet after school so that we have more time. I don't think I am the only one who thinks we will need it," Patricia, so rudely, suggests. I don't have a problem with that so I give a brief nod.

Matthew surprises me when he finally talks, "Are y'all free after school today? We can go to my house. My parents aren't home so we have the house for us."

I turn to Patricia. Honestly, I am hoping to find an answer in her eyes, but she is already looking at me. Probably doing the same thing.

Play it cool, Liam! "Sure thing!"

In my head, Tess and I are hitting myself with chairs over and over again. I can't believe myself right now. Why am I talking like a straight guy? That's kind of embarrassing, even for me.

The bell rings, and as expected we didn't do anything at all. *Is this normal here? Inviting strange classmates to your house after*

33

knowing them for less than an hour? My heart rate barely relaxed in the past hour. Mathew's slightly curled hair and light brown eyes sign a harmony that makes my heart do funny flips inside my chest. *And his cheekbones?! Don't even get me started on that...* He may very well be the most beautiful man I've ever seen.

Instead of disappearing through the door as fast as I can, I wait for Matthew and Patricia outside the classroom, mostly Matthew though because he clearly has no problem with wasting everyone's time by talking to his friends some more before actually packing up. When he finally emerges he just asks, "You guys ready?"

Both of us nod and just follow Matthew through the school to go to his home.

To. His. House.

Matthew doesn't say much all the way there. But surprisingly Patricia and I are hitting it off because neither of us can seem to shut up. It appears that she moved to Georgia from Alabama, two years ago. She hasn't made many friends since. I totally get that. I get her.

"What classes are you taking this year? Besides French?" I ask.

"Honestly, I just went with the basics for this year. Fixed classes I mean," she specifies before she continues, "As an elective, I'm taking French, but honestly only because I've been doing it for two years and it'd be weird to drop it now. For my second elective, I'm doing AP Psych. How about you?"

"Oh. My. God. I love psychology, especially because of my teacher, I think it was Mrs. Usher, or something. What a bummer that we aren't in the same class."

Patricia gives me a genuine smile. Or at least it looks like it, maybe she is just really good at faking.

"I want to continue psychology in College. Although, I haven't thought about whether that will be my major or not," she explains.

I ask more and more questions about school, university, and life. Most of which both of us have an answer for. However, while we talk, I can't stop think about my accent. With every word out of my mouth, I worry whether Patricia can even understand what I'm saying. Maybe she just nods along without getting what I'm saying. I push that thought out of my consciousness as fast as I can.

I can't tell how long we have been walking, but it couldn't have been long. We are standing in front of a door now. The door. The door to enter his home. Matthew unlocks the door and we follow him in. Inside, I don't know what to do with our shoes. At my home, we take them off and leave them near the door, but I can't see a place for shoes. Neither Patricia nor Matthew have taken them off yet.

"This way," Matthew says when he turns to face us.

He doesn't show us anything in particular as he walks through the house with us. Some people, including my own parents, would be offended, but I am kind of relieved. He spares us the unnecessary conversation about how nice this house is. Thank goodness, I'm really not in the mood for formalities. As if I'm ever in the mood.

His room is different from what I imagined it to be. I imagined everything to be on the right side of the room, most of it is on the left instead. The color theme is different as well. I imagined his room to have

35

black everything. Furniture? Black. Walls? Black. Bed sheets? Black. I'm actually glad that I am wrong for once.

Matthew lets himself sink into his chair, waiting for someone to say something.

"Well… This is," Patricia tries, "cozy." It sounds more like a question, but I have to agree, it is cozy. I mean, apart from the shredded pieces of paper all over his floor, the fact that the only source of light is a red lamp that looks like it was made in the 50s. The sound of the electricity in the red lamp makes my brain buzz, but I do everything to look okay, fake smiling like I'm about to announce my candidacy for the presidency. Gosh, I hate it already.

Patricia and I eventually set down our bags and start talking about the presentation. After 30 minutes of hard work, well debatably hard work, we take a quick break and exchange numbers. Matthew eases up pretty fast and includes himself in our conversations.

"My parents won't be home till next week, so if you guys are down, we can come here again in the next few days."

I reply, "First of all, that would be really cool. Secondly, that sounds pretty sad. I'm sorry."

Have I mentioned that I'm incapable of saying something nice without it sounding sarcastic? Though I mean what I say. He just nods, while Patricia gives me a very universal look, but people who get it, get it, and people who don't, don't. I happen to be one of those who do understand and really hope Matthew is one of those who don't. Her eyes scream unmistakable words. *What The Fuck is wrong with you.* I wish I had an answer to that.

CHAPTER 5

Matthew

Dear Diary, today I made a friend. Just kidding, I don't waste my time on diaries. But I think I actually made two friends. Or at least I hope so. We got partnered for a project in French. I suck at French, so I will let them do the speaking. I will try to help with the slides though. If there is one thing I do not want, it is for my new friends to get angry with me. That would be a nightmare. Not to speak of the disappointment with the voices in my head.

That sounds like I'm some sort of psychopath. Maybe I am one regardless.

I wanted to see a psychologist a long time ago after I lost my best friend— Clair moved with her family to a whole other continent. We went from face timing every day, to once a week. Texting everyday hour, to every other day. We thought nothing could break us apart, just like probably every childhood friendship. We never thought to consider distance and time difference, though— but my dad said *Only the weak go to therapy.* I wanted to tell him that maybe I am one of the weak, but wouldn't be able to live with the disappointing look every time he would face me. So of course, I didn't bother to tell him how much that actually impacted me.

As a, not so surprising, result I cried myself to sleep every night, and sometimes still do. Eventually, though, my parents had enough. They left. Left me, here in this house. They didn't bother to tell me before it was too late, I couldn't even say goodbye.

On a random Tuesday morning, there was a note on the kitchen table, informing me that they left and won't be returning. Along with a bit of cash and a credit card. The letter had various things written on it, like the credit card information, the fact that my parents left me and that I couldn't tell anyone that they left. But not a single line indicated that they were sorry about leaving me, nor if they would one day pick me up.

I wasn't an idiot, I knew I couldn't tell anyone that my parents are gone. I knew the potential consequences. Maybe they would put me in an asylum, maybe a shelter. I won't let myself get trapped in either facility. Of course, I've thought about what it would be like to just tell someone, maybe directly inform the authorities and just watch what happens. Over the years I really wanted to let it out so many times, uncountable times, if only to get my parents the consequences they deserve. Hopefully jail for twice as many years as they left me for.

But I've kept quiet all this time. Buying myself groceries, clothes, and stationary. Basically, everything I need to be able to live my life. They at least had the decency to pay the electric, gas, water, and school fees. And I have become really smooth at faking both of my parents' signatures.

On one hand, I want to kill them for leaving. On the other hand, I think it is better this way. Believe it or not, because of them leaving I became the very independent person that I am now. Sure, neglect is a bad thing, but for right now I'm good with who I am.

The friends I made, Liam and Patricia, were at my house. They left roughly 15 minutes ago. We talked a whole bunch more than actually working on our project. Correction, *they* talked. I mostly sat by and listened. I shouldn't have brought them to my house, or at least cleaned up first. I'm actually embarrassed of my house now.

I have plans for events like these, when people come over. I have perfected the art of faking an atmosphere that looks like more than a teenage boy lives in there. Old clothes, used plates all over the kitchen counter, and no dust in sight would fool anyone who comes into the house to believe I don't live alone. But I couldn't prepare anything today because their visit wasn't planned at all. That's why I can't believe that it actually happened.

Those are weird folks. I could have sworn Liam doesn't have any friends in school. And from the looks of it, he hasn't talked to Patricia before either, yet they have this connection. They talked non-stop the whole way here. The conversation never died. I admire that, and maybe, only maybe, I am a little jealous of that. I wish I could just meet someone and have an instant constant with them.

That actually sounds really sad.

That's who and what I am.

A sad human being.

I'm actually sad— which probably makes me even more pathetic— that they are gone. It was nice to have someone beside me in the house. My friends from school are assholes so I never invite them to my house and I never go with them. Their humor consists of two parts, insulting others and doing disgusting straight-boy shit. That includes mostly slapping each other's asses, moaning like fourth graders, and making racist, homophobic, and ableist jokes all in one. They probably don't even realize how wrong that is. I only hang out with them for the social aspect, like having people to do group projects with, *if* we are allowed to choose our groups.

Others might consider that morally incorrect because I am only using them, but I think it's pretty damn fair considering the amount of offensive shit they have said in the past year.
Luckily, I did manage to get both of their numbers for further meet-ups.

Making sure to add the three of us to a group chat, I type the first message, right before I close my eyes.

CHAPTER 6

Liam

I wake up with a single message on my phone, which is one more than usual. I unlock my phone and tap on the notification.

Hey guys! As you can see I created a group chat. Just wanted to say hi.

The text isn't long, but I still don't know how to react. I gave my number to Patricia and I guess, she gave it to Matthew. *Kind of disappointing to be honest, he could have just asked me personally. Especially cause we were already on the topic.*

Would I be happier if he asked me?

Definitely.

Would I have given it to him?

Questionable. But to be fair, I already knew who his friends are and if his personality is anywhere near theirs, I will gladly block his number and never talk to him again as soon as the project is over. Just like all the rest.

I respond with a quick and simple 'hi'. *Nothing to overthink about.* I open Patricia's chat and start typing.

Not to be mean, but WHO DO U THINK YOU ARE? Giving my number off to him without my permission?

She replies within a minute.

Chill. He asked so I gave it to him. Was I supposed to refuse??

I don't respond. Mainly, because I'm not exactly sure what I'm mad about anymore. I grab my bag and leave the house.

Walking is never fun, especially this early in the morning. But I prefer this to the alternative. The bus. I'm not going to put myself through all the shouting and trash-talking at 6:30 in the morning.

I meet Patricia in the cafeteria with still ten minutes to spare. Guess that's our thing now, meeting before class like real friends. Maybe we are real friends. But who knows? She might just be using me for something. Maybe make her ex jealous or maybe because she is as lonely as I am and needs people to vent to. I wouldn't mind if it's either. However, I would appreciate it if she would let me in on her plan.

She tells me that she's sorry about giving Matthew my number, although I'm not sure if I believe her. There's a lot one can say without meaning any of it. I learned that a long time ago.

The only sign of a response I can manage is a soft groan which sounds more annoyed than it's supposed to be, but as one could have expected, I'm not thrilled about having calculus every day at 7 am.

By the start of fourth period, I already had enough of my school. Two kids, presumably 10th graders, decided to have a fight in the hallway on my way to Psych, blocking the whole hall because of the spectators.

When I walk into fourth period, Mr. Lane is already in the middle of instructions before class has even begun. Half of the class isn't even here yet, but that never stops him.

In Creative Writing we usually are working individually anyway so there isn't much to miss if you arrive too late- or on time I guess. The piece we are to write is about the best thing that happened in our lives and how it affected us. Luckily it's only due at the end of the semester, because I have no idea what the best event in my life was. *Certainly not birth.* I know it sounds cliche to say that, but there are only a handful of good events I can list, and choosing from them will be pretty much impossible. There is a reason I'm so obsessed with fictional stories, to get away from the real ones.

On top of everything, one of my classmates has the audacity to ask if we can do that assignment in groups. To my delight, Mr. Lane declined, which shifted a huge weight off my chest.

When the bell dismisses our class, I think about skipping, how relaxing it would be to just sit outside and do absolutely nothing, maybe read though. I will just have to find a spot and then set an alarm so that I can be back for the last period. If it were up to me, I would not go back at all, but I don't want to let Patricia or Matthew down. Besides, I do still want to go back to Matthew's place, no matter how irritated I am by the new group chat. Even if I would not admit it out loud, I like both their company.

Outside, the cold air brushes my face anything other than gently. The parking lot at the back of the school is always full, even though the parking lot by the front is half empty. I cross the parking lot and walk right through the football field, thanking the universe that there is no practice at this time. Behind the field, it is quiet compared to my previous class. Only a few birds and squirrels, making the trees their home. The sun shines high above the school building and yet it's cold.

I choose the tree furthest away from the school, not daring to think about the consequences if I get caught. If that were to happen, I wouldn't even try to apply to Stanford, because I'm pretty sure they don't accept kids who get caught skipping classes.

I would get grounded for the rest of my life.

Nothing would be within my reach anymore.

Suspension, or even worse, expulsion might even follow suit.

I sit on the ground and lean against the tree, my back facing the school. I close my eyes, listening to the wind and birds. It feels like nothing could ruin the moment. *If only it were that easy.*

Can you shut up? I'm talking to myself in my mind, I'm going insane. Stanford isn't going to take me anyway. Not because I might get caught, or am skipping class. No, Stanford isn't going to accept me, because I am slowly, but surely, going insane.

Then I'm going to have to work in some run-down office. Or worse, stay at home with CHILDREN. *Ew. No thanks, I would rather bury myself alive before I get kids.* I probably mean that, but sometimes it's hard to tell what is true and what isn't.

45

I hear the crack of a branch as something shifts behind me. I stop breathing, hoping to see that it's not a teacher, admin, or anyone else employed at the school.

Fuck! Who would be out here at this time?

Both of my hands ball into fists, nails digging into the inside of my palm.

Slowly, I turn my head around the tree to see a familiar face. The light brown of his eyes is staring right back at me. I can't believe who I'm seeing, Matthew stands before me. In the woods behind the football field on a random day, without having coordinated it at all. I would have thought the closest he would get to this point in the field itself.

"Um, " I say, " Hey?"

"Hi." That's all he says to me before a very awkward few minutes of just looking at each other. I look at all the details that I didn't care to notice any time before now. Like the unevenness of his left eyebrow. His head being slightly crooked when he stands like that. The perfect dimple on each side of his mouth.

Nope, not doing this. Absolutely not.

"What are you doing here? Why aren't you in school?" My voice is the first thing that breaks the silence.

"I could ask you the same thing," his reply is too basic.

Not trying to hide it, I roll my eyes.

"If I didn't know better I would think you are following me, stalking me even. So I will ask again, what are you doing here?" I push.

"Relax, I would never follow you without you knowing. I-," I cut him off before he can finish.

"That is even more creepy. But go on."

"As I was saying, I just came here to think. I technically have a free period now," he tells me. I didn't actually expect him to tell the truth.

If that is the truth.

"Don't you have somewhere else to be? Like standing by while your, so-called, friends harass people in the hallways?"

I don't regret even opening my mouth right this moment, even upon seeing his face. His expression. He looks offended, in shock even. But someone had to say it eventually. Because that's what they do. What they almost did to me. My face is unmoved, dead serious.

Josh is the worst. The worst human being I have ever met, in all the countries and schools I've been to. In the not even two months that I've been here, he made it his personal mission to make me leave again. He tried to break the teacher's stationary and blame it on me, he broke into my locker and searched, posting doodle entries from my notes on his story, and so much more. I don't even know why I let it slide this long. My strategy has been to ignore him to the best of my abilities because none of the things he did have actually been hurtful yet. Sure, it's annoying, really annoying, to deal with but eventually, he must get bored of me.

Upon breaking two pencils and one ruler while Mr. Lane was out during my second week, he was so proud to report back to Mr. Lane the next day that I was the one who broke and wasted his supplies. Mr. Lane took me out of class the next minute but surprisingly told me that I wasn't in trouble because he knew all about Josh's tricks and just needed to find people willing to support him when accusing Josh.

About two days later that same week, Josh and a couple of other guys somehow got into my locker and I found them crowding around it after school, taking photos of whatever papers they could find. They left when they saw me approach but left my locker in a mess. Later that same night I made an anonymous social media profile to look at each of their profiles, mainly to look for any leverage, and pretty easily stumbled upon Josh's story that day. To no one's surprise, it had photos of my notes featured as its main attraction. Mostly just doodles or comments I wrote, but all in German so he didn't understand them anyway.

His butlers, Connor and Manuel, are not that bad. They just want to suck up to Josh which entails that they don't try to stop them, mostly, verbal assaults. Somehow I get it, high school is all about popularity and shit. I guess Matthew is pretty lucky to be this popular. *Good for him.*

Finally, he lets out a sigh.

"Are they really that bad?", he asks. *Is he fucking kidding right now? He knows exactly how bad they can be. He himself can be that bad.*

"Look, if you just wanted to make fun of me, then leave. Or better yet, I will." I stand up grabbing my backpack from the ground. I take a step to where he came from, but he grabs my wrist, holding me in place.

"I'm sorry, it wasn't my intention to make fun of you," he hesitates, drawing a long breath, "Don't go. Please?"

This is a first. One of the boys invited me to stay with him, outside of school, in a one-on-one setting. It's probably just some shitty prank, in which I'm being live-streamed on their socials, making a fool of myself. Josh and Co. are probably hiding behind one of these other trees, waiting for me to say or do something embarrassing.

Why me though? There are so many better people in school, why did he have to do this to me?

Not trusting the situation, I shake my head. "No." I don't want to take the risk of being suspended for some bullshit that is not allowed here. I don't know what I think I will be suspended for, but if I stayed I just know there will be trouble.

I've been walking around the school building for almost an hour. I check my phone again, it's only 12:30, lunchtime. Another 2 hours to wait for the 7th period. But after the failed attempt to prank me, I'm not sure if I even want to go back inside to help this bastard get a good grade.

Maybe I should ask Patricia if she is okay with getting a bad grade too. Then we both stop working and fail the assignment, but so would Matthew. *I can't do that to Patricia, though. Gosh, morals are annoying...*

I make a decision. I pull out my phone from the back pocket of my jeans and start typing a message to inform Patricia that I won't be in class. That's the least I can do.

I jumped up at the rustling leaves behind me. Looking around me, I don't see anyone. *Must have been an animal or something.*

I hit send, at the same moment that Josh, Connor, and Manuel emerged from behind a bush. *Here we go.*

49

"What's up Liama? Long time no see." Josh glances at my hand with my phone in it. He elbows Manuel's ribcage and points at my phone.

I realize what they were planning before they come for me. In an instant, there are hands all around me, and no way to run. I hold the phone as tight as I can, not daring for them to get it. They eventually start pulling at my backpack and I fall.

Not caring about the phone anymore, Josh was the first to land a kick, right in my gut. Connor joined in pretty quickly, but Manuel hesitated. It was wrong from my side, to think he would stop both of them. Wrong of me to dare hope. Manuel starts kicking my back as well.

Each kick is harder than the one before.

I spit as Josh's foot hits my stomach.

I hear a car approaching. Luckily they do too and hurry away faster than I thought they could run.

Knowing exactly how it would go, I get up and limp my way away from the car. Whoever it was, would only bring more trouble. I get beaten up, I am at fault. I tell a teacher, I'm at fault for snitching.

"Are you sure you aren't just making this up? Maybe you fell and hit your head?"

"You can't just go around and accuse people of something without proof."

"Even if you didn't make it up, they all got alibis. They were at his house, studying together."

So in everyone's best interest, I stopped trying to report these things and I won't start again now.

When I arrive at home, neither of my parents are there. Mom most likely working, and Dad is off for some appointment.

I go right to my bathroom, throwing off my hoodie and jeans, and putting on shorts. I'm going to have to clean the blood off somehow. From myself, that's no problem, but from my shirt and jeans… I rush downstairs and throw them in the washing machine, throwing it on without giving it another thought.

Before I go back upstairs I grab a kitchen roll, sanitizer, and bandages from the first-aid cabinet Mom set up the first day we moved in. Bandages are going to be major for hiding the injuries from everyone.

First, I sanitize the ripped open skin on my shoulder and knee, then I take the bandages and cover everything as much as possible. While I put on a new hoodie, I hear a knock at the front door.

I take all the supplies and rush them downstairs because I don't want my parents to find a mess when they get back. Which apparently is now. *Dad must have forgotten his keys again.*

"Láile" I scream toward the door. Hoping to put all things back in time. Since my second year in Singapore, I have been using Chinese phrases around the house to practice. Now it's gotten into a habit. My parents were okay with that at first, but now they say it's annoying and I should talk to them in German before I forget that language. Not happening.

I close the medical supply closet and run to the door. Switching to German, I say again "Coming!."

I open the door, but it's not my dad standing in front of me now.

51

CHAPTER 7

Matthew

Maybe this is a bad idea. It probably, most likely, is. Going to someone's house, after lying to the school secretary about why I needed someone's address, even though that someone clearly told me fuck off. And yet, here I am, standing in front of Liam Taylor's house.

I don't even know why I'm here, but after Patricia told me that we wouldn't be meeting today because Liam went home, I couldn't get it out of my head. It's my fault he didn't show, because of what happened behind the field. I don't want it to be weird, so I'm going to have to apologize eventually. I might as well do it today. At his house. Right now.

Thinking about it, I'm pretty sure the secretary of the school broke some law by giving me his address, or at least some school code, if not both.

He opens the door a few moments after I rang the bell. His eyes are wide open when he sees me. *The first sign that he doesn't want me to be here right now.* My eyes go over his face first, chills running down my spine. *What happened to him? Is this why he left early?* When I saw him behind the field, he didn't have these scratches or bruises. Now there is a bandage around his knee, looking as if he just came home from a WWE battle.

"What happened?" I ask, afraid of his answer. What if he tripped when he walked away from the spot *I* interrupted him at?

He doesn't answer. Instead, he widens the opening door, inviting me in, and takes a short look outside before closing the door.

"Phone.", he demands.

"What? Why?"

"Phone.", he says quietly but not weakly.

"Are you just not gonna talk to me before I hand you my phone?" I let out a forceful laugh.

He doesn't look amused at all. He looks dead-serious when he holds out his hand.

"Fine, but don't try to unlock it," I told him. He nods, and I hand him my phone. He gestures for me to stay here while he walks away, through a door right past the kitchen area. A minute later he exits that same door, but without my phone.

He looks me in the eyes and asks, "Why are you here? To deliver a message from your buddies? Tell them I don't give a flying shit about what they have to say."

"What are you talking about? I am here because you didn't show up for class, or for our project," I protest.

53

"Aha. Well, thanks for your *concern* but I just left because I felt like it. Didn't Patricia tell you I left?" he asks, heavy irony laying over the word 'concern'.

"What happened?", I ask again.

"As if you don't know."

He was right. I do know. He practically ran away from me and must have slipped somewhere. I feel myself blushing with embarrassment.

"You slipped when I chased you away." It was more of a statement than a question. He looks at me for a moment, nothing confirming nor denying in his eyes, but nods.

I was right. It is my fault.

"I'm sorry," I tell him, and I mean it.

Liam turns around without saying another word, and I watch him disappear through that same mysterious door.

I still have no idea why I had to give it to him. He said he wouldn't try to open it, but why did I have to surrender it?

The next day I hadn't quite registered what was happening in school. The voices of teachers fade into nothing, while my thoughts keep going back to the home of the Taylors.

The yellow walls, the brownish doors, and the drawers. The oak dining table. Most importantly, the boy who I came to visit yesterday. The things he said, the tone he used.

Realization hits like a brick.

He doesn't like me. He hates me even.

I talked to Patricia during lunch. She assured me that Liam is fine, except for the bruises. Patricia also offered that she would finish the project on her own and share the credit. I tried to refuse, but she said it would be better for us not to meet again.

Ouch. Never had that before, hurt someone so much that their best friend, of two days, tells me to leave him alone, which means completely ditching a project. Hurting him plus having him hate me, is something I didn't think would bother me as much as it does. A pit in my chest clenches every time I think about what I did, and the injuries I've caused.

During French, we can pretend, but outside I won't. I won't pretend anything outside of class anymore. Won't act like I like the people I hang out with, won't act like I'm not sad about Liam being mad at me, won't pretend that I hated having real friends for two days. Things need to change.

After school, I realize that my dad transferred twice the amount of money to the account this morning. Either, he was in a good mood, or by accident. Whatever it was, it brightens up my own mood at least a little, because what's done is done and won't be undone.

I have a choice now. Either I put some of that money to good use by buying an apology gift, or I can not do that and leave him alone as Patricia told me to, but I would probably never talk to either of them again.

It's probably better if I just take the damn advice and don't do anything, even if that means I won't talk to them ever again. They are better off without me anyway, considering all the anger Liam has reserved for me.

I text Patricia a thank you for the project and I leave school without a second thought.

But before I even get home, she replies.

Try to not talk to Liam for a while? Please.

Right now he's not the biggest fan of you or your football friends, so in exchange for finishing the project you'll not contact him until he contacts you.

Understood?

Hurrying home as fast as I can manage, I lock the door behind me before running up into my room, throwing this door shut as well. I throw myself on my bed and feel nothing. Empty.

CHAPTER 8

Liam

The thing about keeping up with long-distance friendships is that it's more complicated than a long-distance relationship. *Yeah, yeah, I get it. Long-distance relationships are almost impossible and all that crap.* But keeping a friendship intact is much more complex than one might think. In a relationship, you know for sure that the other won't just suddenly block you because they grew tired. Well, mostly they won't. But in a friendship or any other form of non-romantic relationship, you never know when the next blocking takes place.

In theory, in a relationship, the opposing partner always wants to talk to you. They try their best to make time for phone calls, face-times, or even just time to reply to messages because they all fear losing contact and breaking up. Meanwhile, friends might reply in a few days, if you are lucky. They don't cancel plans to talk to you. They don't call you when they are in the bath.

They don't answer calls or texts if you decide to call them.

In a relationship, your partner will try to reply as fast as possible. In a friendship, they don't.

My opinions may be a little biased because I've only ever experienced friendships, or what I thought were friendships, and no relationship.

I text Tess, dumping every single thought out of my head into the message. The typing itself takes me more than five minutes, excluding the three twenty-one-minute breaks I take for emotional safety. I hit send, but don't expect a reply, even though they are online right now…

So, I close my messages and throw my phone on the other side of my bed. That side is occupied with human-sized plushies, pillows, and uncountable things including now my phone. It bounces all the way over the other side and hits the floor. *The audacity! Why would that happen at this exact moment? Well, I can do the same thing.* Instead of walking around my bed to pick it up, I fall into my bed and just lie there. No movement. If my phone wants to be on the ground so badly, I might as well let it.

Now I'm talking to my phone, in my mind…Great!

I don't remember the weekend going by, but unfortunately, it's Monday morning all over again. It's 6:32 am and my phone vibrates in my pocket, while I try to sleep on the bus. Tess finally replied to my message. I unlock my phone and read the not-so-long message.

Well, good luck! U know I would help, but cant sry.

Okay, so I write multiple long ass paragraphs, and this is what I get in return?! They didn't even try to comfort me this time. That's exactly how I know things are getting worse.

I'm a little offended. With my phone in the back pocket of my jeans, I exit the bus, with no additional sleep under my belt, and make my way straight to my first-period classroom. I won't stop in the cafeteria to meet Patricia today.

When I moved to the States, this was not what I expected the so-called "freedom" to be. I imagined a ride-or-die friendship, limitless freedom, and a hell amount of fun. I imagined parties, hang-outs, sneaking in and out of our homes, slowly developing a romance with the student who hates me the most- from "I wish you would be buried alive and slowly suffocate under the ground" to "I wish we get buried together, dead or not, I don't care"- that's the dream I had in mind. Maybe that is a teeny, tiny, bit exaggerated, but I have no other way of describing it.

Instead of having that, I'm sitting on my bed, reading non-stop all day long. That's probably why I don't love "freedom" to begin with. How could I have all that, when all I do is sit inside and read?

Well, friends are overrated anyway. Who would voluntarily hang out with a group of humans just to talk, watch a movie, or just breathe? Who would ever want to cancel their plans of reading all night, to have a sleepover at someone else's house? Who, in their right mind, would want to do something totally stupid after school, instead of going home?

Me.

I close my eyes and rest my head straight on my desk in first period.

But, as I said, fun scenarios are overrated, plus, saying that would be unproductive is an understatement. I'm the perfect example of how it works out when you don't have that. I never had more than one friend who didn't verbally and/or physically abuse me, and I turned out fine.

Right?

I know that I don't have to justify myself, especially not to myself, but just to prove my point, I have one last argument. If I read instead of going out, I can't embarrass myself in front of anyone. Problem solves before it even happened.

Sometimes this, right now, is all I do. I don't read, I'm not on my phone, I'm not doing schoolwork. I just lie on my bed, or anywhere really, and have an argument with myself, trying to justify a point, usually totally pointless either way. When I do that, everything around me becomes irrelevant, I don't perceive the sounds and movements around me. Until I'm done arguing in my head.

I won't lie, the space up there can get really loud. Too loud. Too uncontrollable. Too much.

I think too much, and that's an issue, but I'm always okay afterward. At least for a fixed amount of time.

CHAPTER 9

Matthew

I should ignore everything Patricia told me to do. I thought about that every minute for the past couple of days. I could walk to Liam's house, ring the doorbell, talk to Liam, and *somehow* convince him that I want to be his friend.

I have no idea why I want us to be friends, I already have enough "friends", but everyone remotely close to me knows they aren't actually friend-worthy. *If that's not a real thing, it totally should be.*

Just as the bell rings to dismiss us, I determinedly get up from the seat I was, more or less, forced to sit in during lunch because it's the same people I sit with daily- the same people, at the same table, since freshman year. I didn't even bring lunch to school, I never do, but I sit with them anyway.

Where else would I go?

The table is more for the sake of tradition and nostalgia than for the socializing or food aspect anyway- the socializing least of all.

Contributing to their conversation isn't my thing either. They talk about sports, cars, and girls they think are hot. The only things I can even comment on are the football season and theoretically girls, but I don't like the way they talk about people as if they're collectibles, so I stay quiet most of the time.

When it comes to topics of interest, I'm a complete stereotype, not into cars or general sports, it's kind of sad to think about.

Often, I'm embarrassed by the things leaving their mouths. I tried to stop them from talking the way they do, inappropriate and disrespectful to everyone around, by asking them to put themselves in the shoes of others.

Imagine you're a normal teenage girl in high school, minding your own business at lunch, but you overhear some guys mentioning your name and another one pitching in, "SHE'S SO HOT!"

You would be beyond embarrassed and so uncomfortable that you gather your belongings, get up, and leave the cafeteria, and would probably never eat there again.

None of them got my point. They said I was being dramatic, so then I asked them to not talk about girls at all. To nobody's surprise, they didn't respond to that either. I even went so far as to snitch to a teacher anonymously by leaving a note on his desk.

He didn't take it seriously enough to do anything about the issue.

So much to teachers being there to help you out with any school-related concern…

Essentially that led to me being too tired to try anything else, because it wouldn't change anything anyway. Now I do my best to ignore them.

Leaving Josh and the others behind, I walk through the mostly empty halls of our school, trying to find the one place Liam and Patricia would now be settling to host their private lunch. Not once have I heard about anyone ditching the cafeteria just to have a more private setting, but I couldn't find them a couple of times now so I asked around. A few of Patricia's friends told me they saw her sitting in a hallway sitting with a random guy. Some of them even cared enough to question if they may be dating, but at the same time didn't care enough to find out who the guy is.

Because if they had, they would know that Liam and Patricia aren't dating.

I rarely walk through these halls when it's this empty. Surprising to be honest, because the new lunch bell just rang and people should be walking to the cafeteria in swarms, but maybe I'm past that territory already.

There are a few other loners enjoying the quiet while leaning against some lockers to take a nap or call someone, but no Liam or Patricia so far.

What am I even going to say when I find them? I haven't thought that far yet, but at the same time, I can't just show up with nothing to say.

Not when Liam currently has every right to hate me.

63

I take the nearest stair to the lower level of the school, even further from the crowd and cafeteria. With every turn, my heart beats a little faster in hopes of finally finding Liam, but no luck so far. *Am I even allowed to be here right now?* I don't even care. I am going to find them.

Mr. Gaidarov will be mad again when I arrive to his sixth period late again, but this time I actually have a good reason. Not that I would tell him. Physics is overrated anyway.

Just as the thought of giving up pops into my mind, I take one last turn and find them. There they are. Under a staircase in the furthest possible corner of the school.

For a moment I just stare at them, my breath stuck in my lungs, not daring to take another step further.

Neither of them has noticed me yet, so I take another step, slow but steady. And then another, and another, and one more. This feels like walking in a minefield, every step could lead to an explosion.

I feel my face, even my neck, heating up with every step. Never have I been this nervous to talk to anyone before.

Liam and Patricia turn around at the same moment then. *Shit.* The emotion is practically written all over their faces, they aren't thrilled to see me. I halt for a second but then continue walking. After all that trouble to find them, it will take more than one look to scare me away.

When I finally reach them, I sit down right in front of them, a forced smile on my face.

Patricia's death stare doesn't go unnoticed, but it won't be acted on. Patricia opens her mouth to say something, but stops herself, closing her mouth again. *Guess it's my turn to say something then.*

I start with a simple, "Hey."

For a moment neither of them responds. They just stare at me as if they had seen a ghost.

"After all you and your friends have done, you have the nerve to come to our lunch spot to ruin our only break from you?! Seriously, where do all of you get the audacity? Especially after I specifically asked you not to show up again."

You don't need to be an empath to feel the anger rambling in Patricia's voice.

All the while Liam still hasn't made a sound, hasn't moved, hasn't even blinked.

Liam's bruises didn't heal much over the past few days, noting the blue to purple coloration over his forearm. A pang hits my chest upon looking at him, reminding me that I'm responsible for chasing him away, for making him slip, and for the physical pain that he's in now.

"Listen, please? I'm here to apologize," I offer looking directly at Liam now, "I should have left that day behind the field. I shouldn't have pushed you away. I get that now, and I really am sorry." I mean every word that leaves my mouth.

"I… It's fine," Liam sights. Patricia jerks her head in his direction. Apparently, she didn't see this coming either.

I try again, "No, it's really not though. It's because of my ignorance that you got all of these bruises. If I didn't chase you away, you would never have slipped. I'm sorry."

Patricia sounds as confused as she looks when she asks, "Slipped?"

Liam looks at her now and just stares. They stare at each other for what feels like an eternity, before Patricia looks back at me and goes, "Um, uh huh… right."

"So why are you really here? Surely not just to apologize, are you?" Patricia is consistent. Respectable.

"Actually, I did just come here to apologize, but if you were to offer a step into friendship, then "grateful" would be an understatement for what I'd be feeling," I say with confidence, a smile spreading on my face. "But if you can't do that now, or… or ever, then I totally understand and will leave the both of you unbothered," I add assuringly.

But please don't ask me to do that because I'm not sure if I could keep that promise.

Again they face each other and just stare as if they're having a telepathic conversation just with their eyes. Luckily it's faster this time. They turn back after less than a minute and nod in unison. What does that mean? Yes, they accept me into their friend group? Yes, they accept my apology? Yes, I can go fuck off and never talk to them again?

My face must give away how lost I am because Liam finally speaks up.

"We formally accept your apology and you can hang out with us. But I swear to all that's holy to me, including Patricia right here, that *if* this is a well-planned prank, we will come after all of you."

His words sound like a threat, but his tone makes him sound like an elementary school teacher talking to a kid who got the homework assignment right. Meaning, I will have to put effort into regaining their trust.

Before I can even think of an appropriate response, the bell cuts me off and they stand up and walk away, leaving me sitting alone. Finally, I get up and walk to the second half of physics.

When I walk in without any sort of excuse, Mr. Gaidarov rolls his eyes and motions for me to sit down without another word. Only when I sit down in the back of the class do I realize I have one of those stupid happy-grins plastered on my face.

I try wiping it away, but every time Liam pops into my head it comes back.

Nope. No. No. And No. I'm not doing this. Have I mentioned no? I'm not going to crush on the only guy I could have an actual *friendship with.*

Mr. Gaidarov is reciting a speech about how important the basics of physics are in everyday life and how we shouldn't purposefully miss out on that. Feels a little targeted toward me but okay. I choose to tune out and ignore the rest of his speech. Instead, I close my eyes and sink into my thoughts.

Less than 30 minutes until I see Liam and Patricia again. I'm so relieved that he accepted my apology, even when I don't deserve it. I should ask Patricia if she had anything to do with that miracle, even though she really seemed angry before. If she did the smallest thing, I already owe her big time.

CHAPTER 10

Liam

Where do these people get their audacity from? Seriously, how do some people have the nerve to do what they do? And why is it only the assholes with the biggest ego? That seems a little unfair. First, they get all the privileges and additionally, they get such a narcissistic mindset. I don't see how that is fair to the rest of us. How are we supposed to deal with those creatures? Just sit by and watch, while they go out and destroy lives? I try so hard not to give two flying fucks, but eventually, they invade my personal space and I can't handle any more of it. They invade your friendships, interests, and classes, with the only goal to destroy everything they can.

Yuck. Even thinking about it makes me sick.

Like, imagine having nothing better to do in your life than being a gigantic asshole. It's like they are a whole human subspecies, so different from normal humans.

The worst part is, they are everywhere and you can't escape their kind. No matter the age, elementary, middle, or high school, and no matter the country, Germany, Singapore, or the United States, the assholes always leave their mark.

Maybe this is a bit exaggerated, but there should be some kind of solution for this. Behavioral therapy, boot camps, or SOMETHING, to make those people…

Oh wow. Yep, way too far. Just stop thinking about it, get past it.

That's way easier said than done. My whole rib cage still feels sore every time I breathe, all of my organs feel like they're sitting in the wrong place in my body, and the bruises look worse every day. There's a huge spot on my back that's basically green.

I'm lucky my parents haven't found out yet though. I would be in so much more shit if they had.

This is what I do now on Tuesday evenings, it has come that far. I turn around again, facing myself in the bathroom mirror. The white tiled walls stare at me from all around me, like they are judging everything about me. My character, my decision-making, and my behavior. If they could they would tell me how it's my fault that they beat me up in the first place. Because I don't fit in anywhere, I'm too unlikeable, and most importantly, I couldn't have just minded my business.

Pinching my eyes closed, I tilt my head to the floor and release a shaky breath, my chest crippling with the pain. I don't want to think about that right now. What I want to do is forget this ever happened and

69

move on. No more waiting for bruises to disappear, no more flashbacks while I'm trying to fall asleep, and no more being angry about something I can't fix.

So that's what I do. I ignore what's happening in my head and ignore the pain while switching off the lights, unlocking the door, and leaving the bathroom I just spent over 40 minutes in.

CHAPTER 11

Matthew

School is intolerable. Especially when it's seven in the morning and you already have to keep up with your friend's bullshit. Conner and Manuel thought it would be fun to jog in circles while talking about practice. Don't get me wrong, I love talking about football with people. However, I would rather choke on a piece of concrete than talk about it this much at seven in the fucking morning. Every five minutes I nod and say something like "Agree" or "Mhm" to keep from actually interacting.

Why do we even have to talk to each other? Now, I mean. It's seven in the fucking morning!

When the bell rings, Josh still isn't here, which gets me more excited than it probably should. Yes, he is an asshole with no care for the world around him, but he wouldn't skip class. He wants to go to college and all, so he can't afford to skip anything just because he doesn't feel like it. So either he is dead, or preferably he's just sick. Bummer, if he actually were dead. I mean, he still is one of my best friends.

Also a bummer.

Sixth period Physics rolls around in an instant. My mood has already improved plenty over the Joshless day. It's crazy how much a single person can elevate your stress level, and how relaxed you can feel when they are gone. In the good mood that has overcome me over the day, I decide to not let physics ruin it, and instead join Liam and Patricia at lunch.

It sucks that we don't have the same lunch period, because it's not like I can skip physics every day to hang out with them. But maybe it's better if I can't since they would probably get tired of me even faster. I know I can't avoid it, but I can try to delay it.

Surprisingly, I find both of them in the cafeteria today. Both sitting at a table completely empty apart from them.

I slump down into the free chair next to Patricia's and ask, "Heyy! What are y'all talking about?"

"Okay, so, first of all. Hi! We were just complaining about classes, so just the usual." Patricia is in a good mood, as per usual. I look at Liam, who still has his head down. Either he is ignoring me because he still doesn't like, or trust, me. Or, he is about to vomit all over this table. Call me a pessimist, but I believe it's the first one.

"Li, you okay?" Patricia asks after looking back over at him.

"Fine. The psych test tomorrow is just freaking me out." He slams his head onto the table with a low groan. Liam looks defeated and more than exhausted. I'm sure he'll do fine on every test, but it's concerning how exhausting he looks.

He lifts his head, looks at us, and says, "But I'm totally fine." Then lets his head drop again.

"Dude, you should relax for a minute," I suggest.

"Mhm," Patricia agrees, "It would help, you know."

He doesn't even look up, completely ignoring our suggestion. I lean closer to Patricia and whisper, "Is he okay?" She just shrugs. Really comforting.

"Anyway," I change the subject, away from the awkwardness of the situation, "What are you guys doing after school? Because there is this park near the school, which I'm sure you already know, in which we can literally do anything. It'd be fun."

"Bet! Li you in?" Patricia says excitedly, then taps Liam on his shoulder. Again. And again. Until, Liam lifts his head up from the table and says, "Doing nothing for the rest of the day in some random park I've never been to, with people who I barely know, no offense. How is that even a question? Of course, I'm in. But you might need to wait for me, 'cause I need to call Tess right after school."

"Tess?"

"His best, and only, friend in Germany," Patricia explains.

"Ah." I refrain to comment on her word choice, not because it could have been interpreted as an insult, but because I doubt he only has one friend over there. He's Liam. Sure, he isn't the most social person,

73

but he's friendly to everyone that talks to him. So how could he possibly only have one friend?

"Did something happen or why is it so urgent? If you don't mind me asking," I ask, because now I'm intrigued. I want to know more. He has a best friend overseas. Someone from his past that he values to much that he needs to call them right after school. I want to know everything about him, including his past. It's weird because I don't feel the same thing with Patricia. Sure, I would be open if she wanted to tell me something, but I don't crave to know everything there is.

"Actually yes. I don't know many details yet, but apparently, my old principal, Mr. Sauer, suspended them for something they did after school. They weren't even the only one who was there. Four other kids, *white kids,* were there with them, but they only got off the hook with a warning. Now they need to vent, and I'm all open ears for that. Until now, these situations- situations that exclusively happened because they are one of the only black people at that school, weren't as bad. And we always filed complaints and stuff. But now Tess *isn't in the position to file complaints.*" He moves his fingers in the air at the last part, before he lets out a brutally long sight.

"*What the actual fuck?*" Patricia almost screams through the whole cafeteria, as she should. I can't even find words for how incredibly unacceptable that shit is.

"Well, yeah. That school isn't the best… Not even close."

"We can tell. But yes, we can wait. Good luck though. I can't imagine this to be easy, especially because you can't do much from here."

He nods and tries to force a smile on his face before he says "Thanks".

He gets up and leaves, leaving Patricia and me. We exchange a quick look before we leave the table behind.

Classes are as boring as always. Yet, I focus on the voice of my Physics teacher, whose voice is the only thing in my brain right now. Surprisingly he didn't bat an eye when I walked in late again, just continued his class as if nothing happened.

When the bell rings to dismiss the class, it's time for French. I don't even know how I got to French three. My French is bad, like really bad. I do know some of the basics but that's it. It's an honors class, so of course the class has way higher expectations, which is why I am sure I will fail this year. At the beginning of this year, I talked to Madame Veilleux to request a transfer to a standard-level class. Madame Veilleux told me to sleep on it, because colleges and stuff like to see honors classes on a transcript like mine.

Besides, Madame Veilleux told me exactly what I should do when I stay. According to her, I should "Keep up the effort and everything will work out". So here I am, with no clue whatsoever, but at least putting in the effort. Yet, it's barely enough to pass.

I sit down at my normal seat in the front row, waiting for anyone really, to walk through the door so I can talk to someone. Surprisingly, today I am one of the first five people to be here, instead of the last five.

So not talking to the straight boys has its perks after all. They aren't exactly happy that I openly call them "Straight Boys" instead of

75

something else, like their names. But really, what is there to complain about? If I were to call them "Gay Boys" or anything else in that direction, they wouldn't be happier. The opposite really.

Plus, everybody already knows I'm bi so might as well use it to have some fun.

The bell rings before I can even explore the advantage of being early though.

After school, I meet up with Patricia at the parking space at the back of the school. Or at least I intended to. Patricia hasn't shown up yet, but I wait anyway. I sit on one of the benches that have been here forever, but no one really uses them. I watch people get into their parents' car, one after the other.

A minute passes.

Two.

Five.

I stop looking at the time as best as I can because that just makes the waiting worse.

Who knows, maybe they already had enough of me and decided to stand me up. Or maybe they got hit by a car on their way here. Probably not. However, the most reasonable explanation for their tardiness must be Liam's phone call. Patricia probably waits next to him, instead of here with me as we discussed.

I take my phone and start composing a text.

CHAPTER 12

Liam

The sound of the school bell is infuriating. It physically hurts to hear the sound of it. The possibility of getting my eardrums shattered doesn't calm me down at all. I wonder if that ever happened. A school bell so loud and so painful that some poor kid with weak ears got his eardrum shattered. I wonder if the parents of that kid had to pay for the full surgery themselves because insurance in that case… I'm not sure if that's even a thing.

Guessing that the parents would probably have sued the school, they would have gotten all the money they needed if they won. However, in the unlikely event, that they could lose, it would mean that the kid's parents would be in debt for the rest of their lives. Assuming they are average citizens of course. Maybe the kid himself would even be in that same debt. Because surgeries are fucking expensive.

America, where you will get robbed by the government, just to get a life-saving surgery.

That should be their advertising slogan.

I'm sure, or I hope, most people know how different other places are. That healthcare can be free if it's set up right.

The ringing lasts for over a minute, or at least it feels like it. All of my previous schools had way more relaxing bells. Ones that do not give you brain damage. They were soft and harmonic.

This… This is a modern torture instrument.

Either way, we leave the classroom. Matthew taking a right in the hall, while Patricia and I are taking a left. I need to get to a quiet place where I can call Tess. I told Patricia she can go ahead and meet Matthew behind the school as we planned in sixth period, but she declined, saying that she's my emotional support to be an emotional support to Tess.

I'm really glad we can use phones in school whenever we want. Except in tests, but that's obvious. In class, we can choose to listen and do well. Or we can choose to use our phones to do whatever we want, and as a result, do worse in class. Usually, I choose to listen because I believe colleges look at every year of high school, so my grades have to be good throughout all four years. No matter how tiring it is.

The Ivy League doesn't wait for its students to catch up with their sleep schedule. So I will sacrifice as much sleep as I need to. The acceptance rate at Stanford is about 5%, so I have to be in the top 4%. Not only to get in but to feel safe about staying in.

Grades were never really a problem during high school. In primary and middle school, sure. But only because I knew it didn't matter, so I didn't try. At my previous school, we didn't have a GPA, because the grading system is so different. So this semester will show me my first-ever GPA.

Am I nervous? Yes.

Do I hope it to be at least 4.0? Also, yes.

Do I think I won't make it to 3.5? Yep.

Does that steal any glimpse of hope? Kind of.

I slide down the wall, under a quiet staircase, at the left wing of the school. The main entrance is on the right wing, so there aren't many people here. It's not a perfect spot for a call, but the best we got.

I click on the camera signal in the chat with the intention of Facetimeing Tess. While I wait for her to pick up, I walk outside hoping it will be quieter and easier to talk. Without being interrupted by a teacher or a student, of course.

Tess pops up on my screen. They stand in the kitchen, the sound of sizzling onions in the back.

"Hey," I greet them.

Silence.

They probably are just in the wrong mood for this. So I switch to German and ask, "So what happened exactly?"

They drop the knife onto the counter and look directly into the eye of the camera. That look kind of scares me, but it's nothing I'm not used to.

They sight loudly. I already know that's just for the dramatics of it all.

"Okay so… Remember Luis and Simon? The twins. One in A, the other in B. Anyway, they invited me to hang out after school, to study for a test. I, of course, didn't think much of it. Yes, it was kind of weird to ask me when they rarely spoke to me since fifth grade. But I thought they wanted to get in touch again, maybe even apologize for *the incident.* Damn! I shouldn't have been so stupid to believe them in the first place!"

I cut them off, "Tess, breathe. It's not your fault that they're assholes. I thought we went over this?!"

"Either way, I texted my moms to not wait for me for lunch. After school, I went with both of them to their car and let them drive me to their house. We didn't talk much on the way there, but that bitch, Luis, just had to play country music. You know how much I hate country music."

I nod, knowing exactly how much passion fuels their hatred of country music.

"When we finally got to their house, I almost didn't recognize it. It's still the same house, but they changed a lot. Everything is painted in different colors. The chairs out front are gone. Nothing looks the way it used to. We went inside. I wanted to say hi to their parents, but they weren't home. So instead, we went upstairs into Simon's room. That, unlike everything else, doesn't look much different. Still has the same shade of yellow walls and all. I sat and pulled out my Latin homework and vocab, with the obvious intention to study. But Simon and Luis just looked at me and didn't move. I asked them if they were just going to watch me study. Then Luis suggested we go for a walk before we study, to clear our heads or whatever.

Again, I didn't think much of it, so I was like 'Okay, sure!' Fast forward, we walk by the school's soccer field. Around the fence at least. I thought it was weird they brought me here, especially after we had just left school, but whatever. But then Luis suggested, out of nowhere, that we go in. We could play tag for a bit, he said. I didn't think it was a good idea then, but peer pressure, you know? We climbed over and did… I don't know what that was. We just ran through the whole field, from one end to the other. With no care or goal in mind.

Except when Mr. Sauer came toward us. I thought we should run since he couldn't possibly have seen our faces from that distance. But when I attempted to run, Luis kicked my right leg, and Simon my left ankle. I fell to the ground, and by the time I got up, Mr. Sauer stood next to me, starring down at me.

I told Mr. Sauer, and everyone who asked, that Simon and Luis were with me. My moms thankfully believed me but the school kept pushing. Eventually, I got suspended and the twins only got a warning. The security footage of the field even proved my point. It clearly showed all of our faces. But that Nazi of a principle thought it would be fair to only punish me. The only girl in the school who looks like me. What a coincidence," they emphasize the last sentence with a bitter tone.

My knuckles are white from the pressure of my anger from that story. I don't know what to say so I stay silent. Tess picks up their knife again and continues making their food.

81

"So what did you do after that? Did you go to the board about it? Did your moms sue? All of the above?", I ask eventually, realizing that Tess is completely done.

They sight and make a sound. Something between a laugh and a sob. I'll take that as a no for any of my hopeful suggestions. Switching back to English I say, "You have to answer me at some point, you know?"

That made a clear difference between the sob and giggle because now it is only their laugh that remains.

"Uh, no. We didn't do any of that. We considered it of course, but my moms say we don't have enough evidence to go to the board. So now I'm sitting at home, using this time as an excuse to finally catch up on all the shows I have to watch. I started this show yesterday and I'm already on season 5. I think I may have a problem." They tell me about the show for the next two or so minutes before their mom calls them for dinner.

We end the call without coming up with an idea to get revenge on the twins. Of course, it can't be obvious that Tess did it, which makes getting revenge harder. In the past we would find something to do that would make people, other students who backstabbed us, furious without knowing it was us. I would help them the two times I've been in German for the past nine years. But I would also do it alone in Singapore, and Tess alone in Germany. With each other on the phone.

In eighth grade, I went to this kid's house and stole all of his chargers. I pretended to forgive him and that I want to repair the friendship. Gullible little bastards. I went to his house for multiple hours after school. Making sure to put every charger I see into my backpack.

He didn't even think about me as a possible reason for the missing cables. His parents ended up buying new ones, so I would consider that a successful mission.

Tess did almost the same thing. But instead of chargers, they were batteries. Batteries from the TV remote, the LED remote, and any other remote they could find. Or basically, anything that ran on a battery. All suddenly stopped working on the same day. Again, what a coincidence.

Neither one of us ever got caught getting revenge, nor do we ever plan on it.

My phone goes back into my pocket and Patricia has a concerned look on her face. I utter a quick "Sorry" to her and motion to go back inside.

Logically going through the school to the back parking lot is faster than walking all the way around, but I'm not sure if we are even permitted to be in here. This school, unlike my old one, is not an open campus so we can't just walk around whenever and wherever we want.

There is some sort of after-school activity going on behind almost every door, so even if we get stopped, we can come up with a good excuse. Even if we are not really walking to a school-sponsored after-school activity.

Going to Matthew's house after school is an activity, but compared to school-related stuff, this could actually be fun. If all three of us allow it to be.

It's strange, knowing you will spend your day after school at someone else's house and in my bed reading or doing pages of homework like I usually do after school.

If all goes to waste, I, of course, have a book in my bag. I might just sit in the corner of Matthew's room and read, or end up catching up with homework with all three of them. Won't be as fun but better than doing it alone.

Or I'll just leave. That's always an option. But Patricia will do anything in her power to not let me. I don't know if I should be worried about that.

The parking space is almost empty.

Wow. Did the call last that long?

Usually, this space is crowded even 30 minutes after school ends. Matthew sits on a bench near the back entrance, his back facing us. Patricia looks at me and I nod.

I stop walking on the spot and watch as Patricia sneaks up behind him.

She waits a long moment before resting both her forearms on Matthew's shoulder, all while she screams her lungs out. Matthew, however, doesn't even look so much as pull out. He looks up, unimpressed.

"Hello to you too. Took you a while."

I continue walking now, "Yeah, sorry about that."

I say nothing more because his eyes meet mine. In an instant, my blood rushes through my whole body. His eyes are clear. Then he smiles. His stupidly cute face is fogging my brain. I force my head to look at Patrcia and away from his stupidly cute smile. I do not want to stupidly crush on someone just because he smiled at me once. I fully look at Patricia now, who is already starting to walk away from the both of us.

Matthew gets up and we try to catch up with Patricia. I noticed he glanced at me a few times, questions in his eyes, but I pretend not to notice. Mainly because his presence in itself makes me nervous. I would hate for this to be any more awkward just because I can't keep myself together around a cute guy.

Totally not crushing though. There's a fine line between admitting a guy is conventionally attractive and falling head over heels for him. I'm still behind that line and it will stay that. Totally.

We arrive at his house and he leads us to his room once again, the rest of the house is still as clean as it was before, besides a few used plates in the sink. Matthew throws his backpack next to his bed with a loud thumb. Patricia and I just watch as he does the same exact thing again with his own body.

"So, uh, when are your parents coming home?" Patricia asks, probably just trying to fill the silence.

He shrugs from where he lies, "I'm not sure. Sometime this or next week, I think."

I take in the room one more time, this time scanning for something important. Important to me. Disappointingly, there is not a single fiction book anywhere in sight. Only school books, but they are no fun to read. Crying at the kitchen table at night because your dad tried to explain the homework to you, typically math homework. Absolutely not.

Those school books are always present for any type of frustration or sadness, usually, they're the cause of them too.

I turn back to Matthew, who is still lying on his bed. Though, he did turn on his back so that he is facing us now. My eyes almost automatically fly to the small spot of his stomach, which is uncovered now, right where his shirt lifted just a tiny bit. Enough to uncover his smooth, slightly tan skin.

I feel a strong pulse going through my whole body. When I say my whole body, I mean it.

I don't know how long I've been looking at that incredible spot, but I force myself to look back up, hoping he hasn't caught me staring. When I look up though, it's not Matthew who's looking at me, but Patricia. Her eyes tell me she knows what I was thinking. Hell, she probably thought the same thing.

I take out my phone and type. When I hit send, both of them are staring at me.

I shrug and don't say anything. I just take out my homework, place them on the hardwood floor, and start to write.

The text was to Tess. Just a quick vent about that little slip-up, to get it off my mind.

I finish rewriting my psych notes, the primary goal I had for today, and wait another 20 minutes in silence. While I am waiting for the others, I pull out my book and literally sit in the corner of Matthew's room.

Matthew had moved from the bed to his desk about five minutes after we officially started working, and hasn't moved since. When I look up at him, he looks so concentrated, like he's fully emerged in his work. Patricia is sitting next to him at the desk. She pulled herself an extra chair from one of the other rooms, but I gladly stayed on the floor.

"Hey, Liam? You're done with your stuff, right? Can you come over real quick?"

Matthew has now turned around looking at me in expectation. I nod, stand up, and slowly walk over to the desk. Patricia takes the moment and gets up from her chair, making space for me, and says, "I'll get some water, you guys want?"

I shake my head but Matthew says, "Yeah sure, can you carry three glasses or do you want help?"

"Nah, I'll be fine. You stay focused. Three glasses of water coming right up." With that, she's out the door.

"What's up?" I ask when I settle beside him.

"I don't get this and you're like the smartest person I know, so I was hoping you could help me?"

My stomach drops into my legs and does a little cartwheel. I'm sure of it. I will need surgery to get that corrected. I swallow down the feeling and snap back into focus.

87

I look at the problem. Luckily it's French. Homework that I did two days ago.

He points at the problem he needs help with. Just some conjugation. I read the text and scan the word bank before deciding on an answer. It's technically pretty easy but I can see why he's unsure. I explain my whole thought process and hopefully clear up any confusion he has.

When I'm done I turn to him and he's already staring at me. My breath stops in my throat and I just stare back. His eyes struck me by surprise every damn time. They're so unique. Crystal clear, deep, breath-taking, and the most calming brown tone.

When I peek down, Matthew's hand is next to mine. I must have moved it too far by accident. He moves, his hand now covering mine, and says, "Thank you. You really are the smartest person I know."

Have I mentioned that my heart is two beats away from stopping altogether? It's beating so fast as if I had just run a marathon. I wouldn't be surprised if Matthew can hear it thumping against my chest.

I'm probably just reading this wrong. I must be.

There are multiple explanations for why he is doing this though.

The first one could be that he maybe had this tragic accident where his nerves were damaged and now he has involuntary muscle movements.

But no matter what, he's not moving.

A more likely explanation is that he did this out of reflex. The football guys all look very touchy with their constant hugging and jumping, so maybe this is standard for him.

Or, the most unlikely explanation could be that he did this on purpose. That he placed his hand on mine, on purpose. I don't know how to interpret that though. Is it a romantic move? Is it immense gratitude? Is it a sign that he's just a friendly person?

After a minute or so, I can't take it anymore. I brush off his hand, stand up, and excuse myself to the bathroom. Though, I have no clue where the bathroom is, so I just walk around until I can't feel the warmth of his hand anymore.

I stop and lean against the wall of what looks like a bedroom.

There is a bed and a closet door. This room is huge compared to Matthew's. The bed is made but there are a few clothes on the ground and not made nearly as neatly as the bed. This must be the room of his parents. Maybe they were in a hurry to pack their suitcase and that's why they left stuff just lying there.

I leave the room as quickly as I can without being too loud. I don't need Matthew to find out I've been in his parent's room. It would look like I was trying to steal or snoop around or something.

Back in his room I avoid eye contact and am surprised to see Patrica back with 3 nearly full glasses. Weird that I didn't see her on my walk.

going to stop me, as long as Liam seems to be okay with it, I would like to have more moments like that. Deducting the running away, I mean.

I'm unsure why he stands out so much. We barely know each other. But I really wat to find out.

I take off the suit and change back into my black sweatpants and an oversized hoodie. Great comfort comes from baggy clothes, and that's a fact. Nobody will ever convince me otherwise.

School has been exhausting recently. Not the assignments, homework, or study time. But to fight the constant urge to go over to Josh and just punch him in the face. Just once, but really hard. Because a guy like him deserves that. I know I'm not some ruling power over who deserves what, but I deeply believe he needs to be punched. It would ground his character a little. I like to think of myself as a pacifist because I avoid violence when I get the chance, but for Josh, I would definitely break that. Or any of the guys.

When I walked to the first period this morning, I saw how Josh and Manuel making a freshman give them all his money. Bullying as it's written in the books, yet the teachers don't do anything.

From what I could tell it was just a few coins, yet I want to smack both of them into their next hospital visit. The worst part was the look on that kid's face. He looked so unbothered like that is just part of his routine now. I wouldn't be surprised. Something went wrong with this school. Actually, not something but someone. The kid hasn't been in this school for more than three months and has already had enough of it, because of Josh and all the other guys.

I can't believe I used to be friends with those people, can't believe I used to just stand by and let them do stuff like that.

I confronted Josh during lunch, but neither he nor his buddies had any idea what I was talking about. How convenient. I don't even blame the others, only Josh. People like Connor, Manuel, and Tyler are social gold diggers. They befriend whomever they believe is most popular and use that person for social status. They don't want to be on that person's, Josh's, bad side so they do whatever is asked of them. Lie, steal, deal drugs, do drugs, harass people, and even become violent. It's a silent agreement within the group, to protect Josh at all costs, so I don't expect any of them to speak up.

But what do I really know? I mean first, I used to be part of their friend group, so I kind of thought like one of them. And secondly, it doesn't take a genius to look right through them. Lucky for them, Josh is anything but smart enough to figure this out himself. Evidently just showing that he hasn't for the past three years, at best.

Exhausted I get home not long after school ends and fish a letter out of my mailbox. I recognize the handwriting immediately. It's from my mom. She used to write a lot of letters right after they left. At least two in a week. But then it got less and less. From twice a week, to once a month. Maybe they moved further away and that's why they take longer to arrive, or maybe she just doesn't want to bother anymore.

First I was naive to think that the letters meant she still cared and would come back to get me. Deep down I knew they wouldn't, but I made it hard on myself to let that hope go.

93

They won't come back simply because they are afraid of the consequences. If they weren't criminals before, they became criminals the moment they left me. It's better this way for all of us. Who knows what they might do with me if they ever came back? They obviously don't care about me, so what would stop them from harming me even further?

Good thing they never had a good enough reason to get back.

I cringe at the thought of seeing them again. If they ever were to come back, I will call a lawyer. They left a bunch of numbers, at least two of those must be for lawyers. Of course, I can't use their own lawyer against them, but I can ask that lawyer if they have a friend who can help me out. However, I won't be able to pay them on my own, and in that scenario, my parents won't pay for their own lawsuit.

So, public attorney, it is. Would be.

I throw the envelope on the kitchen counter, somewhere in between lots of crumbled papers and a glass that's been sitting there for about three days. I should probably clean up sometime. I really, really, should. The problem is time. I can't be a full-time student and meanwhile manage a whole household. Usually, I clean up on the weekends, and it worked so far because it's never been this bad.

Determined, I bring my bag upstairs and turn on the sink, finally starting to wash some stuff.

My phone vibrates in my back pocket just as I am about to start scrubbing the glass. I take it out of my jeans and open the message. It's from Liam.

Hey, you're probably busy, but if you aren't, do you wanna come over?

And another one follows right after that.

Sorry if im disturbing, im just really bored.

I would have to clean up later if I go now. If I do it on the weekend, I would be following my routine which is way more comfortable anyway. So it's decided, I type back that I will be at his house in 20 minutes. I hurry to get upstairs and change into something I can leave the house with without looking like a depressed mess. My school clothes would work, but I don't want to give off the wrong vibe.

When I lock the door behind me, I'm wearing a sky-blue hoodie, gray sweatpants, and sneakers. I would have worn a T-shirt if I had called an Uber for myself. The walk itself is about two miles though. So no shirt this time.

My headphones die about halfway there, so I'm stuck with my thoughts again. I should have charged them right after school. Damn it. Will it just be Liam and I or will Patricia be there? His parents will probably be there, so I have to be on my nice behavior today.

I knock at the door as soon as I arrive, and to no surprise, Mr. Taylor opens the door.

"Hey, uh, Liam invited me. Hope that's okay?"

"Oh, yes right. Matthew was it?" His thick German accent catches me by surprise. Liam's accent is audible, but not that heavy. I would have thought his whole family would speak the way he does, but I was proven wrong.

I nod as I step inside, glancing behind Mr. Taylor just to notice Liam isn't there yet.

"He's upstairs. Can I offer you something to drink?" he asks enthusiastically. I shake my head. "No, thanks. Can I just go upstairs or do you want me to wait?"

"Go ahead, but shoes off."

I smile, because I know exactly how he thinks I operate. He thinks because I look like a normal teenage boy, I don't have manners or any care for respect, but he's wrong. Since I live alone and have to clean up alone, I wouldn't dare to get prints on the floor or carpet.

It just hit me how sad that would sound if I were to say that out loud, maybe old even.

Out of habit alone, I take off my sneakers and leave them at the front door, then walk my way up the stairs. The hallway is empty. Three of the four doors are closed and the fourth is only open for a small gap. I haven't been upstairs before so I just assume the one with the gap in it is Liam's. Not taking a chance, I knock, letting the gap widen.

Inside it's dark. The only light source is a dark blue LED strip around the room. In the middle of the darkness lies Liam. His bed is huge compared to mine, it's king-size. I wish I could afford to get one. Or be strong enough to single-handedly switch the mattress from my room and my parents' room.

His head is flat on the mattress with his headphones in. Liam doesn't look like he noticed me yet. Without waiting for him to look up and invite me in, I walk to the other side of the bed. It's fortunate for me that his eyes are closed, it makes this even easier than it could have been.

In one motion, I lay on the bed next to him. He finally opens his eyes, surprised by the extra weight next to him

He takes out his headphones and looks at me. "Hey," he says.

"Hi," I respond, too lazily to say much more.

I look at him as he shifts on the bed to face me. His eyes look black in this light. My skin begins to heat up and the tips of my fingers prickle. I don't want to look away, but I should before my heart explodes. My eyes wander from his eyes to his mouth. His thin lips look smooth but dry. I want to change that.

After a minute or so, he finally says, "You came."

"Yea, I did. You asked and I came."

Our voices are barely louder than a whisper. I should have at least put a shirt under my hoodie so that I could take it off, because of that rush of warmth that won't leave me alone.

"Did you want to talk about something or..?" My voice trails off because he shakes his head.

"Don't be mad, but I asked you over because I had really nothing else to do."

I'm speechless. *Maybe in a good way..? Should I be flattered?*

He continues, " But I wanted to see you either way." He opens his mouth to speak further, but he closes it again.

"Why?" is all I manage to breathe.

"Because I like you," he follows up with a short, "duh."

I laugh. Yes, I definitely should be flattered. All I want to do now is reach out to him and hug him and maybe never let go. He looks so incredibly hugable laying there. I just want to touch him, run my fingers through his hair, hold his face in my hands, and so much more. It's so tempting to just go for it, but after Liam ran out on me last time, I can't risk that again.

Another pulse of that desire rushes through my body, but I try to push it down, though his words aren't helping. Especially because those five words keep playing in my head. Over and over, like a loop.

Because I like you, duh.

He likes me!

I look at his eyes again, full of something I can't place. He looks sad, but excited. Disappointed, yet happy. Happy, but yet so scared.

I whisper, "Aww. I like you too."

Liam moves in closer to me. His body is merely 5 inches away. Another pulse of heat rushes through my nerves.

Fuck it.

When he rolls over once, closer to me, I lose it. I can't keep it down anymore. I lean in and land my lips on his. Short and sweet. He smiles and leans back in. Our lips meet for a second time. This time slower and with more meaning, in a rhythm I didn't know exists. My hand goes through his hair while the other cups grab his neck. Making sure to get even closer. If that's even possible. Doing everything I thought about in the past few minutes.

I can feel his hand lightly on my neck, giving me the best goosebumps of my entire life. I don't want them to end. I'll drop out of school and live in this bed, right here with him.

I have kissed someone before, my ex-girlfriend Chloe, at the end of eighth grade. It was ground-breaking to me at the moment. The perfect kiss with the perfect woman. I never thought it would get any better than that, but this experience just set up a new definition for the word "ground-breaking".

After Chloe broke up with me, I didn't think anyone else would meet my expectations and I didn't want to ruin my kissing experience by making out with the girls that approached me during the last two years. Not to sit on a high horse, because I'm sure the girls might have been great, but I just didn't want to risk it until I was ready.

That's why I never gave in on any girl in school. It sounds cliché, but some of Josh's girlfriends and other friends have tried to kiss me. Three to be exact. Each time I made up another fake excuse to not do what they were about to.

I have to get to class.

My dad will be home soon, I should go.

I actually have to study. Alone.

I'm more than glad to be proven wrong though.

Just as I thought this couldn't get any better, Liam turns on his back. He lets me take control over what's happening. Which would be great, if I knew what I was doing. With my eyes closed I do what any guy in a movie would do now. I pin his hands with mine behind his head. I lower myself down on him, still slightly hovering above his body. I can feel his body heat. It's comfortable, but I couldn't fully lay on him.

99

mad at us, I would be mad at you, you would be mad at I don't know who. And everything is going to be ruined."

Liam inhales deeply. I'm too stunned and still trying to process what he just said. Does that mean he doesn't want this to happen? Was it a mistake for me to kiss him? Did I just read the conversation wrong?

No, that can't be it. He kissed me back. That's a fact and there is nothing to overthink there. My face must look empty, because Liam says my name like it's a question. As if to check if I was still in my body.

I lift my head to look at him but instantly miss the comfortable spot I had moments before. I open my mouth to respond, but I can't. After a slow and shaky breath, I try again.

"So, uh, you — you don't want to continue this?"

He doesn't answer, which says more than enough. This obviously was a mistake. I should have known. I shouldn't have come here in the first place. I also knew this was a bad idea, but I did it anyway because he would have been worth it to me. But he didn't think the same thing about me.

"I'll go," is all I'm saying before I stand up and walk out his door. The last piece of hope within me dies when I don't hear him protest. As irrational as it may be, I was hoping he would scream my name, or run after me, or something. But that only happens in happy movies.

CHAPTER 14

Liam

I watch him leave my room, hear him walk down the stairs, and finally close the front door. I adjust my shorts and get up. I'm sweating because of what just happened. Yet, I don't know if the sweat is a sign of how great the kiss was, or is it because of how afraid I am of Matthew being mad at me for the rest of my life.

If it comes down to it, I know I can count on Patricia to stay on my side. I know she would… I hope. If she doesn't, I would still have Tess. I know I will always have Tess. No matter what. They once even told me that if I were to murder someone, they would help me cover it up. *What else are friends for?*

My body is cold at the places where Matthew was touching me, not even five minutes ago. I can still taste him on my lips. I can still smell him. And I miss that I can't touch him anymore. It obviously wasn't the best idea to say what I said right there and then. I meant everything I said, but it still wasn't the best moment.

Classic Liam, always ruining everything.

I could have at least waited to let him know about my concerns after we were done kissing. Guilt clenches itself in my chest and makes it hard to breathe. *What if I hurt him?* I know I didn't really hurt him, because for that to happen, he would have needed to have feelings for me. Which he obviously does not.

Even if I didn't hurt him much, I still feel like crap. I am crap, that's why I feel like crap. If someone were to describe me based on my actions, the word garbage-human would be mild. 'A waste of sperm' would be mild. Anything anyone can think of would be too mild. At this point in my life, I might as well kill someone. It would fit right in with my current pattern of life choices.

I used to be a good kid. I used to just sit there and be quiet. Did I ever talk to someone?

No.

Was it fun to just sit there and do nothing, whether I liked it or not?

Nope.

Was I happy?

Absolutely not.

Did I have a proper childhood?

Also no.

Did I deserve to not have a proper childhood?

Probably not either.

But did that at least keep me out of trouble?

A hundred percent.

So now that I have my own brain and make my own decisions, I mess everything up.

Go me!

Getting up from bed takes more energy than it usually does. And that says a lot. Usually, I am already exhausted as soon as I leave the comfort of my bed. But now, now it feels like I am ready for the reaper to pick up my soul, and spend the rest of eternity locked up, possibly tortured, in a cold cell in the firing pits of hell.

Awesome, that's the spirit to make things better!

I could just go after him, or call him. Or maybe just text him. But I meant what I said and I don't want him to think otherwise. As much as I might want this to happen again, it can't. Ever again. I probably won't even tell Patricia, otherwise what good does it do to avoid this from happening again? If she finds out, everything is going to be destroyed.

If it isn't already.

It feels weird, the next Monday in the cafeteria, talking to Patricia. Practically, lying to her.

"What did you do over the weekend? Why didn't you answer any of my texts? I thought you were dead! You can't do this to me!"

"Damn, no need to be that obsessed," is all I can manage. *I started making out with the third in our group and I want to do it again, but don't want to ruin our friendship. So instead, I ruined Matthew's and mine when I told him, all that wasn't a good idea,* stays unsaid.

If I don't talk at all, is that considered lying? Or is it just keeping important information to myself?

Either way, I don't like it. I actually hate it. I haven't told Tess either. *Yet.* It doesn't seem like the kind of thing I want to text them but rather tell them in person. But, of course, they don't have time to Facetime. Not yesterday evening, not today morning. They texted to call when school is over, so I'll see then. Tess is probably hanging out with their friends. My former friends, actually. But that was so long ago, they all wouldn't even recognize me.

Hell, I don't think I would recognize this version of me either, if I were myself from two years ago. Everything about me changed. Characteristics, looks, spirit, and everything else. I used to be outgoing and fun, but now I'm just the embodiment of a cliché depressed teenager. Physically, I grew taller, changed my hair at least 20 times in the past year, and all the silver-looking jewelry I can find. Two years ago, I wouldn't even have dreamed of it.

I wonder how my parents kept up. How they didn't just say *enough* and forbid me from doing much more. They haven't said it, but their expressions do. Every time I buy a new ring or dye my hair a new color, the looks on their faces shine with a sort of annoyance if not disgust. Probably not even annoyed with me, but with themselves, in each other. For not raising a "better" son.

I sometimes feel sorry for them. I know I shouldn't but I can't help it. It's better than to feel sorry for myself, after all.

"You usually answer texts within an hour. Respect by the way. If you don't answer and then can't give me a reason… It just feels off."

"So what?! I have to answer you every single time you send me a simple text? I have to always react a certain way, so that *you* feel comfortable? Why can't you just live with the fact that I want to have a weekend alone?" I yell, not caring for a second that people around us are starting to stare.

I suddenly notice the too-bright lights, the too-loud conversations around us, the tightness in my right shoe, and the nasty itchy feeling of fabric against my thigh. I want it all to stop. But I know it won't. I need to leave right now. I stand up, grabbing my backpack and ignoring the eyes on my back as I, almost literally, stomp through the aisle of tables. I look down at the floor, to avoid the lights above. The fabric at my thighs feels even worse now that I'm walking. I want to rip it off my skin. But I keep moving.

Out of the cafeteria. Away from the noise, away from the bright lights. The lights in the hall are dim, soothing to my eye. I get faster with every step until I'm almost running by the time I reach the doors of the school's side entrance. The cold air hits my face and I take a deep breath.

Looking at my phone, I realize there are still ten minutes until class starts. Which gives me five minutes out here to calm down. I lean against the cold stonewall of the west exit and let myself sink to the floor. This seems like the right moment to cry, but the tears don't come. Nothing does. It feels blackened. It feels like nothing.

Instead, the images flow through my head. The images of how I screamed at Patricia. Of the hurt in her eye. Of the look on Matthew's

107

face that night. Neither of us tried reaching out to the other. Not once. Not a simple *Hi! How are you?* Nothing.

The students passing in and out of the entrance don't give me a second look before continuing on their way, which is exactly what I wished for.

Still three minutes 'til I have to get back inside. Going into Calculus will be fun. Especially after being emotionally overwhelmed before 7 am in the morning.

My eyelids fall shut and my neck muscles fail to do their job, resulting in my head hanging in between my knees. My head is empty. No thought to be found. I'm fully lost in the depths of my mind when the sound, of someone sitting down next to me shakes me out of it. I lift my head the slightest bit but refuse to open my eyes. I'm sure I don't want to see or talk to anyone right now. Especially not Patricia or Matthew.

When they don't say anything, I give up on my mission to ignore them and open my eyes. Next to me sits Matthew. Expectfully looking at me he says, "Hey, whatcha doing out here?"

He must have noticed I'm not in the mood to answer because he continues a second later, "You know, I haven't stopped thinking about what happened last night. And I won't be able to stop thinking about it anytime soon. I don't want to."

A layer of sweat gathers in my palm with the fear of what he might say next. It would ruin things. The temptation of getting up from the hard cold stone and just leaving him behind looks more and more appealing with every second. But I know I can't do that without messing up the rest of the friendship we have left. I hate sacrifices for the sake of friendships.

"Yes, it will change the friendship we have right now, but it's for the better. Don't you think?"

Every muscle in my face is unwilling to move, so I just stare at him. My expression must be unbothered, but he isn't fazed by that. The noises around us get quieter as it's only one minute until school starts. I should already be back inside, or at least get up now and run as fast as I can to not be late. A few clueless kids wander outside with their earphones and music in, enjoying the cold air. I wish I could be that uncaring for school and the world.

"Just so you know, if it were up to me, we would be doing *that* again. A lot. It's not just up to me though, so if you want to bury this secret for the rest of eternity, so be it. Just please let me know what you decide, because I can't keep waiting for long. Anyway, I have to get to class and so should you. See you after school!"

When he is gone, so is the sweat in my palms. I'm stunned that he can just brush all of this off within a second. He is right, though. I take a few seconds to gather myself internally, stand up, and get back into the building.

Calculus isn't nearly as exciting as I thought it would be, even though being late was a first for me. I imagined something like the movies, which I can see now is a mistake on my part, again. We have 12 students in the class, two of them didn't come in, four of them are asleep,

109

and only three are actually paying attention. The other three, including me, are doing something completely off-topic.

I'm in the backseat with my laptop on my desk, pretending to be taking notes. As if I didn't already know most of this stuff. Besides, my grade in this class is surprisingly 98%. That should be respected given I rarely pay any attention.

Mr. Brunting is very much aware of the lack of discipline in his students but isn't going to do anything about it. We all know that if they fail, it's their own fault, and he doesn't get paid enough to educate us on anything more than what the district tells him. Which, personally, I think is kind of badass.

I never thought I would be describing a teacher as "badass". A lot of firsts this past seven days, I guess. First time calling a teacher a badass, first time kissing a guy, first time kissing a friend, first time running from the consequences of that kiss, and first time really regretting something I said.

I'm afraid of what could happen if I let myself listen to Matthew. I already hate how things are and it's not even been 24 hours since I kissed Matthew. I want to give in. I want to be able to kiss him even more. I want to be able to be there for him. I want him to be there for me, like he was just now. I want us to be able to meet up and make out on a bed, or anywhere really, without it being weird afterward.

Letting people in has never been my strength so who knows if I would even be able to do that with him. If I don't, but I do give in, who can say what it would do to Matthew? He would want to know more stuff about me. Some of which I'm not at all comfortable sharing with anyone. When I don't, he will get angry and disappointed. Over time even devastated. It would kill him to be my partner. I'm not doing that to him, or anyone.

It's old-fashioned, but I believe I will be alone for the rest of my life.

Everyone must have thought that at some point of their lives, but only a fraction really believe it's true. And only for another fraction, does the belief become reality. Either being part of those, or ending up working in an office and with kids at home, is my worst nightmare. Hot take, but I would rather be alone for the rest of my life than have kids and an office job.

The bell rings to dismiss the class and I leave the room without a look back. It's been two months since I enrolled in this school, and yet every day is the same. Every class is the same. Yes, we learn different materials, but the classes are still the same. Some care, some don't. Our teachers really don't, which makes class fair but boring.

Weeks passed by one by one. No comment from Matthew about anything. At least not to me. And not to Patricia, because otherwise, she would have blocked me out entirely. I guess Matthew really meant it when he said he wouldn't tell anyone if I didn't want that.

I want it to stay that way, although, all I can think about is the night it happened. The feeling of his lips pressed against mine, moving in that very enjoyable rhythm. The weight of his body against mine, the tingly feeling in my gut right before and after it happened. I have tried my best to forget about it, or at least not to think about it all day long. Obviously, I failed.

Matthew is still my friend after all. Every single time we meet after school or on our days off, his face reminds me. The depths of his eyes throw me right back to that evening. If I were to get lost inside his eyes, destined to never emerge again, I would thank the universe.

But I should not be thinking about this. It only makes it more difficult for me to ignore everything. It's pure desire and it won't stop. I should lock myself up in my room without internet access, to prevent myself from ever contacting Matthew again.

It's 7:36 pm on a random Friday and I'm sitting at my desk, alone. I'm typing the start to a new project. It's not even for school, which makes it even sadder. Or at least I should be typing and not thinking about Matthew. Again.

The project is something new. It's for a local writing contest of short stories. I saw it online this morning and thought that it would look great on a college application. So here I am writing, or trying to. I've written many short stories before, so this shouldn't be as difficult as it is. There's a major difference here, because no one ever read any of my texts, so I don't even know if they were any good. To my luck, it can be any genre we like and there are no restrictions on topics. I doubt that's true though. They can disqualify people if their story is offensive or threatening. Or at least I hope they can.

My first idea was to write a fantasy short story about a gay assassin. I wrote the first paragraph, read it over again, and deleted the whole thing because it was really bad. The second idea came to me during APUSH. A young and ordinary, bisexual adult dies and goes to hell, where he falls in love with the prince of hell, the son of Lucifer.

I wrote almost two-thousand words before I threw it into the corner of my mind. It was great, but I couldn't see myself writing a short story out of it, because there are so many details I want to add. Though, the maximum is ten-thousand words. I didn't delete the document in case I ever need to write a longer story for a competition.

At last, I decided to drop the fantasy and just leave the romance. My current draft consists of 200 words about a bully-to-lovers, high school romance. I have a month to get this finished and submitted.

I don't think I will even make it to the 10,000 words limit, because they are already falling out of character and getting too close too fast. But who knows? I still have that whole month.

My nerves are on fire when I think about winning this competition. I want to win so badly. Winning in the contest would really set me apart from a greater part of applicants. But for that to happen I need to write the best damn story in my damn life.

With my fingers on the keyboard, I finally let the world around me fade and start to type.

CHAPTER 15

Matthew

I don't get why he is avoiding me like this. I made it perfectly clear that I support any decision he would make. Yet he hasn't made any decision at all. I really wish he would just tell me what the hell is going on in that brain of his, wish he would just tell me it was a mistake and let my hope die.

False hope is never a good thing when it comes to relationships. It will just shatter my heart for wanting more than I could possibly have. Not something I particularly look forward to if I'm honest.

Of course, I understand why Liam would want to keep the kiss a secret, but if I had to choose between him or the friendship with Patricia, I would choose him. Wish I could say the same about him. Besides, maybe Patricia won't hate us. She might even be happy about it. Happy for Liam at least. Or both of us.

That's not to say that I don't value Patricia as a friend, but there will always be a barrier between us because she'll always choose him over me as well. Which is fair enough. But that also means we'll never really be *that* close.

The kiss was the best kiss I ever had. I made out with a couple of the girls in middle school and one in freshman year, but none were ever this great. Bad isn't what I would describe them with either, they were okay, good even, just different.

None ever made me want to get more, as much as he does. None would ever be able to live up to that.

Which is why I want more, why I need more.

Liam, however, has been taking every opportunity to avoid me. When we are in a group with Patricia, he wholly ignores me as if I weren't there. At first, I wanted to tell him how rude that is, but then I thought better of it. If he wants space, he'll get it.

I just don't know how long I can give him that, without going insane.

The old Matthew would now be out somewhere, at some person's house, who he never met before. Probably drinking that person's alcohol and partying around. But instead, I'm lying on my couch and scrolling through my phone. A quiet Friday evening, at my own house. I don't know when the last time that happened was.

Considering that I still have light means my parents paid the bills. *Yay.* They only missed a payment once, right in the first week of this year. It was great. No water, no light, no heat. Everything was great. It took them three days to get it back to work, but that was enough time to make me consider moving out and living under a bridge or something.

115

At least then I wouldn't be so dependent. They have food and showers in school, so I could show up an hour before class starts and take my time to shower. All of that wouldn't be a problem. One meal a day would not be so great, but it would carry me through the day.

But then I thought that this house would be empty otherwise. That would be such a waste, wouldn't it? I would enjoy knowing my parents still pay the bills even after I left, though. My 17th birthday is coming up in two weeks and I doubt that they will make any effort to "congratulate" me.

I turn on the TV and put my phone back in my pocket. Yet my thoughts overtone the voices of the TV. My neck muscles fail me as I close my eyes and let my head fall back onto a pillow. Even with the TV on, it's quiet in this house. I thought I would get used to that silence after a while, but that never happened.

It could have been an hour or just a minute when the vibration of my phone wakes me. Sitting up, I pull it out from my pocket to see a notification pop up. It's from Liam. I look at the time and realize I napped for 40 minutes. When I get up from the coach, I grab the remote and turn off the TV. I unlock my phone and read Liam's message while going up the stairs.

My phone is the only source of light in the hallway, so I use to shine the way. The thundering of my heart is like a heavy weight on my chest. I open the door to my room and let myself fall onto my bed.

Turning the phone to face me I finally read his message.

Can we talk?

The weight on my chest just got even heavier, but I don't hesitate to reply.

Of course. When?

It takes him a good minute to respond. The bubbles on the bottom of my screen appear, then fade. It feels like my nerves are on fire. *Where did he get the audacity to leave someone waiting on a message like that?!* Fear ripples through every fiber of my body. What if he is finally ready to tell me to leave him alone for good? Or maybe he just wants help with homework.

That's definitely more reasonable than the first thing. Okay who am I kidding, Liam is an academic genius, he doesn't need my help with homework. But what if it really is about the *situation*? I'm not ready to give up Liam, and Patricia of course.

Now?

I stare at his reply for a second before I type back.

What do you mean now? Like now-now?

This time he doesn't hesitate.

Yes. I'm outside. Are you even at home?

I lock my phone, get out of bed, and practically run to the door. Before I open it, I take one last look in the mirror, hoping not to look like a goblin. In hopes of fixing my hair, I run a shaky hand through it. It's hard to see if anyone is actually outside, so I switch the light switch for the light in front of the door.

I grab the handle and pull it open. There he stands. Liam. At my front door.

117

A smile makes its way up my face when I say, "Hey, didn't expect you to actually be here. Come in."

He steps inside.

"You know the drill, shoes off, coat on the hanger." He does as instructed. I walk through the narrow hallway into the living room, where a dim light fills the room. The muddled blanket from earlier is still lying on the sofa as if I just stood up from there. The glowing lamp was enough before, for one person watching TV, but not for two people having a conversation. Before Liam emerged from the hallway I flip the switch for the overhead light.

When I turn back, facing the room, Liam stands there waiting for something. Waiting for *me*, I realize quickly. I make a gesture for him to sit down, which I'm glad he does.

"Can I get you anything to drink?" I ask. By the way, I ask, I feel like I'm having a proper adult, invitation-only party. Liam shakes his head but I walk to the kitchen regardless.

I return with a glass of water in hand, finding Liam to be standing again. Not standing, but rather pacing around the room. I put the glass on the nearest cabinet and walk towards him. With a creak in the floorboard, he turns to face me. My breath feels like it's stuck somewhere in my throat. Unable to take a proper breath, I wait for him to say something. Anything would be just fine, or at least better than the constant dread of silence we got going on here.

My heart is going to explode when I think of this moment in the future to come, no matter the outcome. The fact that Liam just stood outside my house to talk to me, in the middle of the night, would be movie worthy by itself.

I write down a mental note, reminding myself to ask about Tess' suspension. By now, they must be back in school otherwise I might just suggest Tess and her parents sue the school. Although, that might not do much good. After all, the court might not be better than Mr. Sauer when it comes to fairly solving problems.

Liam, who still hasn't moved, takes a deep breath and finally says, "Okay, so, I know it's not fair for me to make you shut up about what happened. You should be able to tell anyone you want to. And I get how selfish I have been for being scared of you telling people, specifically about me. I've obviously thought about it and I realized I don't actually care if people know that I'm gay. With that said, I obviously also don't want things to change with Patricia. As I'm sure you have gathered by now, she is my only friend here."

He took another long breath. This one is more shaky than before.

"But if she is angry about it, then she can just leave. I've been without friends for the past eight years, so I can handle going back to that. However, I think I like you. Like really like you, in a way I have never liked anyone else. Everything I think about is you. Gosh, sorry, that's creepy. Anyway, my point is that I like you and that I want to kiss you again."

My jaw hangs wide open. Liam sees the obvious shock on my face and goes on.

"Of course, you don't have to respond right now, or ever really," Liam forces a laugh. I was so wrong before, apparently, he does know what he wants.

There is a single tear rolling down Liam's cheek, but he doesn't turn or walk away. Not so quickly, I realize that he is waiting for me to say something. Instead of saying anything at all, I step closer, and closer. Eventually, my face, and my lips, are an inch away from his. I don't want to make him kiss me, just because I leaned in. But Liam doesn't pull away as he had the chance to but he does the opposite.

I shut my eyes and feel his lips against mine. *God, I missed this.* I take in everything at once. The light pressure and rhythmic movement on my lips. The little jump as my pulse increases, the almost instant urge to feel him. My hands now reach out to his body. His chest is warm against my hand. I want to be consumed by it. Liam pulls away first, and almost whispers, "Before we continue, I would prefer to ask you a question first. If that's okay."

I nod, anticipating his question. "Actually, it's a couple of them. So uhh, what exactly does this make us? A couple of platonic friends who make out from time to time? Or boyfriends? Or something in between? And who are we going to tell about it? Are we telling people about it? And please don't even try to give me one of those bullshit vague answers like *Whatever you want*. Thank you."

Oh.

OH.

I haven't even thought about that yet.

I don't think too hard before I sigh. Overdramatically sucking air into my lungs to create support for the cinematic effect has always been an underappreciated favorite of mine.

"I think I would be offended if you were to go around and tell people that we are, quote on quote, a couple of platonic friends who make out from time to time. I can't tell you what we should do though, only what I want us to do. I want you to be my boyfriend because I really-really like you. In case that message wasn't clear already."

There. I said it. There's no taking it back now.

I close my eyes with the intention to never open them up again, to just stop existing. What I just said is true, I want us to be boyfriends, but what if he doesn't feel the same? Waiting for a response, I open my eyes again. The dim light doesn't do much to hide Liam's openly shocked mouth. He's just looking at me with his jaw practically on the floor. Chills and sweat run down my back when he steps closer. Even closer.

I register the warm feeling of his hand on my neck first. Then his lips brush against mine. Soft, as if he were afraid of spooking me away. I close my eyes again, but this time to concentrate all my energy on remembering this exact moment. The exact feeling of my hand brushing through Liam's hair. The pressure of his hand on my back, pulling me into him. I want to remember it all.

Liam stops moving which I take as a sign to pull away, but his hands have other plans.

We just stay like this for at least twenty minutes and by the time I stop kissing him, my lips are sore. My forehead stays leaned against his and I can feel him smile into me. The warmth of his breath makes me want to lean in again, but that's probably not the most productive thing we could be doing.

It takes more willpower than I am willing to admit, to release my hands and pull away from him. I look into his eyes, for real this time. Something in them has changed, there is something in them that wasn't there before. Something good.

CHAPTER 16

Liam

Today might have been the best day of my life. The dream I didn't know I had came to life. I kissed Matthew. Matthew kissed me. And this time nobody ran away. I'm standing in the spot where it happened not even two minutes ago. Even if I wanted to move, my legs would give out after about three steps.

"It's dark out. Do you have someone who can pick you up?" Matthew asks when he looks out the window. He's right. We must have spent more time here than I thought we did.

"Nope, but it's okay. I'll just walk. It's not that far."

Matthew turns to face me.

"No. It's too dangerous. You can't walk home alone, in the middle of the night. You could get kidnapped or murdered or who knows what."

Chills run down my spine because nobody has ever been this concerned about me walking home.

"Seriously, it's fine. I often walk home, even in the dark. And as you can see, I'm still alive and not kidnapped, so there's no point in getting worried about this," I reply but Matthew doesn't look convinced.

"Well, you won't walk home today, then."

I breathe out a short laugh, "Honestly, you are getting way too worked up about this. I'll be home within 20 minutes."

I take a steady step, then another, and start walking toward the front door. Matthew grabs my wrist when I'm about to walk past. I stop and turn to face him.

"Please. If you're not going to get picked up by someone, in a car, you can stay here overnight," he says, but the rest of the words fade away. My throat closes up at the thought of staying here, in Matthew's house, the whole night. If I were to stay I would do something really stupid, embarrassing, and/or unforgettably humiliating right in front of him and he will never want to see me again. So that's also not an option.

Blinking myself back into reality, I look at Matthew's eyes and swallow.

"I'm sorry, what did you say? I just blacked out," I say, as if hearing all this again would make a difference.

"I was just suggesting that you can stay the night. I have an extra toothbrush and you can borrow my clothes if you want. Then you can walk home tomorrow when there's actual sunlight."

I swallow once more. Matthew invited me to stay overnight. It's not like I don't want to, but I have never done this before. There are just too many possible scenarios in which I wouldn't know how to act. Would I be sleeping in one room with Matthew or in a separate room? Should I assume that I sleep in his room? How long would we be staying up? Would I have to say 'good night' and all that? What if his parents come home and find a random guy sleeping in one of their rooms?

He looks at me with helpful eyes, to which I apparently can't say no. I sight and nod.

"Sure. I mean what could go wrong?" I laugh to hide the uncertainty in my voice.

Every cell in my body feels uncomfortable. I'm going to be sleeping in the room across from Matthew's, the guest room. In a house that technically belongs to strangers since I haven't even met his parents yet.

"Are you sure your parents are okay with me staying over while they're gone?" I ask, but he just shrugs me off. After showing me the bathroom he gives me a spare toothbrush and toothpaste which I just put on the cabinet of the guest room for now.

I haven't said many words besides the occasional thank you, but when Matthew leaves the room I take the chance to text my parents that I won't be coming home tonight and to call Tess. They probably won't be helping me at all, because the best thing for me right now would be to calm down, which Tess naturally is not capable of doing.

"Tess!!! I'm going to cry!!"

"Hello to you too," they say sarcastically, "the good or bad kind of crying?"

125

Switching to German I start filling them in, "Not sure yet. Matthew invited me to stay over. Not only that, he insisted because it's dark out already. I did not prepare for this at all. Like, how am I supposed to sleep if a guy I made out with 30 minutes ago is lying right next door?"

I tell them about everything that happened leading to this moment.

"Li, relax. Maybe he just doesn't want to feel guilty if you really would be found dead the next morning. But maybe he wants you to stay because he likes having you around. Maybe he wants things to go further than just kissing if you know what I mean."

"Actually, I do not know what you mean. So, please elaborate. And tell me what the heck I am supposed to do!"

"Okay maybe, just maybe, he wants to get a piece of you-" Tess can't continue as I cut them off with my really dramatic gasp.

"Like sex? No. No. He wouldn't want to do that. Right? I mean we are young and have barely even had a conversation after the making out part. And even if he wanted to have sex with someone, why me? I mean have you seen me?" My voice is barely a whisper now, hoping Matthew doesn't overhear any of this.

Silence. "Liam. RELAX. There's literally nothing to worry about. If you don't want to do what he wants to do, you can say no and/or set his house on fire. Which of those is more appropriate, depends on his reaction."

"Very helpful, thanks," I say sarcastically before hanging up. Their so-called advice won't do me any good and neither will screaming at them.

A message pops up on my screen. I half expect it to be Tess being mad about me hanging up without even saying bye, but it's my mom.

Alright! Let us know if you need anything. Love you!

I think it's funny that Mom tells me to let her know if I need anything, but if I actually were to need something, she would rather burst into flames than leave whatever comfortable spot she's is right now. And what if I would have been kidnapped and the kidnapper wrote the message to my mom? She didn't even ask where I am or when I'm planning to get back tomorrow, not that I have an answer to the latter.

I pop my head out the door into the empty hallway. For an instant, I think Matthew might have already gone to bed, but then I hear noises coming from downstairs. With my phone back in the pocket of my jeans, I walk downstairs. Matthew is standing there in front of the stove, the smell of it hits my nose faster than my brain would have figured it out. Matthew is making eggs, scrambled I assume because he moves his spatula like his life depends on it.

I sort of freeze because my mind goes off again, imagines popping into my head of a future I'll never get. A future I haven't deserved yet, and probably will never deserve. One of these images is similar to the situation painted out, in front of me. I'm watching a guy, who I just know is my partner, stand at the stove, cooking something for us, and I'm just watching him, admiring almost.

I don't know why I sometimes even bother thinking about these things. Thinking about the future is useless, especially if it involves someone other than myself. I might move again in less than a year and won't ever see Matthew again, or stay anywhere long enough to really start anything with anyone at all. I will never figure out why I keep imagining all these things.

Sometimes I don't know why I do anything, ever.

"You hungry? I'm making eggs, as you can probably see. I made a lot because I didn't know how much you wanted. But if you aren't hungry that's fine, no pressure."

I only stand there, still frozen as his voice rips me out of my own imagination.

The only sounds during our meal are the occasional clattering of forks against plates. I keep my head down as much as I can with the goal to forget that someone, a whole ass boy, is sitting right in front of me, at the same table, eating with me.

When I'm done I stand up and bring my plate to the sink in the kitchen. Grabbing the utensil in the sink, I start washing my plate. Manners and stuff.

Once that's done I sit on the floor and lean back against the wall, waiting for Matthew to finish up. My first instinct was to go back to my room and not come out until tomorrow morning, but rapidly decided against that. If Tess was right about one thing, then that this whole night is more of an opportunity than anything else.

My heartbeat doesn't make it easy for me to just sit and relax. Although, neither do my eyes. They keep staring right at Matthew, still sitting, eating, and occasionally scrolling on his phone, which brings me to notice so many small things, and with that encouraging myself to keep staring. Like his veins slightly being visible through his arms, the one-sided dimple on the right cheek, and the unevenness of his eyebrows. And now my brain does this thing where it will keep thinking about these details for no reason whatsoever.

It's not like I'm in love with him or anything.

It just gets in the way when I'm actually trying to be productive, or do anything else really.

Matthew is still busy with the tenth chore of the evening, which is unloading the dishwasher when his voice fills the room.

"So what do you want to do tonight? We could watch a movie or play games or something if you want? It's fine if you want to sleep though. I don't want to keep you up."

I haven't thought about that yet, but I do know that sleeping isn't in the cards for me tonight. Even if we don't talk all night, I wouldn't be able to get my brain to shut up and let me sleep.

About twenty minutes later, it's 9:32 pm and we are upstairs. Matthew insisted on giving me a pair of his extra pajamas because he says sleeping in jeans is a crime against humanity. I wait in the hallway because Matthew is also changing into his pajamas inside the bathroom.

He emerges wearing an oversized t-shirt with, whom I assume to be, his favorite superhero and a red-black checked pajama bottom. The

129

boy has never screamed more American than at this moment. Although, the combo really does make him look more handsome. His dirty blond hair illuminates in the light, making it look as fluffy as a stuffed animal.

"I've left your pants in there. And a shirt if you want to change that too. It might be a bit large but I hope that's not too big of a problem. Warm water in the shower is on the handle on the right, but I think you can manage."

I nod my thanks and step past him into the bathroom.

"Oh and," I turn my head to look over my shoulder.

"Sorry, last thing I promise. Towels are on that shelf right there." He points at a shelf above three silver hooks on an otherwise empty wall. The shelf is made of white oak, fitting to the rest of the room. The sink and bathtub are made of white ceramic. The white wall only adds to the vibe. The sorry excuse of a bathtub doesn't surprise me anymore, because our house had a similar one.

I step inside and close the door behind me.

Then I just stand there for a while before I turn on the water and take one of the longest showers I have had in a while.

Before I even put on the pajama pants Matthew left me, I realize what he did. He left the same pants he was wearing. Same colors, same square pattern. At least the T-shirt looks different, not that I have anything about his hero.

It's 10:47 pm when I find Matthew downstairs, lying on the couch in the living room. He is reading a book, but I can't make out the title before he puts it down and looks up at me.

"Considering you just spent over an hour in the bathroom, I'm assuming you enjoyed your shower?" It sounds more like a question than a statement.

I nod and say, "Sorry, I kind of lost the time in there. Didn't mean to use that much water."

"No no, I'm glad, because I was hoping we could talk about, you know, everything?"

I walk down the remaining steps and sit on the other end of the couch, barely an arm's length away from Matthews's legs. I turn to find him still looking at me. His eyes almost shine in this light which makes my stomach feel weird. Not yet sure if that's good or not.

"I was hoping the same thing, to be honest. We kissed not even three hours ago. And like I said, I really like you so I hope that makes things clear. Also, before we get too deep into this, I want to say thank you for letting me use your shower and borrow your clothes." I exhale deeply, then try to smile up at him. As if my nerves aren't actually pulsing, waiting to explode out of my own skin.

"Of course," he says gently. When he smiles back I can see his dimple.

It makes him even more perfect than he was before.

I might just simply pass away because of heart failure if I'm honest. The most perfect person on the freaking planet is looking at me, in a way nobody has ever looked at me before. I know it sounds crazy, but *damn.*

131

I swallow, anticipating what comes next. To prepare myself for what may or may not happen, I think of the worst possible scenario. Of course.

"So I was thinking we should probably stop seeing each other altogether because I can finally see how disgusting of a person you are. I don't want to be your friend. I don't want to be your hook-up partner. I don't want to be your boyfriend. I don't even want help in French anymore because I'd rather fail the class than spend any more time with you!"

Instead of letting the fear take over my body, I smile up at him again. Or at least I try to.

Matthew turns his head, then looks at me again, his eyes wider than before.

Oh god. That can't be good.

My breath catches in my lungs as Matthew says, "I actually wanted to ask you if we can be together. As in, more than just friends or hook-up buddies or whatever that was. I mean like an actual relationship? If that is okay with you?" It's like his voice jumps up an octave in the last sentence.

His body is relaxed as ever, but I can see the slight blush on his cheeks and neck. I exhale, thinking about how I answer this. Of course, I want to be his boyfriend, that's not even a question, but I just still can't believe he asked me this.

I start laughing uncontrollably. The sound of my voice is the only thing filling this house. Matthew's smile disappears as if I said no.

Two minutes passed and I still haven't stopped laughing. My cheeks hurt but I can't bring myself over the irony of this entire situation.

"You know, you could just answer something that is actual words. As much as I enjoy your laugh, I'm kind of dying on the inside until you give me a reply." He exclaims, looking at me expectfully.

I inhale deep and long, trying very hard not to start laughing again. Once I have that covered I say, "I'm sorry. But I just think it's funny because I was so sure you wouldn't be into me, at least not for longer than making out. No offense. And I guess I just assumed I would be the one asking you if you want to be my boyfriend. Yet here we are."

"So is that a yes?"

Rolling my eyes overdramatically, I say "I thought that was self-explanatory after what I just said, but yes."

I feel awkward after saying that, not because of the content though. I know it's because of the way I pronounce things. The difficulty with words like 'this', 'though','through', and basically any other word with a 'th' sound, has plagued me ever since speaking English. I know I shouldn't be ashamed, but I can't help it. Accents sound cool in almost every other language, but not German. It's just embarrassing and uncomfortable. But I force myself to not think about my accent, but rather about the beauty of this very moment.

My cheeks still ache but my mouth turns into a wide smile. I can't even remember the last time I laughed and smiled this hard.

133

Matthew settles down next to me, reaches one arm behind my head, and pushes his lips on mine. I close my eyes as my lips touch his. His lips are soft and warm as if I could sink into them and never leave.

To my disappointment, he breaks the kiss first and I pull away. He holds my hand as he sits up and wordlessly guides me back on the couch, he lies down all the way, only this time I lie down with him.

Please don't let this be a dream.

CHAPTER 17

Matthew

Liam is still lying on me when I awake. It must already be after 8 am because the kitchen is lit by sunlight.

He looks so peaceful and I don't want to wake him, but I can't feel my legs and have to get up and move them.

Yesterday's events circle back to me. The most important one hitting first and fastest. He is my boyfriend. I am his boyfriend. We are together, actually together. Which is why I can't wake him up. Good boyfriends don't do that.

If the circulation to my leg is completely cut off and they have to be amputated, then that's a problem for later.

His breath and his body are calm and relaxed, maybe the most relaxed I have ever seen. Getting him to loosen up even the tiniest bit is complex, but I always suspected that he's never fully calm. His shoulders are always tense, his back always straight, and his mental shields always up. As if he's afraid of moving a certain way or sharing a personal secret.

If the latter is true, then I get it, but if it's not it would have to mean that he doesn't feel safe enough to talk freely around other people, including me.

But what do I know? I'm just overcomplicating things probably, besides, assuming stuff like this about other people never works out.

It's been at least two hours and this boy, MY BOYFRIEND, still hasn't woken up. And I'm certain that I will have to get new legs by the time he wakes up. Not only that though. About, what feels like, 20 minutes ago, I started to feel the urge to go to the bathroom. The universe is really trying to test my abilities on being a boyfriend. I will not wake him up.

I closed my eyes a couple of times now, but I just can't fall back asleep. Gathering the confidence to move something other than my eyes, has not been part of today's accomplishments so far. I lift my right arm, from in between the couch cushions, to Liam's back. Gently, I lay my hand on his back and start moving in slow circles, listening to every breath he takes.

His shirt, which he borrowed from me, is moving along with my hand. It has not been a minute before he huffs a short and low moan. Which means he is awake, physically at least. I do my best not to be too sudden when I whisper, "Morning Li. I am sorry for waking you, but it's almost noon so we should really get up and be productive or something."

The only response I get is another huff.

"Look, it's fine if you want to sleep but can I at least get up first, my legs are dying."

Liam doesn't respond, instead, he rolls to the side, off of me, and into the crease of pillows.

I stand up from below him, my legs aching even more than after practice. Instead of walking right away, I turn slightly, to see Liam with his eyes closed lying on my couch with an oversized t-shirt and pants. His hair is all messy and every muscle in his body is calm. It is the most adorable thing I have ever seen with my own two eyes. Almost makes me want to ignore the pain and lie back down.

Something about knowing that he feels comfortable enough to wear my shirt and pants is making my heart warm up.

After way too long to be healthy, I walk away, doing my best to ignore the ache in the first few steps.

My first stop is the bathroom, then 20 minutes and a warm shower later, I'm in the kitchen. Making food has always been part of my routine at least once every single day, so making breakfast is basically just muscle memory.

When I'm done I bring two full plates of scrambled egg with a few strips of fried bacon into the living room. Liam is, of course, not bothered by any sounds and just continues lying there with his eyes closed. I walk back into the kitchen, grab two forks, two knives, and two glasses of water. When I'm back Liam is already sitting up completely, as if he'd been awake this whole time.

"Morning! Look who's awake."

Liam yawns, blinks twice, and says, "Morning. You made food."

"Seems like it, doesn't it? I thought I would wake you with something nice."

"Aww! You didn't have to do that. But thanks," he says, glancing down.

I sit myself down in an armchair to the right of where Liam is sitting on the couch. I wait for him to fully wake up before he starts eating before I dig into it too.

About an hour later we both finished our food and I stacked the dishes in the sink, leaving them for the evening. Which I know I will regret later, but at this point it's routine.

As I walk back into the living room I ask, "So what do you want to do now? Go home or just rest on my couch for the rest of eternity?"

He frowns, "Actually this is a really comfortable place, so if the offer stands I'll stay until I die. Thank you very much."

"Ha! Ha! Did you ask your parents to pick you up yet?"

He shakes his head but I'm not sure if what I feel is disappointment, because it's supposed to be right? Liam should go home and change into his clothes and eat his food because he doesn't live with me. And I shouldn't enjoy sharing all my stuff with him as if that's the entirety of my life's purpose.

Though, I'm obviously just trying to be a nice boyfriend.

BECAUSE WE ARE FREAKING TOGETHER NOW!!

"I can walk you back if you'd prefer that," I say. A careful way of testing the waters, because I don't want to be too clingy, but if he's okay with me walking him home, then it should be fine. Totally fine.

"Nah, that's okay. How about I'll stay for a bit longer and then worry about the rest later."

His lips go up into his adorable smile which enlights something in my chest. It's strange to have this feeling. It physically aches, but somehow I don't want it to disappear. Yet there's this slight sting behind the ache, a reminder that maybe he doesn't want to spend any more time with me after all.

Hopefully, that's not true. Otherwise, he wouldn't want to stay any longer.

I have a game this evening, which I haven't told him about, so he will have to leave sooner or later. Can't let Coach down, or my future.

Football may be the only way into college for me, with a full ride or something just as good. I can leave the house and won't have to be dependent on my parents who basically left me to die. Sounds really cliché now that I think about it. Senior football player with no hope for the future except the sport. Doing everything he can to stand out and impress colleges. With a dad, if this were a movie, who is so proud and probably the only reason why he still plays. Good thing that this isn't a movie.

I could quit football at any given moment, and just go to community college and get a decent job to not starve. My grades are okay enough for that. But I'm not sure if that's okay enough for me. Without a scholarship, I'd have to go into debt for the next 30 years of my life. So that's a hard pass.

About an hour later, Liam finished his food and now comes back down the stairs after changing into another shirt I let him borrow. It does look way better on him than it does on me. On him, it's a baggy dark red shirt with a stitch of a gray baby elephant right above his heart. On me the red looks way too rusty and it's not nearly as baggy. Although it's technically not supposed to be worn this loose, it does wonders for Liam.

"Wow," I laugh, "Look at you, looking better in my clothes than I do"

"Of course I do," he says rolling his eyes, "but maybe you just need to get new clothes. I mean, some that look better on you than on anyone else."

I blink. Don't I have those already?

I blink again. "What… What exactly do you mean by that?"

He drops in the chair right in front of me, and elaborates, "I didn't mean to be rude. It's just… how do I say this? I've never seen you wear anything that makes you look like you feel like the *baddest bitch* in the world. Correct me if maybe I just haven't seen that look on you, but I think everyone should have something."

I never even considered that and now that I think about it, 90 percent of the clothes I own are very similar to one another. Hoodies and jeans in different colors, a few T-shirts with silly designs on them, and socks in exactly three shades. That's about all I can think about before Liam goes on.

"We should go shopping for some clothes for you. No pressure of course. But you could try to see what clothes you like, hate, and which ones make you feel like the baddest bitch in the world." I can tell he's excited to do this so who am I to say no? Besides, he's right, maybe a bit forward about it, but he's right.

"Fine, but not tonight. I have a game so it'd be too late."

Liam uncrosses his legs and stands up to look at me.

"Ooh, that's fun, right? Can I come?"

"I mean, I guess, but you totally don't have to. I can tell football isn't really your thing."

He gasps, way too dramatically. "What gave you that impression? Okay, you're not wrong. But since I'm officially dating the hottest guy on the team, I can adapt for it to be my thing."

"Please. For one, you don't even know how it works. And secondly-"

"I'm a fast learner, so not a problem." He steps closer, still smiling enthusiastically. I don't know if this is weird to think about, but his teeth are really beautiful. Slightly crooked, but also unique.

"And secondly, I wouldn't call myself the hottest player on the team. Have you seen Dylan?! Phew, what a smoke show.."

We're looking into each other's eyes for no longer than ten seconds before breaking down laughing, again.

"Okay, okay. You're right though. Dylan is gorgeous, such a tragedy that he's straight."

My shoulders go up and down in one swift motion. "Meh, his personality ruins him though. I can totally see him being the kind of person who, as a kid, would blow out a candle, on your cake."

Not a lie. Dylan is definitely a piece of work.

141

"Believable. But you still haven't really answered my question. Can I come to the game? Because that didn't really sound like you wanted me to be there. I can just not go if you want me to, not a problem."

"Honestly, I'm good with either so you can surprise me with your choice," I say, backing away. "Either way, I think you should go now because if you stay any longer, I won't be ready in time."

"Alright, fair. I'll see you tonight, or not. Who knows?" Liam chuckles and walks back upstairs. Not even 15 minutes later, he stands before my door and puts his shoes back on. We stand in silence for about three minutes before a car parks outside. I doubt Liam would have told me anything more anyway.

"Bye," I wave as he exists.

"Tschau, text me after the game in case I don't show up."

I nod, and with that, the door closes behind him.

CHAPTER 18

Liam

Of course, I was going to show. Sure, I'll hate it, but… sacrifices have to be made. *Why am I such a cliché?*

My dad picked me up from Matthew's place, which meant that the car ride consisted of my dad asking two basic questions, "How are you?" and "Did you have fun?", and the rest was silent phone time.

I haven't reported back to Tess after yesterday evening, which meant I had a lot to tell them. Though I couldn't just text all that, so instead I go with a simple: You have about 10 more minutes to get ready before I am home and will call you. I have news!!!!!

Mom isn't home when we arrive, so I just walk straight upstairs and into my room. With no further warning, I click on the call button and the ringing begins. One ring. Second ring. Third ring.

"Heeeey, give me one minute to go to my room and we can start." Tess' way too familiar face pops on my screen, background moving in the also familiar house of the Forbes. Though one thing is different. About halfway down her braids, the natural brown fades into a radiant red. I hear a click and see Tess drop dead like a stone onto their bed. The sign for me to start.

"Okay so, first up, you dyed your hair! It's gorgeous. Second, this will take a while, and I don't want to be rude, so I will ask you now: How are you? Any news? Do tell or hold your peace until I'm done."

"Thank you for noticing, I wanted a dark green, but the lady said it would take a while because it's a longer process, so I went with this red instead. And nope, nothing that can't wait. Let's go."

It takes me over an hour to explain the whole night in as much detail as I possibly could. I've been talking in a mix between German and English, usually known as Denglish, which didn't save me any time whatsoever because every two minutes I had to stop and think of a specific word in either language. Spoiler alert, I usually just skipped over it because I wouldn't remember anyway.

This is what we do. Tess and I have always done it this way. We greet each other, then spill our news, then react to the news, and then move on to a normal conversation.

I finish my vivid description with a sight and say, "You know, I miss the older times, when one of us could simply walk over to the other's house and we would stay up all night, instead of having to do this in a stupid call."

"Firstly, me too, duh," I see them roll their eyes, "and I don't even know what to say. I'm happy for you of course. I mean, it took you a hot minute to find someone like him. No offense. But at the same time,

I feel obligated to tell you to be careful. If he hurts you, I will run over the stupid ocean and take a sharp swing at him.”

I inhale sharply, “Tess, I thought we’ve been over this? You can’t just hit people who have hurt you, or someone you care about.”

“Yeah, yeah. Fine. But I mean it.”

I stand up from my bed and walk toward my closet. Tess doesn’t say anything else for a while, and neither do I because I'm too occupied with trying to find an outfit that I can wear to the game. On top of that, I have to leave in a little more than an hour, or else I’ll be late.

“Okay… Tess… I need your help right now. What do I wear to the football game? You know that I don’t own anything remotely sporty or anything that screams ‘Supportive-Boyfrined-of-a-Player’. HELP!”

Tess immediately snaps back at that, “Okay so, you know that I don’t have a clue either, but show me the options and I’ll help you decide which one is the least horrific”

I hold into the camera what I believe to be outfit number one, a red-black checkered flannel, black jeans, and a three-part chain for the jeans.

“Okay,” Tess acknowledges this in a monotone voice, “It’s a little basic. It’s a safe outfit though, it fits any occasion and none of the kids at the school would judge. If you can’t find something better, you’ll go with this. Next.”

It takes me a good few seconds to come up with an alternative. For my second option, I chose light blue jeans, a jean jacket in the same color and some tiny but sparkly earrings.

"No," they reject immediately.

Feedback can be a tough aspect of life. I know I asked Tess to do this, and I knew what I was getting myself into, but it's frustrating to be unable to get a decent outfit together right this moment.

Four outfits and 27 minutes later, we both collectively agree to go with the first one. I tell Tess that I love them and that I have to go because I still need to shower. There are 24 minutes left for me to shower, put on the outfit, and drive to school. The game starts at four, but it won't matter if I get there a little bit late. I hope.

It's so loud. Unexpectedly loud. The bleachers are full of people, with hardly any space to move around. Most people on both sides are screaming and cheering, following everything that's happening on the field.

I find myself at the bottom row of the bleacher furthest to the left, leaning against the fence. I would try to find Matthew in that exact field if I knew where to look. Truth be told, I'm not even sure which of the teams is ours. Plus, with those helmets, every single one of those players is unidentifiable.

Time passes slower than I'd like it to. I expected the game to be about an hour, plus 30 minutes to wait for Matthew to get changed and to leave. Wrong. I've been standing here for almost two hours now, but I think I've figured out which team is ours. The sun has almost set and it's close to being completely dark, except for the bright spotlights which illuminate the whole field, and the bleachers.

If someone were to trip and hit their head open right here, on one of these bleachers, I'm almost positive the majority wouldn't notice. So far it is a mystery to me why American Football is so popular. From what I have gathered over my almost two hours here, it's just two teams full of people throwing a ball, running with the ball, and colliding with each other.

Really doesn't appear to be the most entertaining thing.

I texted my dad that I would let him know when he can pick us up. It's a Saturday, so neither of my parents have a problem that a friend will be staying over. Now only Matthew has to agree. Assuming I find him.

When someone, who I assume to be some sort of referee, blows the whistle again, everyone shouts even more than before. After a while of that, the players start heading inside, which means the game must be over. I ignore all people in my way, as I slither through the crowd towards the front of the school.

Heeey! Great game. I'm waiting near the front entrance of the school, see you soon.

That's all I text him.

How long does one take to shower, change, and walk here?

It feels like an eternity before Matthew finally walks around the corner of the building and looks around. I take a step forward and wave at him. When he spots me, the corners of his mouth twitch up, and he falls into a slow jog for the last few meters.

"Hello there, stranger."

I wave again. It's strange, do I go in for a hug? A kiss? A handshake? Nope, not a handshake. How do I do this?

147

"I would congratulate you on your win, but to be totally honest I'm not even sure which team ended up winning. So, did you win?"

Matthew laughs. The tone sounds almost like back at his house, but not quite the same. I enjoy making him laugh. He's holding his left hand over his face to cover his open mouth as he is almost completely curled into himself.

"Come on. I'm serious. Did you win?"

He only shook his head while drastically trying to catch his breath.

Once Matthew has gotten back steadily on his two feet, he finally gives a normal reply.

"I told you that you wouldn't understand much, but apparently I've overestimated you if you can't even decipher the colors of the team."

"For the record, I was aware there were two different color patterns, but how would I know which belongs to our school and which doesn't?"

Matthew lay his arm around my shoulder, pulls me closer to him, and starts walking.

"So, what are you doing tonight after someone picks you up? At least I hope someone is picking you up because we are not having this conversation again where you'll just walk home," he states with a playful tone to his voice.

"Relax, my dad is picking me up, and I was hoping he could pick you up too. I know it's a little.." I go silent while trying to think of the right word, ".. spontaneous. But it could be fun, right? It's a Saturday so there's no school tomorrow either and my dad would drive us to your house first so that you can get some stuff."

The weight of Matthew's touch on my shoulders is warm. I can feel hot blood rushing into my neck and face, bringing a level of excitement and comfort along. All I can do is smile. Turning my head, I can see Matthew looking my way, grinning.

"Uhm. Heck yes! Let's do that! It'll be fun, and maybe I can even teach you some basic, very basic, things about the game. You'll see, once you understand it, it's actually pretty easy.``

"Sure. Totally doubt that I'll understand anything at all, but sure. Give it your best shot."

We walk like this- Matthew's arm around me, we both talking, smiling, and laughing- until we arrive at the parking spot where my dad usually picks me up. It's cozy, only the two of us with the only light around us the street lamp, and the only sounds being some people and cars further away. It may be creepy to the point where we might both get kidnapped, but that would be totally worth this exact moment.

CHAPTER 19

Matthew

The game was worse than expected. We lost by 30 points. The whole team was off, even before it started. After the slaughter was over, Coach basically threatened to quit if we didn't put in more effort. He was mad. Most of the guys on the team already knew as much or had already given their best. Whereas others, obviously Josh and Connor, blamed everyone and their mothers, before even considering themselves. Such as blaming the rest of the team, accusing the other team of using steroids, or, my favorite, Connor come up with the genius excuse that his helmet was too loose, and that distracted him. Coach didn't buy any of the crap they were pulling.

I would even go as far as to say that their inability to play as a team is part of the reason we did so badly, if not the entirety of it. Though I have to admit, knowing that Liam was in the audience kind of distracted me. Just a little bit, so I can't blame the whole thing on them either.

Coach had taken at least twice as long to scream at us while we were changing, but when he was finally done and I had found Liam waiting outside, things were fine again. Until I saw his text I wasn't even sure he was coming. I mean, I suspected it, because who asks to come to something and then chooses not to go? But something inside me was kind of doubting it. Just a little bit.

And now I'm inside his house for the first time, and already staying overnight. Surprisingly enough his parents don't hate me… I think. Liam introduced me to his dad before I got in the car and to his mom when we got to his house, but to both, he introduced me as a friend. Totally fine. Yeah. Maybe a teeny tiny bit disappointing, but totally fine.

Liam's dad, Eric, is really talkative and has a somewhat better understanding of sports than Liam. Eric had asked me how school is going, how I know Liam, how today's game went, and we generally just talked a lot more about classes. It was relatively hard to understand him sometimes because of his accent, the same accent Liam has just thicker, so I had to ask him to repeat himself. I hope I didn't make him uncomfortable because of that. It sometimes feels like that with Liam, I don't always understand him but don't want to make it worse by asking him to repeat himself.

Liam's mom introduced herself as Iressa right before Liam practically hauls me upstairs. He leads me upstairs to his room where he tells me to put my stuff down for now and is about to show me around the house. I'm sure Iressa and I will have a proper conversation when we go back downstairs.

With a strong sparkle in his eyes, he exclaims, "As you can see, this is my room. A bit untidy but I did the best I could in the little time I had."

I look around, place my bag against the wall and take a few steps, taking in the entirety of his room.

"Feel free to look around of course."

His walls are in a light yellowish color with a black corner table stuffed to the right of the door. In the opposite corner is a king-sized bed. Many different-sized pillows and stuffed animals are placed in an orderly fashion. Some are almost human size. The other side is empty. Across the bed is another door, assumingly the closet, and the rest of the wall is covered in shelves. White frames, with books in every single one of them, all illuminated by dim shining fairy lights. Looking at it makes me see how boring my own room is. But it also makes me wonder, how does one have the time and will to read this much?

"Wow, I clearly underestimated you when you said that you read a lot. Tell me, how long does it take you to finish one of these?" I ask, pointing at a book.

"It obviously depends on the book. General length matters of course. But one of these," he pulls a book from the highest row to the right, "is going to take me much less time to finish, than one of these." He pulls out another book, this time from the middle area.

"Both of these are about 400 pages, but this one is a gay enemies to lovers fantasy book. Whereas this one is a horror book, which I personally don't enjoy as much. Therefore, I'll probably like the first one more and finish it faster. It mostly depends on how much you enjoy the book you're reading. Anyway, I don't know if that makes any sense so ignore me if it doesn't."

He puts the books back to where he took them. I'm not sure how to respond to that. It makes perfect sense. I stay quiet and wait for him to continue.

"Anyhow, would you like a house tour now?" he asks, opening the door to the hall.

"Yes please," I reply nodding. I follow him out the door and into the hall. He doesn't turn left to the way we came from, but instead opens the door to the room opposite of his. He switches the light on, illuminating the pitch-black room.

It's a bit smaller than Liam's. The bed is to the wall in the center of the room and the closet door is practically jammed into a corner. Across the bed is a small cabinet with a TV on top of it. Looks cozy. There are no clothes, nothing that looks like a personal item, and the bed looks too neat to just be made this morning. I know what Liam is about to say. This is the guest room.

"This is the guest room. You can stay in here if you like and carry your stuff over after we're done with the tour. Or don't," he shrugs.

And suddenly I forget everything around me. I think I completely froze up because he just invited me to sleep in his room. At least I hope so! I should try and act like I didn't hear anything in case I misheard. I swallow once and force my limbs to move. I switch off the lights and close the door behind me.

Before we arrived here I knew it was going to be fancy, but this straight-up undermined my expectations. His house feels gigantic but alive all at once. Liam leads me back to the hallway we came from, but doesn't descend down the stairs. Instead, he stops dead in front of another door, turns around, and says, "My parents' room. Do not go in there. Ever."

I nod, imagining some sort of scary illegal drug lab behind the door. Obviously an exaggeration but what am I supposed to think? I continue to follow Liam down the stairs. As expected, Iressa and Eric are both still downstairs. I can hear them talking from what I assume is the kitchen, but Liam leads me into a different room.

A couch and two large armchairs are facing the middle of the room, where a small glass table is displayed on a round carpet. An oven in the middle of the wall, neighboured by large shelves on either side. Each shelf has its own aspect to it, making it look immaculate. It takes me multiple moments to grasp everything on display.

On one side there are various vases in all sizes and colors, below there are so many adorable carved wooden figures, all of which are facing each other as if they're having their own interactions in a whole different universe. On the other side, there are cute little plushies spread all over the shelf. It kind of makes me feel weirdly under surveillance.

Even when I turn around I swear I can feel those tiny eyes burning into my back. Liam doesn't say anything upon entering the kitchen area. It's smaller than I thought it would be based on the dimensions of the other rooms. No fancy kitchen island or thousands of built-in cabinets.

Eric is leaning against a countertop with his side, while Iressa is with her back to the fridge. They both turn and smile at us.

"Hey, guys! We just met but again, I'm Iressa. Nice to meet you. Can I get you anything to drink or dinner?" Her accent catches me off guard, so different from Liam's or Eric's. More like Madamme Veilleux's, but not quite the same either. She must have French roots, that's for sure, but also something else.

"I'm Matthew and it's nice to meet you too. Actually, I think I'm good for now, thank you though. If I want something later I can just ask Liam so it's not like I'd starve," I answer nervously. *If they knew how I lived for the past few years, they'd know that I wouldn't starve. But then, if they knew, I would be sent to away. So this little charade is worth it.*

"Oh yes of course! You know, we're so happy Liam brought a friend over! That hasn't happened since primary school so we're really glad you're here," Iressa exclaims, the enthusiasm basically sprinkling out of her.

Liam, still standing quietly beside me, drops his head in a swift motion. When he lifts himself up again he slowly opens his mouth in reply.

"Mom, there's no need for you to say it that way but thanks. I'm actually just showing Matthew around so wrap up your conversation because we're leaving soon."

"Aha. And where are you going?" This is Eric, contributing to the conversation for the first time so far.

Liam sights, "Nowhere, just upstairs."

155

Now Iressa jumps in again, "Okay, well. Have fun guys! Let us know if we can help you in any way and it was lovely meeting you Matthew."

I smile, "Yeah, thanks. You too."

Not two minutes later we are back in Liam's room, the fairy lights still illuminating the majority of the room. He sits on his bed and smiles up at me, but neither of us say anything. I maneuver around his bed to see what else he has in his room.

I want to see every single detail to find out as much about him as I can. And not in a creepy stalker way, but in a caring *boyfriend* way. Wow, I still need to get used to that word, even in my own bed.

When we first stepped into this room, I remember the bunch of posters and images standing out from the rest of the room. They seemed way more out of order than everything else here. Or maybe 'out of order' isn't the best way to describe it. Everything has a certain harmony to it, except for the posters. There's no pattern or any sort. I'm closer now and still don't recognize anyone or anything?

"Hey Li? Who are these people?" I ask, pointing at some of the art.

Liam turns and smiles as he sees what I'm looking at. It's a faint smile like he's somewhere in his thoughts, only sightly aware of what I asked.

"Those are book characters I really liked. I know, shocker. The other photos on the very right," he says motioning for me to follow his gaze, "are of my friends and I back in Germany. I could tell you our origin story if you want but I'm warning you because it's long."

I grin back at him, "Then I guess it's a good thing that I'm here all night."

With that, I find a free wall space and sit down under his window. I lean my head back and close my eyes, ready to visualize everything he wants to tell me. "I'm ready."

He snorts, "Don't fall asleep, otherwise I would be telling you all of this for nothing. However, because I am such a generous human being, I will give you the shorter version."

I still have my eyes closed when he takes a deep breath, in and out.

Then, "Okay so, during primary school, I never fit in with any of the guys there because they would talk about sports or whatever and I obviously have no clue of that, so I would usually just hang out alone at lunch. Until, one day in second grade, Tess came up to me and gave me a card. It was a birthday invitation. I first thought it was a prank or some sort of joke to invite me so I almost didn't go. Because why would I, if they were just going to make fun of me?"

Damn. I thought this was going to be a happy story of friendship, but instead, Liam's tone inflicts a sudden ting of sadness in my chest. Imagining Liam in that situation really isn't hard because he was as quiet when he came here, before he talked to me and became friends with Patricia.

"Anyway, long story short, I went and didn't get pranked and actually had fun there. Tess introduced me to some of their friends, Luca, Alice, Vanessa, and some more. After that party though, we never really

at first, then he lifts his head again and starts replying at a higher level than a third grader.

"First of all, *"somewhere in Asia"* is Singapore. Now, to answer your first question, many things there were cool and unique. For example, the amount of nationalities in the population, or the architectural way the city is built. And something I miss. Oh, easy! The food! If I ever find something here that gets close to what it tastes like over there, I will drag you there in a heartbeat." He chuckles, no doubt meaning it very literally. "Your turn," Liam declares.

With a smirk that lets the green of his eyes stand out like poison ivy on a brown tree's branch, he announces, "One question each. Back and forth until we grow bored. My first question is, what is something about our school that you think I, as a relative newcomer, should know?"

"You know, I expected many questions, some more cursed than others. So I didn't see that coming, but it is actually an interesting question. Off the top of my head, I would say to stay away from the counselors. From my experience, and from what I've heard others say, the counselors are only here to teach us to be independent."

CHAPTER 20

Liam

It continued all night. Question after question, until the morning sun illuminated the room. Every answer gave us a little more insight into each other, even as sleep tried to claw its way into our bodies. It may not be the greatest feeling in the world to know you missed every opportunity to get some actual sleep, but it sure as hell was worth it.

Eventually, around seven now, we decide to pause, what Matthew called "very insightful research" and I tell him to go shower. I demonstrate how to work the shower and hand him a towel.

"Two last things," I say in the most serious tone I can muster, "do not drown in here, because that would make it very hard for my parents to sell the house when we leave. And, just knock against this wall if you need anything."

I demonstrate and close the door behind me. I hear the water pounding on the ground of the shower as I step back into my room. My legs give in right as I come close enough to my bed to fall face-first into the mattress. I'm just closing my eyes for a short second, nothing too long.

Everything is dark.

There's nothing around. No up or down. No left or right.

Until there is something, someone. Four silhouettes, instinctively I know who they are.

Three of them I hated, and the remaining one being myself. A kid who went by Bobby and his two friends surrounded me. Suddenly we're back on the schoolyard where I spent almost all of my elementary years and they're once again picking on me.

It's strange, I'm watching myself get bullied, knowing exactly how it feels because I have already experienced this, but also being disconnected from my own body. I can't do anything but watch.

With every word that came out of their mouths, my chest heaved harder, fighting for air, and my eyes transformed into fountains, a non-stopping flow of tears rolling down my eyes.

I remember this exact moment. It almost made me switch schools during third grade. Back in Germany, I quickly learned that anyone, especially little kids, can be very mean if given the right motivation.

Usually, they would just hit, kick, or scratch me, and I could endure that because the pain faded. But that time, they focused on vocals, probably because teachers couldn't just look the other way anymore at that point. I vividly remember almost every single word from that day, because they really hurt me. These eight-year-olds managed to make me hate life. I don't want to watch anymore.

If I were to meet them today, I don't know what I would do.

Crawl back in my own imaginary safehouse, like I did back then? Probably not, because now I know how wrong they were.

They said that nobody would ever like me in any way whatsoever. Now I have friends all over the world and THE CUTEST GUY AT SCHOOL IS MY OFFICIAL BOYFRIEND.

They said I would never succeed in life. I have accomplished three times more than all of them combined because I would bet the life of a firstborn that they are all sitting in the small little High School in our hometown with the worst grade average and no plan for the future. Meanwhile, I have traveled to so many countries, learned fucking Chinese, and am at the top of my class in the hardest classes I could take, even though school isn't even in my native language. Yet the feeling in my chest doesn't lift.

The setting changed. The school grounds and the boys are gone. And again there was nothing.

I wake up with a headache piercing through my skull, but my mind is clear. I'm in a great spot in life right now, so I should finally move past all the bad things that happened before. What matters is now, and my miraculous boyfriend. Who had spent the night at my house, and is now using my shower.

Speaking of, I should probably go check on him to make sure he doesn't need anything. I don't hear the water running anymore so I guess he should be out relatively soon, but I knock on the door anyway. A gentle knock, trying my best not to wake up my parents.

163

"You good in there?" I ask, my voice barely louder than a whisper. Matthew however doesn't reply, excelling at not waking my parents. Instead, he unlocks the door and cranks it open a little, motioning with one hand for me to step inside.

I guess now I know one of the very possible and common disadvantages of being in a relationship with someone you actually like. With every move, you feel like your heart may explode and splatter against the inside of your body. Along with that, your blood usually starts heating exponentially, and there's the constant knowledge that that can happen at any time all day long.

After pretending to think about it, for a solid two seconds, I follow his arm through the door and into a room that is semi-filled with hot steam. Matthew is in fact nearly done dressing and *holy mother of Jesus fucking Christ. He really is not only the hottest dude in the school but in the whole wide Milky Way.* I think my heart actually misses a beat as my eyes meet his.

The normal light brown of his eyes appears way darker than usual. For once, it matches with his hair, now a dark blond tone. A sight I didn't know I needed. The same moment that my eyes meet his, they leave his again, scanning over the rest of his body. He's wearing the same sweatpants from last night, but no shirt yet. If he were to even put his hand on my shoulder right now I would faint for sure.

I feel two surges of electricity flow through me, one from my chest and the other from elsewhere. I can feel that he is everything. Everything I would ever need in life. Not food or money or electricity or water, but him.

A voice in my head starts to come forward, but I do my best to ignore it because how often do I get to see Matthew with no shirt and wet her in my bathroom?

Exactly. Not that often.

"Hey," he says, as if it's the most normal conversation in the world, "Sorry, let me put on a shirt first." He reaches his hand behind his head, scratching his neck. He reaches for his shirt on the space next to the sink. I have to put every last effort into not telling him not to.

To my luck, a shirt doesn't cover his dazzling eyes or his incredible smile. I must have a certain look on my face because Matthew cooks his head to the side and smiles at me.

"What?" he asks snickering.

"Nothing. I'm just so glad you're you and that you're here."

That makes him smile even more. Our stares lock with each other and while I try my best not to get sucked too deep into his eyes, he blinks once as if to say *I'm glad you're here too.*

"Well, I'm done so you can go now," he declares.

And before I can say anything else he closes the door again.

Probably better that way, because who knows what would have come out of my mouth. He doesn't need to be rushed, or else he will leave. I can not let that happen.

After he's done it is my turn to shower and change, and when I come back to my room I see Matthew lying on my bed.

165

And since neither of my parents had barged in within the past hour I'm relatively sure that we have succeeded in letting them sleep.

"Morning, you didn't fall asleep did you?" I ask in a mockery voice.

"Morning indeed and no, I resisted the temptation," Matthew admits.

Lying down next to him, I ask, "So what do you want to do now?"

He rotates his whole upper body to properly face me and suggests, "How about breakfast? Talking all night has got me famished."

I stand back up, my legs groaning from exhaustion, and motion for him to follow me. We're quiet all the way down the steps, making sure to walk slowly on our tippy-toes.

The whole morning, until around 9:30, we had to keep up with this sneaking and whispering unless we were back in my room. My parents took their time with falling out of their beds this morning.

By the time we finished eating lunch that my dad had made, Matthew wanted to go out for some time, and how could I deny him? We leave the house without a plan and only a small bag with essentials including water, a power bank, and cash. We walk for a while, mostly through my neighborhood, but neither of us had a particular goal. Until I mention that there's a park not far from the neighborhood and Matthew, naturally, gets more excited than I would have expected from anyone.

Even though we had walked for over an hour in total, the image of shirtless Matthew moving through my bathroom never left my mind.

The way his abs contracted and his damp hair covered his forehead in strands. *It makes me want to... agghhhhhhh! I don't even know.*

CHAPTER 21

Matthew

It's a beautiful day. It has been all night, but it just keeps getting better. I had assumed I'd be unable to move if we stayed up all night, but after that shower, I proved myself wrong. Especially after what happened almost immediately after the shower, which is why I have the energy of three days' worth.

For the beginning of March, the weather has been on our side for the past few days. It started last Tuesday, but before it was freezing cold, 60 degrees when the sun was out, but all of a sudden it rose over the 60s. Not as hot as the 70s though. That makes it the perfect time of year to walk through nature without freezing to death or overheating.

There also aren't any bees, mosquitos, or other creatures of hell outside yet.

So basically, it's ideal.

Birds are singing their own little melodies up in the trees as we strode through the park. There are lots of people in the park, predictable given it's prime time on a Saturday. From kids playing and screaming at each other on the playground to teenagers our age playing basketball, to parents watching over their kids, to a field full of dogs mostly just running all over the place.

I haven't said much to Liam since we left. He led me all the way here, which wasn't that far but every single second that his hair was shining with sunlight, I wanted to reach out and grab his hand. Liam is the best thing that has happened to me in years, probably even ever, so I can't risk actually taking his hand before I know that he is ready for the publicity of it.

But how do I ask if he's good with that?

Liam breaks the silence by stopping and pointing to a wide fallen trunk right ahead of us.

He explains, "That's the spot I usually go to to read in the summer, just on the other side of that branch."

Understanding I say, "From what it looks like it's not a branch but a trunk, but yeah." I can almost feel him rolling his eyes, but I do my best not to react.

"But why on the other side? I'd assume it's just more dirt and bugs and stuff."

"Mostly for the view. My own and others. I don't have to see people when I'm trying to relax and people don't see me either, meaning they can not even get the idea to get any closer."

169

He smiles, but I don't. Does he really hate people so much that he gets out of his own way to avoid them? I can't imagine how much time and extra energy that would require.

"Do you want to sit a little? Because my knees could kinda use a little break."

Without waiting for a response I start walking over there, my knees begging to sit down. I don't hear him object so I guess that's what we're doing now. Neither of us has the energy to climb over the trunk so we make a long turn around.

Finally sitting, my whole body relaxes even though the dirt under me is ice cold. I watch as Liam positions himself next to me. It's not as bad as I thought it would be. It's been about thirty seconds and I haven't seen a single bug. *Which doesn't mean they're not there.* So that's great. But Liam was right. Not a single person in sight, but of course still audible from the rest of the park behind us.

If it weren't for the noises, it would really be a relaxing place to be.

"How come you haven't even been in this area for a year, but already know better spots than I do?" It's supposed to be some sort of joke, but now that I think about it, I really don't know that many nice places outside my home to chill. Much less in nature.

"It's a talent. Everywhere I go, I find a place, where I'm away from people and can just be. You know?" I don't really but don't say anything.

He sights but continues," Okay, so for context, you are aware that I'm not the most social person, yes? That's because I get really anxious around random people. I know, shocker." This conversation is supposed to feel serious, but that joke makes it really difficult not to laugh out loud.

"Anyway, so because of that I essentially changed my whole personality to appear antisocial, to avoid people and therefore avoid the anxiety. Because as you might have noticed, I do talk *a lot* when I'm around people I like. Then boom, changing your whole personality all day every day does tend to get exhausting, believe it or not."

"I do believe that, it's just… that doesn't feel like a healthy thing to do… at all." Is he doing that now too? Is this maybe not him, but a fake version of him he wants me to see? I really hope not.

"C'est la vie," he says clearly, yet I have not a single clue what it means. Awesome.

Liam must have read the confusion on my face because then he follows with, "It means 'that's life'. We're in the same French class, how do you not know this?"

I'm baffled by that. What is that even supposed to mean?!

"Li, forgive me if I'm being too forward, but what in the actual fuck is that supposed to mean? Last time I checked, life wasn't about making up new personalities to avoid your own feelings."

I look at him, searching for any kind of sign to figure out if he's offended or not.

He swallows, "Damn. That was uncalled for, but even if you're right, it wouldn't matter cause I can do what I want."

Liam's jaw doesn't fully close this time, physically gaping at me.

171

"We're not done with this conversation yet, but I really want to kiss you right now," I say, my lips drying out at this exact moment.

"Yes please," he nods, the hunger in his eyes becoming more and more visible. Which just makes me want him more.

Not being able to wait another second I lean and he meets me halfway. I will never be tired of this, the pressure of his lips on mine. The movement that connects us, if not in sync but still perfect in its own way. I take in the radiating heat of his body as we lean more and more into each other.

To my dismay, the kiss ends as fast as it started and we just sit there looking at each other. Just as I'm about to protest, Liam leans his head on my shoulder and I have no more reason to complain about anything. If I could choose any moment in time to be forever stuck in… Never mind, it wouldn't be this one. The ground is the only freezing thing around us.

However, the moment I would actually choose is a random Thursday, when I first saw Liam in Madame's room. It's cheesy but true. I will never forget the mixed feeling of excitement, attraction, mystery, and just very good energy. I surely didn't expect this to happen, but I'm more than happy that it did.

Ever since that day, I have always been excited for seventh period. French has always been the class I did best at, which is why I even have one class with Liam. He told me that this year he is doing four APs, which from my point of view is just crazy. Where do you find the time and energy to do all of the work?!

As for me, French is the only higher-level class I'm taking because I just don't understand any other classes. So I'm lucky that we have at least one class together.

"Thanks for that," I whisper, "but can we please start moving again? I'm freezing my ass off. But we can definitely continue this very lovely activity when we're somewhere inside."

That made him audibly chuckle. All the tiredness and pain in my bones is so worth it.

"Back to my house? We can ask my dad to drive you home… or you could stay until tomorrow?"

"Not a question, I'm staying. But can we still drive around my place? I need to get more clothes, and dispose the old ones while I'm at it."

As soon as I'm standing upright again, I offer my hand to help Liam. He takes it and our hands don't part until we're back at his front door.

Ms. Iressa was more than happy to drive us to my place because she had some errands to run, she said. So she would drop us off and pick us back up after she's finished. Iressa is such a good mom, friend, and person in general. All of his family that I have met is. I really adore that.

I have my bag of old stuff, just a t-shirt, underwear, and socks, on my lap in the back of Iressa's car. Liam is in the back with me but just quietly staring out the window. No doubt lost in his thoughts again.

Iressa takes the opportunity and asks me, "Hey Matthew, is it alright if I drop you off at the entrance of your neighborhood? That way I wouldn't have to drive around trying to turn or find another exit."

"Of course, we can walk the rest. It's definitely not far," I joke.

"Okay great. So what did you do while you were gone? And where did you go?"

"We walked to a nearby park. Liam said he went there sometimes during the summer, so I wanted to see what he meant. It's a beautiful park for sure, though I think it'd be a lot better when it's sunnier."

"Yeah, I bet. Eric and I haven't been to that park yet so maybe we should go once it's a bit warmer. If it's really that nice."

"Yeah, you totally should."

And that's the end of that conversation apparently.

Iressa drops us off, just like she said she would, and tells us it'll be at least an hour before she can pick us up again.

Liam and I walk down the street, turn right once, and walk around the corner of the street before the panic sets in.

I stop dead from walking, practically in the middle of the street, because of what I see at my house. A police car is parked in front of the driveway. *Why are they here? Do they know? I don't want to live somewhere else with strangers. No. No. No. No.*

This can't be happening. Not when everything is so perfect right now.

Liam turns to me, worry in his eyes.

"What is it? Matthew? Hello?"

I don't reply. I don't think I could if I tried. My body feels stuck. As if paralyzed. I don't feel the arm Liam puts around me as he slowly guides me to the side of the road. I don't want to go over there. I can't go over there.

"Matthew. Please talk, with your words… What happened?"

I concentrate on my breathing and sit down at the edge of someone's front lawn.

"Okay, I can see that talking isn't your thing right now, so how about we try something else? I say a sentence, and you shake your head for no and nod for yes."

I think I can do that. Even if I'm only half listening because images of cops, and random families, and group homes, are actively swirling through my mind.

"Do you need medical attention right now?" I hear his muffled voice.

I shake my head.

Maybe if I keep Liam occupied with me long enough, the cops will leave and we can continue on with our day. But I can't use Liam like that. He doesn't deserve it.

"Okay that's good, that's great even," he says as he lowers himself next to me. "Are you scared of something?"

Breathe in. Breathe out.

Breathe in. Breathe out.

I nod.

175

I look up at Liam this time, there's so much worry in his expression. That just makes it worse. How dare I cause this magnificent son of goddess so much trouble?

I want to tell him. Everything. That my parents left, that I have lived alone for a long while now, that I have been keeping that secret since, and that he can't tell anyone. But that's the problem, he will tell someone. I know he cares about me, which is exactly why he would tell someone. It's what most people would do for someone they care about.

He stands up and glances in the direction of my house, no doubt seeing the car this time.

"It's because of the police, isn't it?"

I nod again and look away immediately. I just can't handle how he must see me now because he must think I'm a criminal, and it's not like I can deny that because then I'd have to explain.

Instead, the next few of his words bring my heart to literally melt inside.

"Tell me if you did something bad, because I'd probably help you hide a body so I'll help you with everything else you could have done. But you have to be honest."

I shake my head.

Honesty is exactly the one thing I can't give you.

"If you didn't do anything, they're probably not here for you then. Maybe someone broke in while you were gone? Not that I'm saying someone did, but it would explain the visit."

I shake my head. I know they are here for me, I just know.

What should I do? Wait here until they're gone or go and find out for sure why they're here? If I wait, they're going to come back eventually and now I have Liam with me in case something happens, so I should definitely go find out why they're here.

I stand up, look at Liam, then back at the house, and I start moving.

"Li, I'm good now," I lie, "and everything will be just fine. You're right, they're here for some other reason, not me." I'm mostly trying to convince myself than him, but he follows me nevertheless without another question.

As we get closer to the house, I can decipher two silhouettes at my front door.

So they're not here for a neighbor then.

When I step foot in my driveway, I try not to act weird, so I raise a hand and yell, "Hey there!"

The two of them turn, as if in sync. One of them, a blond woman in her mid 40s, yells back as we get closer, "Hi, how are you doing?"

I look her in the eye and say, "I'm doing well, how about yourself?"

"We're good. Do you happen to know who lives here?"

"I live here actually. Is there something I can help you with?"

My pulse is at least at 120 beats and the sweat in my fist is killing me. I wish I could just stop the time, not hear her answer, and make it so they never came here.

"That depends. We got a call last night that one of your neighbors saw someone suspicious on the property and since last night no one opened up, we thought we'd try again today."

A GIANT weight fell off my shoulders. *They don't know. THEY DON'T KNOW!*

Now all I have to do is get them out of here so that they won't come to find out any time soon. So I smile at them, playing my part.

"I'm sure it's nothing. Probably just an animal," I try to convince them.

"That might be, but we'd still like a quick tour of your house to make sure it's safe."

As if. I don't believe a word they're saying, but I go along with it anyway.

I had prepared for this moment, in case someone wanted to see inside my house. I had always kept the dust off all the things in every room, including my parents' former room. I had kept all the clothing in their closets and even moved some stuff around so that it would look like someone was still living there. Mainly the reason I didn't take the master bedroom.

I have spent days placing and moving things around, every single detail is perfectly laid out.

Yet I still respond with a distrustful tone, "Respectfully, I don't think I'm allowed to let you in. You see, my parents are on a trip for work, and I'm still a minor. And as far as I can see, you don't have a warrant either, so I'll have to ask you not to come in."

I'm so dead. The second officer, a younger guy, looks like he's about to violently bite me.

"That's fine. If you see or notice anything suspicious please don't hesitate to call," the woman says and they're gone.

Liam stares at me with an open mouth. I start laughing. It's the adrenaline for sure because I know I don't actually feel like laughing right now.

"You just basically told a police officer to fuck the fuck off!!!"

"Yeah, I think I might have," I say still violently giggling and Liam joins in. We just stand there, laughing in front of my front door.

I took Liam through the garage into the house, because soon after the police left I realized that I didn't have my key. It's either still with my bag in Liam's bedroom, or it's lying somewhere inside and I had never brought it with me in the first place.

We stand right on the door swelling to the garage and just stare inside. Neither of us daring to step any further.

"Quick question, what if someone was actually in here who wasn't supposed to be?"

I had thought about the same thing, but after many seconds of carefully examining every piece of furniture, decor, and household items, everything looks normal. I take another few steps into the kitchen area, just enough to glance around the corner into the living room.

Again, nothing looks abnormal there either. Nor have I heard anything besides our breathing and my footsteps on the wooden floor, much less anything strange.

"It looks fine to me. Everything is how I left it, no broken glass from breaking in, and I don't see anything that shouldn't be here either."

I turn around to Liam, who is looking at me, but still hasn't moved any further. I smile, walk back over, and reach for his hand.

"Come on Li! It probably really was an animal."

I pull Liam after me but only hear a low grumble from him.

"See? Everything looks normal, and besides, the officer said they got the call last night, so it was most likely dark. Which makes it even more likely that someone just saw something, didn't know what it was, and called the cops just in case."

Liam turns around himself to make sure that everything indeed does look normal, yet he still doesn't look too convinced.

"And let's say that someone actually broke in last night… they wouldn't still be here so there's no reason to be afraid now," I continue.

"Yeah, you're right. They wouldn't still be here," he mumbles, though it sounds like he's more trying to convince himself than agreeing with me.

"Okay well, I'm gonna go upstairs and grab some stuff. You can stay here if you want," I offer but Liam just shakes his head and follows me eagerly.

Upstairs, everything looks normal but I check behind every closed door if something is off, but again there's nothing. Finally getting to my room, Liam sits on my bed and I empty my bag of old stuff in the designated corner of my room.

Laundry isn't due till Thursday, so I have multiple, two, baskets in that designated corner of my room for dirty laundry, which are barely filled. That reminds me that I should be getting money from my father tomorrow and need to get groceries after. *Having adult responsibilities is draining.*

Without spending too much time deciding what clothes I bring, I just grab one of everything, a t-shirt, boxers, jeans, another hoodie, and a pair of socks. Then I stop and consider, what if they allow me to stay another night after? I turn to Liam, who apparently had decided to explore a little bit because he's not on my bed anymore, but sitting on the chair in front of my desk.

"Li?" I ask.

He turns to me and makes an "Mhm" sound.

"Any chance that I'd be spending more than one more night at your place? Because I don't want to come back here again in case that suddenly is an option, you know?"

Liam nods, and says, "I'll call my mom to ask. Just so you know, I'd love it if you stayed longer, but you really don't have to if you don't really want to."

"I am well aware, thank you. Oh and, if you don't mind, could you not tell your parents about the police? I don't want them to worry and call my parents, because then they'd worry too and I don't want to be the reason they have to cancel their work trip," I lie, but I know they wouldn't care one bit.

The way I see it, if I were to get kidnapped and/or murdered, my dad would be relieved that there's one less person to waste money on.

181

If Liam's parents were to call my parents, they'd not really call them. They'd call their old phone with their old number, which they left here and is now in my possession. Therefore it would lead to unnecessary troubles that nobody wants.

Liam already has his phone out and up his ear, calling Iressa.

"Hi Mama. Kurze Frage, kann Matthew von Sonntag auf Montag auch bei uns bleiben? Weil falls ja würde er jetzt für zwei Tage packen, und so weiter."

I didn't understand a thing besides my name and the word "mama", and I realize that I had never heard him speak German before. Now, the only thing I can think about is the way his native language sounds intriguingly attractive. His accent has turned me on countless times, but this is a whole other level.

"Oke, danke, Mama. Hab dich lieb."

Oh hell. I want more of that. I need more of that.

I turn around as Liam hangs up the phone because I don't want him to see the obvious bulge of my boner. I didn't know it was possible to be turned on by words you don't understand.

"She said she's fine with it, just bring your stuff for school on Monday."

"That's cool. Thanks for the reminder," I say because I would have forgotten for sure. I put the second shirt, pair of socks, underwear, and t-shirt in my bag as slowly as I can. Maybe if I take my time, my boner will calm itself down.

It doesn't. Partially because I keep replaying the sentences in my mind. Turning around I hold the bag, now again full of clothes, in front of my crotch, doing the best I can to hide it. I walk over to my table, where Liam now gets out of the chair and back on the bed.

"Thanks," I whisper because he made space for me.

I hadn't unpacked anything on Friday after school, because I had to get ready for warm-up practice before the game. So I swing my backpack over my shoulder and look at Liam.

"Should we stay up here until your mom comes or wait downstairs?"

He shrugs, I guess we're staying here then.

"I'll be right back, I'll grab a toothbrush," I say because the idea suddenly popped into my head. That wasn't a lie, I wanted to grab a toothbrush, but right after I close the bathroom door behind me, I glance in the mirror and use my hand to try and hide the boner in my pants as much as I can.

It wouldn't be the end of the world if Liam found out about it, but I'd still be kind of embarrassed. I mean, we haven't done anything more than kiss yet. It hasn't been that long since we've gotten together, not even a week to be exact, but with my latest girlfriend it didn't take more than two days.

I'm not mad about that of course, just worried. Maybe he doesn't want to do more with me. Maybe he sees me as a player and thinks that once he does something with me I'd drop him. Which I would never do! I had three girlfriends before Liam came along. Naomi, my first girlfriend in middle school, of course we didn't do anything besides kiss

183

and hold hands, but she's the only exception. She broke up with me because apparently she liked another guy, which was fair enough.

Then there was Joey, who gave me my first blowjob in my freshman year. I broke up with her two months after that because it just didn't feel right. Lastly, last year there was Chloe, who I lost my virginity to, and that, I still regret to this day. We broke up after five months because I had finally figured out why it didn't feel right, that I hadn't truly known myself yet.

To my own delight, thinking about my exes did help with my boner situation, so I grab my toothpaste and toothbrush, stash them in my bag, and return to my room.

"Got it," I shake the bag in front of my face, emphasizing that I do in fact have everything I need.

"My mom texted while you wandered off, she said it's going to be another 15 minute wait."

"That's fine. How about we do something other than sitting around? How about we play Never Have I Ever?"

I crook an eyebrow at his idea, "You do know that that is in fact a drinking game, intended for a group of people, yes?"

"Obviously, but we have spent the whole night just asking questions, at least this is a more creative way to do that."

"Fine. You go first," he sights overdramatically.

Uhm… I hadn't thought that far yet. I close the door behind me and settle on the ground, leaning my back against that door.

"Okay so, never have I ever joined a cult?" Absurd question of course, but we have to get into the game spirit first.

"By choice or by accident?" Liam asks. I'm more than surprised.

"Uhm, both?" I respond with a question because I am unsure of myself. How would one even join a literal cult by accident? That just doesn't feel possible.

"Then no," Liam replies, "I have never."

"THEN WHY WOULD YOU ASK THAT?!" I half scream, still in doubt that he actually said that. He just shrugs in reply.

"My turn," he looks around the room as if searching for some sort of script with questions, "Never have I ever been drunk."

"How drunk is drunk? Like tipsy drunk or full-on drunk?"

"The latter."

"Then I can safely say that I have not. Next question, never have I ever had a crush on a straight guy. I mean straight guy by your knowledge."

"Obviously, everyone has," I can practically hear Liam roll his eyes. Is that true? Has everyone except me had that universal experience? Not that I particularly want to have it, but I don't want to miss out on shared experiences either.

From the empty expression on my face, Liam must have sensed something, because he almost falls off the bed when he jumps up and screams, "You haven't?!"

"I mean, not an actual crush, no. I only just realized I was into guys last year so there wasn't that much opportunity to fall for a straight guy. That is, if celebrities don't count."

"Damn, that's recent!" He exclaims, looking more and more invested in the conversation because instead of lying on his back, he is now sitting on the mattress with crossed legs and a semi-straight back.

"Can I ask you something?," he continues with a much calmer tone, "You totally don't have to answer if you don't want to, but I'm just curious."

"There's nothing that you could ask me that I wouldn't answer, Li." I can feel myself blush, from the neck up, as the cheesiest sentence of the year comes out of my mouth.

"Good Grace, I will die soon. Like, I swear if you keep this up, I will cry first and then melt into the ground," he uses his hands to act out the scenario which makes me laugh.

I'm still not done laughing when he says, "Anyway! My question was, if you want to tell me, how did you come to find out that you were not straight?"

"Long story short, things just didn't feel right with my girlfriend at the time, so I tried *looking* at men more often and suddenly it all clicked. How about you? Same rule, you don't have to tell me if you don't want to."

Liam just blinks into nothingness for a good few seconds, before he catches himself and responds. "Oh, uhhh. I guess I kinda always knew? I always felt different from the other boys but didn't totally fit in with the girls either, but back then I just didn't have a word for it."

Wow, that must've been scary for him. Knowing he's different but doesn't know what it is and no one would explain it to him. My chest aches just from thinking about it.

"I-," I want to say something to help, but I can't so I do the next best thing I could think of. "Thanks for telling me."

I hear a vibration from where Liam sits, his phone I realize quickly.

"Perfect timing, my mom is five minutes away from where she dropped us off. We should probably start heading there."

Nodding in agreement, I wrestle myself from the floor.

I open the garage for Liam and me to step outside, but remember one last thing to check before I leave. I have to check, alone.

"You should go ahead, I think I left my pencil case upstairs." Liam doesn't question me as I drop the bags to the floor and return inside. Careful to close the door to the garage.

It was a lie. I know I have packed everything I would need, but I want to make sure to have an excuse to go back into the house alone.

I don't walk up the stairs either, but walk straight past them into the open office. Going straight to the bottom drawer stashed under my desk, I aim and pull it open.

There's a blank and empty space where the letters have been only a day earlier.

How? How did someone find them? Why does everything look normal if someone searched through the space to find the letters? Why the letters? To frighten me or to get to my parents?

This can not be happening right now.

CHAPTER 22

Liam

Mom had picked us up like she said she would. Everything was perfectly fine until we left his house. On the two-minute walk, Matthew didn't say a word to me. He didn't seem himself.

Usually, he looks around when walking outside, I noticed it in the park and thought it was really cute actually. Even on our way from the car through his neighborhood, though he has probably seen all of the houses thousands of times.

But now he just looks ahead, straight ahead. He looks sad or empty even. As if he's lost behind his eyes, trapped in his own mind. It feels like more than just a random mood swing. There has to be something that caused it.

Maybe if I can find out what it is, I can help him. Or me finding out will completely break his trust and I'll just make everything worse, as evidence I present every movie about teenagers ever. So that's probably not the best idea.

We got into the car and Matthew greeted my mom and again stayed quiet for the rest of the ride. I told my mom that we played a game while we waited for her so it's no trouble at all that she took longer.

When the car was standing in our driveway, I offer to take Matthew's school bag so that he didn't have to carry two bags at once. He just nods and exits the car.

Now we're upstairs and had brought all of his stuff into the guest room because we both didn't exactly want another night with no sleep. Maybe it's that. Maybe Matthew is just tired and the sleeplessness was tugging at him.

But suddenly? And such a drastic change? Doesn't seem plausible.

"Matthew," I say his name, no reaction. Then again, "Matthew." This time he turns to me.

"I have to do some homework now, so if you want you can join me. But you are also extremely tired, so you can sleep a bit if you want and I'll wake you when I'm done or if there's food."

He nods and leaves my room. Just before he closes the door completely, I verbalize a "Byee" and as expected get no reply.

Doing my homework was maybe an excuse to get him to sleep, because I hope that resting will lift his mood again, and I have a lot of work to do so I guess it's a win-win. I open my laptop and start on a discussion board that Mr. Lane had assigned days ago.

It's due on Monday so it's best that I do it now. I'm halfway through reading the prompt choices— my favorite so far being to write a

189

discussion on whether you agree or disagree with the statement that "children's books are the easiest genre to write" and I know that I do of course disagree— when Matthew comes back into the room. He changed from his previous clothes to what looks like pajamas. *Huh? Is he here to tell me something before he goes to sleep?*

I observe him, about to ask if something is wrong when he slumps into my bed, takes my blanket, and yanks it over himself. *Unexpected but better than okay.*

Not wanting to disturb him any further, I turn back in my chair and start typing.

The discussion took me 40 minutes to finalize and then I spent another 50 minutes on Math homework, trying not to throw up every time I saw a new function.

Were we technically supposed to do it last week?

Yes.

Did I do that?

No.

And now I can feel the consequences of not doing it right away.

Sometime in between limits I texted Tess but they haven't responded yet. I was planning on catching them up with the Matthew situation while he was asleep, but I haven't heard back from them.

Matthew took a good while to fall asleep, at least 30 minutes because he stopped staring at the ceiling right before I finished the discussion.

Had I taken multiple breaks from work to watch him sleep in my bed?

Obviously.

Was it worth it?

Sure… but it also made me remind myself of a weird stalker and I just couldn't do that to myself. That means that I haven't looked at him for longer than five seconds in over twenty minutes and have tried my best not to make any sounds at all. I even concentrated on typing with less pressure on the keys to reduce possible noise.

Matthew slept through dinner, which didn't bother my parents because apparently they had heard us, their words not mine, "squeaking all night" and totally understood that we'd be tired now. I made Matthew two slices of bread— actual bread, not what people outside the US would call toast— with butter and ham, then filled up two glasses of water, one for him and one for myself, and brought everything upstairs. However, I had to walk twice because the last glass of water didn't fit in my arm without spilling all over the floor.

I should wake him up. He has to eat, right?

I had set the plate on my desk moments ago and am now standing in front of my own bed, where Matthew was still sound asleep. Not for much longer though. I reach out and push my right hand steadily on his exposed shoulder. When he doesn't move, I do it again with a little more force. Luckily, this time he opens his eyes slowly, one after the other.

"Hm?"

"Good morning to you too. You just slept through dinner, but lucky for you, I have brought you something so that you don't starve."

191

I turn and point at the plate on the desk.

"Thanks, but I'm not hungry," he rasps.

"That's not an option. You're sleeping in my bed right now so the least you can do is not starve."

Happy to see that I have convinced him to at least start to get upright, I sit back on the chair behind me and reach for the plate. I hand it to him when he has successfully opened both eyes and is sitting upright.

In the time he is eating, I turn around and look back at my work. Not much left, meaning I can try to do everything now and have free time tomorrow. Or I can finally go to bed as well and do the rest in the morning.

After not so much thinking, I finally decide that work could wait. I leave the room and change into my pajamas, which I usually don't wear because boxers and t-shirts are the most comfortable things ever, but if Matthew is going to stay in my bed then not wearing proper pajamas might make things uncomfortable.

I come back and am surprised to see Matthew not asleep again, but still sitting on the bed's edge. He looks so shallow, empty even. I don't know what I'm supposed to be doing, what he wants me to do. Logically, I can't change his mood, and I can't try to help if he doesn't tell me what the problem is. However, what I can do is try to comfort him to the best of my abilities. For whatever it is that he's so obviously upset about.

I walk over and sit down with crossed legs right in front of him. He's already looking at me when our eyes finally meet, but this time I don't see the sparkle that was there before, the life within his eyes. *Maybe that's a little dramatic but that does come very close to what it feels like.*

"Matthew, you seem different today. Since we left your house. You don't have to tell me anything, obviously, but just know that if you want to tell me eventually, I will always have open ears for you and I promise that it'll stay between us. Because you know… privacy is a thing."

That wasn't so bad. Not bad at all considering I don't have any prior experience.

That's the breaking point. Almost immediately after that speech, Matthew squeaks and tears flow down his face. He just starts sobbing right there and then.

HE'S SOBBING! WHAT DO I DO?

I jump up and run to my bag because I always have tissues inside the small front pocket. I fumble it out of the pocket and run back to Matthew, offering him the pack. He takes it and actively tries dabbing tissues under his eyes to stop the tears from coming.

He's still sobbing, maybe dry heaving, or something in between, but at least the waterfall of tears has stopped. Slowed down at least.

"Sorry," he sobs, "I think I may have gotten some tears on your bed." He laughs. That's a good thing. I think.

"Eyyyy, he's still got some humor in him! That's awesome."

He doesn't say anything more and just stares at the tissue in his hand.

193

"You know…," I start, then stop and take a few seconds to reconsider what I was about to say.

"You know, you don't have to apologize for having feelings. I would even encourage you to cry and scream and do whatever you have to make yourself feel okay. And my offer still stands, so do you want to talk about it or should I just shut up before I make it worse?"

Now that- that was bad. Why couldn't I have stayed at the same level as before?

He sniffs, then replies, "I want to tell you, and I mean everything, but I can't. I'm sorry."

"No," I protest, "you're not sorry because there's nothing to be sorry for."

"Okay. I have a weird question though. Can you maybe hold me, please? At least until I am asleep? Otherwise, I think I'll cry again and I don't want that to happen again. If that's okay," he whispers in between sniffs.

That makes my heart do the funny little jumping thing again. That's so much more than I had ever hoped for. So of course I just nod and wait until he's laying in bed again. From the other side of the bed, I lift the blanket and crawl into the same bed. Next to him.

His body heat meets me with a welcoming radiation. I scoop closer until I can wrap my arms around his body and close my eyes. Matthew is almost quiet now, except for an occasional sniff, so I try to be as still as I can. Just to make sure I don't accidentally bump my legs into his or anything that would disturb him.

But suddenly his leg brushes mine and it takes us less than ten seconds to fully entangle each other. It's so warm and calm and I wish we would never have to get up again. Ever.

CHAPTER 23

Matthew

I have never felt this bad in my life. Not even when I read the first letter my mom had left. Not even when I realized a couple of days later, that Dad hadn't signed it because I was probably too irrelevant to him.

I wanted to tell Liam. I wanted to explain everything. That my parents aren't actually on a work trip, but in reality I have no clue where they are today, or ever. That my mom had sent me occasional letters and that they're gone. That, if I don't get those letters back, I will most likely be sent away.

But I'll also be sent away if I tell Liam. I have thought it through, and in every possible situation Liam ends up heartbroken and I'm trapped with random people, in a random house, in a random city.

It's better if no one knows.

Either way, I have to find out where the letters are, who took them, and why they took them. Did whoever stole the letters know about them and came to retrieve them, or did they just look through everything until they found them? And most importantly, what might they plan to do with them?

I've been thinking about it all night, although I did get more sleep than I originally thought I would. Liam's arms were around me almost all night, keeping me warm, comfortable, safe, and yet my mind was screaming, racing through every possible scenario.

At first, I thought maybe it was a random house looter and they had picked my home from straight-up bad luck. But then why bother with the letters and nothing else? Then I thought about the people I know. Who had a bone to pick with me? Josh and his buddies were the first obvious answer, but again, why bother with the letters? On top of that, they wouldn't have the self-control to not break or steal anything else. After nobody else came into my mind with an actual motive I went over to another theory. Maybe my parents hired someone to get every little piece of evidence I had of their vanishing because they don't wish to have any sort of connection with me anymore. This one scares me the most, but also the least of all theories I came up with.

Fortunately, I stopped myself before thinking about all the effects of all this. If those letters go public… bye-bye life. Bye-bye house. Bye-bye friends. Bye-bye Liam.

I had wiggled myself out of bed early in the morning, 7:23 am to be exact. I haven't checked my phone since yesterday, and I don't think I will anytime soon. There's no point in seeing everyone's totally normal and happy social media, while I might lose everything. The only task that I will perform soon is to shower.

I'm trying to be as silent as I can possibly be, but a shower is naturally loud and there's not much anyone can do about that. I just have to hope that I don't wake anyone up. I'm standing in boxers looking in someone else's mirror, brushing my teeth, and I can not wait to get under warm water. Ever since I had gotten out of bed, the warmth of Liam's body was gone and it left me freezing.

The water was so helpful to just calm down and not go feral, for now at least. It's soothing as it flows all around me. I focus on the sound of the water hitting the marble shower floor. I breathe in and out. Over and over again.

Which is good enough for this exact moment.

It's still early so I take my time to dry myself, dress with the new clothes I brought, and get back into Liam's room. He's still sleeping, which is great. It gives me time to not talk about what happened

day, and why I acted the way I did. It wasn't fair to Liam and his

only

y it can't be

bag out of the corner behind Liam's door,

e. Since I slept through most of the time

ly be logical if I do mine now.

gain, like an endless

else, but I have to read a lot

o make the words make sense.

n doesn't really register them. I

don't know if I'm the only one who unwillingly does this, but I very much don't recommend anyone to do this.

The time goes by and it feels like hours of work. I'm exhausted already, but at least I'm being productive. Kind of… I mean, I'm trying. In what feels like hours, I have only finished a document analysis, a picture to be exact, for history. Before I can get any more frustrated, I hear a rustle from behind me.

"Hey," Liam whispers, "you're awake."

"I am," I'm feeling bold, "why, is there a problem? I can come back to bed if you want."

"Actually, that sounds like heaven," he's smiling now. A new kind of smile. A very adorable, sweet, I-just-woke-up kind of smile. How could I resist?

I leave my pen and notebook behind and climb into bed. Lying next to each other again, I reembrace myself in that familiar warmth.

The sun shines through the split of Liam's curtains, which makes it feel like it's afternoon, and it might be. I didn't check the time since before I started my work. I don't care what time it is, I'm here, in my first-ever boyfriend's bed. I block out every other word in my mind, repeating one phrase over and over.

It came true.

I haven't heard a sound from outside either. Logic? afternoon yet but it wouldn't change anything if it was.

Liam shifts around to face me. We're lying eye to eye, staring into each other's souls. I just want to reach out and kiss him, maybe even more, but kissing is a very good start. Or… it would be.

This is almost all I ever wanted. It came true.

Now that I think about it, that first sentence isn't even correct, I didn't know I wanted this until about a year ago. The second part, however, that's the truth, it did come true.

Time passes within the blink of an eye. How much, I don't know. It could've been years and I wouldn't be able to tell the difference to a few hours. We just stared deeper and deeper, eventually I may have gotten lost in the forest green of his eyes.

That's very cliché of me. Be more creative next time.

My consciousness is not in a good mood today, but it's right. I have to do better.

If it were up to me, this bed would become our private little island where we can stay unbothered from the rest of the world, for all the time we have left. Tess and Patricia could eventually visit for an hour or two, his parents too, but the rest of the time would be ours to make the most of.

To my disliking, we can't actually stay here forever. At most until his parents wake up and come searching for us.

As if on cue, I hear a door open down the hall. I sigh, then smile at Liam while I get up. He grabs my arm and asks, "What are you doing?"

I look to the door and back at him, "Didn't you hear the door? I was going to get back in the chair before your parents catch us. I thought you didn't want them to know we're dating?"

Dangerous territory for sure, but if he's going to keep quiet about our otherwise public relationship, then I think I deserve some sort of conversation about it at least. Besides, focusing on this will keep me from thinking about the letters.

See, it's already working. Totally not thinking about the letters… At all.

"You're right, I haven't told them yet. I'm sorry, I know I should have. But I also know how they'd react. They would never let you see one of them again without being drilled with questions about yourself. And about us. I know it might be selfish, but for now, I want you all to myself."

That was the sweetest thing anyone has ever said to me, and though the interrogation doesn't sound quite as sweet, I cannot wait for it to become a reality. "It's really okay," I say, putting as much confidence as I can into my next few words, "I want you all for myself too."

"So I'm guessing you haven't told your parents about me either," he says it more like a statement than a guess, but he's technically right. They don't know about him…

I'm caught off guard nevertheless, "Um," I try, "They don't even know I'm gay, so no, I didn't tell them." *Not that I had much of a choice on that one.*

201

"That's fine. Take your time and do it when you're ready." He soothes my arm with his hand as he sits up next to me. It's so sweet of him to say, much sweeter than I ever deserved, but again it's not like I have the choice to tell them.

Even if they had stayed, I don't know if I would have told them by now. My mother would probably be happy for me, and my father would've been indifferent about it. At least I can believe with certainty that he wouldn't have kicked me out. Although, I'm not sure which is worse. Being hated or being indifferent to someone. But who knows, if they had stayed maybe they would've changed with me. If they had stayed, everything would be different. *Would I even have been able to meet Liam?* I'm glad everything happened the way it did. After all it showed me that being raised by my parents would have been worse if they had stayed. With all that potential in their characters, to leave their child to fend for itself…

My body feels numb, too heavy to really move. All I crave to do is fall back into the mattress and hug Liam. But with his parents in the haul that might be too risky.

I get out from under the cover, stand up, and stretch until it feels like I almost tear a muscle. *Refreshing.*

Liam does what I should have done a while ago as well, he turns on his phone. By the look on his face, there's either a huge celebrity scandal, or he's received so many messages that his brain couldn't handle it all at once.

He's typing and typing and typing so I can safely assume it's the latter.

Since I'm already dressed, I go downstairs without waiting for him. My guess was right, Eric is in the kitchen preparing breakfast while Iressa sits at the table not even 3 feet away.

I stand there awkwardly for a few seconds, the embarrassment from last night sinking into my skin, but eventually, I step forward into a spot where Iressa immediately spots me. The sunlight streams through their board window, shining a spotlight on the wooden table just in time for breakfast. Everything feels so harmonious and peaceful, so happy.

Iressa sets down her cup, steam still rising from its surface, and waves me over, "Matthew! Good morning, come sit down!"

I walk over to the table, where plates had already been set on their red tablecloth, but before I sit down I look over at Eric and ask, "Do you need help with anything, Eric?"

He just shakes his head and motions for me to sit down. After that reassurance, I look at the remaining spots and choose the one diagonal from Iressa. This kitchen is fancy. Not like overly-rich-people fancy, but cozy yet shining with… I can't think of anything better than fanciness.

"Morning, Iressa. How are you today?" I ask with the nicest voice I could bring out.

She smiles at me, "I'm good so far, thank you. How about you? I hope you didn't stay up the whole night again." Her tone is almost playful and not at all angry. They really are the coolest parents I have met so far.

"Haha, no we actually got some sleep this time. Myself way earlier than Liam, which I actually wanted to apologize for, since that made me miss out on dinner. Liam brought something up for me though and it was delicious, so also thank you for that."

"Don't even worry about it. We know what it's like to be teenagers. Anyway, how is school going? You're taking French with Liam, right? I'm from France actually, but never had time to teach him much so I'm happy he's learning now."

"Thanks, and that's so cool. You're from France? That's so surprising because your accent doesn't sound French. Not in a bad way obviously. I just meant that it doesn't sound like it does in the movies." *Great job. Offending my boyfriend's mother during the third conversation.*

"Yah well, what can I say? My family moved from France to Germany when I was six and learned German before I started English, which is why my accent is now somewhere in between."

"Wow," I start, "and you still speak French then? How many languages do you guys speak?"

"Well, I speak French, German, English, and some Latin, although I forgot most of it. Eric speaks German and English, but we're both still learning of course. And Liam, he speaks the most but I'm sure he already told you."

I shake my head as I realize that I had never asked him how many languages he speaks. That's a mistake I should've corrected by now. Damn it.

"Oh, he hasn't? Okay so, from my knowledge, he speaks fluent English, German, and Mandarin. But he also speaks conversational French and Bahasa Malay, and he also started learning American Sign Language a while ago but I'm not sure if he's still doing that."

My mind is officially blown. I knew Liam spoke a few more languages than the average American, but this… wow.

"Wait, why did he learn Malay? You guys lived in Singapore, right? Did the school offer it and he wanted to take it or was it like out of school?"

Iressa sights and smiles again before she continues, "Neither. You have to understand that schools over there aren't like they are here, they mostly don't let you choose classes until you're in grade 11, and we left right before that. In his school, students had to take both, Malay and Chinese. Liam didn't exactly want to learn the language, but he still did in the classes he had over the years."

"Oh, that makes sense. I'm still so flabbergasted about how you don't confuse all these different words in different languages."

My jaw is still gaped open when Liam walks into the kitchen. He sits down next to Iressa, right opposite of me. I smile at him and he smiles back. Suddenly it's like everything is how it was supposed to be from the beginning, and the letters never went missing.

"You should ask Liam about that, he knows best," Iressa motions a hand between us.

"Right, yeah he probably does," I mumble, "Your mom just told me how many languages you speak and I am more than impressed. But I

205

was just wondering how you don't mix up all those words in all those languages?"

He laughs, "Trust me, every polylingual person mixes up words. Sometimes I don't even know a specific word in a language and try to google a translation from a different language and then I realize that I don't know that word in any other language either. It's frustrating but funny at the same time."

I laugh now too, and Eric starts setting up all kinds of food around the table. From four different types of bread to six or seven jams, to cheese slices, to honey and chocolate spread. Unbelievably many options.

I bite into the breakfast that I chose, whole grain bread with gouda cheese and strawberry jam upon Iressa's recommendation, and listen to the lively conversation around the table. Or at least the bits that are in English.

The last time my family had a breakfast similar to this was when I was about four or five. Even before they left, they didn't have much time for family meals or stuff like that. It makes me hate them, but I know that it wasn't their fault they had to work a lot. Yet I still hate them for that. Almost as much as I hate them for leaving.

When we're done eating I carry my dishes to the sink and offer to help wash up, but again Eric refuses and insists on me to go have fun. Whatever that means for today because as far as I know, we have nothing planned for today.

For starters, Liam and I walk back upstairs, back into Liam's room. Right after I close the door behind me, Liam asks me, "So what do you want to do now? We have the whole day for ourselves."

I shrug because I still do not have the slightest idea of what we could do. Liam walks to the end of his bookshelf, and quickly looks out the window and back at the books, as if scanning for some grand idea.

"I got it. We can invite Patricia and just go somewhere. To the mall or the cinema or something else that'd be cool."

That doesn't sound too bad. "Yeah, but I think we should call Patricia first before we make any decisions on her behalf."

"Already ahead of you," he says and indeed, his phone is out and ringing on speaker, waiting for Patricia to pick up.

"Hey, what's up?"

"Patriciiiaa," Liam almost sings her name as a conversation starter, "As you know, Matthew is staying at my house for the night- Say hi Matthew."

"Hey," both of us say at the same time.

"Anyway, we were wondering if you wanted to join us in doing something. Please?" He asks somewhat nicely.

"Uhm, sure. What were you thinking we do exactly?"

"That's the problem," Liam responds, "we don't actually have a plan yet. We were thinking about the mall or the cinema or anything outside this house. I think we'd both be fine with what you'll choose, right?" He looks at me and I give a reassuring nod.

"Okay, give me a minute," Patricia says and goes quiet for a few seconds, "There's laser tag, malls, a bouncy house, and movie theaters pretty close so we can do one of those for sure. Anything else would probably be too far."

I chip in, "I think laser tag would be fun if we had more people, malls, and movies are kind of basic by now, so my vote is for the bouncy house."

"Matthew is right, can you send me the address for the bouncy house?"

"Just did, I'll see you there at… Now it's almost 10, so I'll see you there at 11 or 12? Whatever is best for you."

Liam looks at me again with the question in his eye. It's cute but I shrug again because either is fine for me.

"Let's do 11. Do you want us to pick you guys up? I'm sure my dad wouldn't mind," Patricia says.

"Nah that's fine, thanks though. See you at 11." And that's that. Patricia hangs up before either of us can say goodbyes.

CHAPTER 24

Liam

I was happy to wake up to a bunch of unread messages from Tess, yet unhappy when I realized that Matthew wasn't in my arms anymore. Last night, I didn't text them about much that happened, only that I needed her advice because Matthew was staying at my house again.

Before breakfast, I had spent at least half of my bathroom time texting instead of getting ready. At first, I filled in on minor details, such that Matthew wanted to stay another night, that we didn't sleep the night before because we both wanted to keep learning more about each other and so on. Tess, as hoped, reacted with lots of imaginary screaming, disbelief, shock, and above all, almost the same excitement that I had felt for the past few days.

That is part of the reason our friendship still works so well, we are always on each others' side. By screaming for the other when excited, or crying with the other when heartbroken. Although so far the heartbroken one was always Tess, for me it was mostly just despair that I never had a boyfriend. Until now.

After the basics, I filled in more details, like the different things he said that made my heart flutter and where we went. And of course, I told them about the cops that showed up, but that Matthew believes nothing happened. Really spending a majority of the conversation on trying to figure out why Matthew acted so weird when we left his house.

Tess said that's weird, too. They speculatively suggested that Matthew might have lied about nothing being missing, and that whatever was missing had value to him. But that couldn't be it. Right?

He's acting normal-ish again, so if something important really went missing, wouldn't he try to get it back? And wouldn't he have told the police if it was that important? Something doesn't add up here.

But Tess also agreed that I shouldn't worry about that now, because now all that Matthew wants to have a good time with me, and Patricia, so I will focus on that.

Tess and I are still actively texting while I get Patricia's text with the address. I look it up on google maps and it's about 20 minutes by car, so I'm already on the stairs to where Dad is still sitting at the kitchen table with Mom.

I smile and come up as politely as I can.

I speak in German because I didn't hear Matthew follow me which means he stayed upstairs and wouldn't mind not understanding now.

"Dad, can you please drive Matthew and me down to a trampoline park in 40 minutes? Please? We're meeting Patricia there because we have nothing else to do here. Please?"

He looks at my mother, as if silently waiting for her approval. When she nods, I grin even wider and thank them with an awkward hug.

When I'm back upstairs Matthew is standing in front of my shelf. It looks like he's admiring the books. Relatable.

"Whatcha looking at?" I tease.

He turns to me, slightly startled, and asks, "So did your parents say we could go?" Avoiding my question. But I don't feel like pressing for an unnecessary detail.

We have 40 minutes to get ready, meaning we have to hurry. I walk past Matthew and the shelves to reach my closet while I remember that Matthew doesn't have much else to wear if he gets his clothes for today full of sweat. Abruptly I stop searching through the piles of clothes and turn around.

"Matthew. Did you pack more than two days' worth of clothes? Because we'll be sweaty and you'll want to change but then you may not have clothes for school tomorrow."

"Uh, I did not. It'll be fine. I can wear the same thing to school tomorrow that I'll change into today."

I couldn't let him do that to himself, so while I speed through everything I own, trying to find something comfortable to jump in but also something that can get sweaty, I make sure I grab another T-shirt and pants that are usually too large for me and toss them at Matthew.

"You can see if these fit and wear them if you want, and I should have another pair of socks if that becomes a problem."

Matthew nods, grabs the clothes, and leaves the room. He left to change, which makes it the best possible time for me to change as well. It feels weird, the possibility of the best person ever being able to walk in and out of my room at any given time.

It's going to be awesome, my two favorite local people and I are hanging out together. The only thing missing is Tess, well… human not a thing but whatever.

If they were here, today could end up being the best day of my life, but like today, Tess will always be missing and I hate that. I despise it even. The only logical action to take now is to sit on my bed, wait for Matthew to come back, and text Tess.

We didn't stop texting since I woke up, but we both have outside lives and had to check on that for a minute or two in between. It's currently 5:07 pm in Germany and Tess is still out with their friends. They told me how one of her friends organized this really big proposal for the other girl in the group, except the proposal wasn't for marriage but for a relationship in general.

Most romantic thing EVER. Not to sleep on many other great gestures, but I have yet to witness one myself, and hearing it through my bestie is the closest thing to that.

Selfishly, all I can think about is wanting to get one myself. I know it won't happen because well… I'm already in a relationship. Yet, the way that went down was definitely something.

I had turned off my phone and threw it in a bag where I had also stored water, ibuprofen, a charger, a power bank, and my wallet. I keep the bag in that exact condition at all times in case I need to go somewhere and don't have time to pack. Comes in handy a lot.

Matthew is back in my shirt and sweatpants. He's as handsome as always, but luckily my stuff fits him. When he gave me his spare pajama it was no problem because he's bigger than I am so it was just a bit floppy, but if my stuff didn't fit him, Matthew would look like a... I can't think of a better expression than *Pellkartoffel.*

Yes, it means potato, but in German, it's an expression used to exaggerate how tight something is. I swear it's a thing.

"How do I look?" Matthew's voice rips me out of my thoughts. I take a second to properly scan and assess him before I reflect on an answer.

"You look amazing. As always. But that outfit just has a special flare to it."

He smiles. As if he reads my mind, he's already walking over before I can take another step. I more than happily embrace him as he leans into me, and our lips touch. My face flushes immdiatetly but the outside world disappears with it.

I break away for a moment and breathe, "We should do this more often."

Matthew doesn't reply, but immediately puts that plan into action. We stand there for a great amount of time before my dad calls us down. We grab the last of our stuff and head downstairs.

213

It's 11:04 am when we arrive at the address Patricia told texted me. We're late, yes. But not too late, which makes it acceptable. I texted Patricia two minutes ago, and she said she was already inside.

The park is in a separate building right across a mall, so if neither of us like it, then we can still go there as a plan B. We thank my dad for dropping us off and head inside.

Patricia was inside, waiting at the counter, as she said she was. I have money in my bank account, thanks to my mother this morning, enough to pay for me and Matthew since I doubt he has any money on him right now. He can pay me back later if he insists, but I'd be happy to pay overall. But I know Matthew well enough that he won't let that go unless he pays me back, so I don't argue when he whispers in my ear, "I'll pay you back by the end of the week, promise."

I just smile and search for a free table between all the parents. We're probably the oldest people here who want to go jumping. It's full of screaming little kids running around after one another, so we just stand out a little more than usual.

I turn to both of them and say, "I already feel judged." Of course, Matthew replies with the most perfect response of all time, "You just have to ignore them. They don't know how to have fun if they're judging us."

He's right, obviously. But that doesn't change the feeling of all the eyes, of parents and children alike, burning holes into my back.

CHAPTER 25

Matthew

We went from one attraction to the next, from normal trampolines, to mini games, to trampoline-dodgeball and so much more. We didn't stay at anything longer than ten minutes because we only paid for an hour and apparently needed to see everything.

It's funny because we look so old compared to the kids around us. Technically we could already be working here which makes it even stranger. But the employees are all really nice, and so far we haven't accidentally jumped on a kid, nor did any of us hurt ourselves by accident, so that's good. The parents only shoot us with weird looks but don't say anything, better that way.

After we've been everything at least once, Patricia leads us back to her favorite area. It's a trampoline that's kind of angled to the wall. It's like a wall of trampolines. Who knows what you're actually supposed to do on them.

Liam and Patricia run down the trampoline wall at least four times, each, before either one dares to jump. I jump once before I decide that I'm just not built for this type of sport. After my very pathetic attempt at a jump, I sit myself on the ground next to the air pad. Watching Liam have fun is one of the best things today, so far… who knows what else will happen?

Pretty much all of us are exhausted when we leave the park. Unfortunately for me, I didn't think of bringing water even though I knew we were going to need it. Patricia was apparently the only one who planned ahead.

"We can go to the mall and get food, then you can buy drinks along with that," Patricia suggests. And again, she's apparently the only one who has any sense of planning ahead.

"Yes, please! I have water in my bag, Matthew if you want, but at the same time one bottle of water won't be enough for both of us.," Liam says. I just agree I take the bottle.

The parking lot around us is pretty empty except for an occasional car that drive by, probably also trying to get to the mall. So we walk, continuing along the sidewalk all the way around the lots to, finally, the mall's main entrance.

It looks like it has come down quite a bit, at least outside. The paint is pealing off the walls and the sign above that reads *Entrance A,* has mold almost completely covering it. However, the inside is lively enough to move past the appearances and go on.

None of us hesitate though. The first thing we see is a tiny bookstore to the left, and a clothing store to the right. In front of us, the hall is divided into two paths. One left, one right.

"Which one will bring us to food faster?" I ask, looking at both of them. Liam shrugs and Patricia doesn't respond. "Okay, perfect. Right it is," I wave them to follow me. We don't walk for a long time before a food court becomes visible through the crowd. Just a bunch of tables surrounded by two rows of restaurants.

That feeling in my stomach right now isn't hunger, but relief as we step into heaven.

The three of us had decided to get Japanese food and ate it there. Of course we got drinks too, so we did in fact not die. Patricia's dad graciously picked us up and dropped me and Liam back to his house. Hours had passed since we left the trampolines behind, so it's nearly dark when we walk through Liam's front door.

Neither of his parents were downstairs so we wordlessly walked upstairs and straight to his room. We're both still exhausted, me less than him, but I think that's because Liam isn't really a people person.

He falls straight into his bed and groans.

"Didn't have fun?" I ask.

"No, of course I did!" He yells defensively, "but it's exhausting too!"

Trying to show understanding, I respond, "Yeah. You should rest."

Liam looks up and turns, staring me down.

217

"What?" I shrug, "You said you're tired and now I'm telling you to rest so that your problem won't be a problem anymore. Some might call that Problem Solving."

Liam sights drastically and falls back on the mattress.

"Can I get you something? Water maybe?" I try again, forcing my voice to be as gentle as possible.

"Dude," Liam cranks, "You're the guest. I should be getting you something, not the other way around." He stands up and walks back out the door. In the hallway he says, "Rest, I'll bring both of us water."

Very determined of him but I honestly wouldn't have minded. He's obviously more exhausted than I am, so I just wanted to do something for him but that kinda back-slapped. Though, does it matter now? Not really because it's just one trip downstairs, and he insisted on it.

He comes back not two minutes later with two glasses that are filled to the top. I'm surprised he hasn't spilled anything yet, or at least it looks like it. I'm already lying in bed when Liam claims dibs on the shower, and as soon as he closes the door behind him I fall asleep.

Waking up Monday morning feels like sleeping in… well not really, but we wake up 20 minutes later than I usually would on a school morning. Yet we got to school around the same time. Eric drove us, which was almost a luxury experience.

School went by fast. After first period I barely saw Liam again until seventh. But even then we didn't talk much because Madame Veilleux decided that Monday is the perfect day to introduce another verb tense for us to memorize. Amazing.

After school I waved goodbye to Liam, who by the looks of it, has something planned with Patricia, and got on the bus. Surprisingly, the drive is mostly calm. Nobody is screaming or squeaking, just casual conversation. I don't listen to any of them though, because I have my eyes closed and am almost fully immersed into the song drumming in my ear.

Since Saturday, I haven't allowed myself to think about the letters again. So far I haven't been contacted by anybody about them, which I guess is good considering that also means I'm not being blackmailed. Yet.

I'll just hope that whoever has them now, doesn't know what to do with them and therefore won't do anything at all. Burning them would be nice though. That would be way less trouble for everyone involved.

What isn't easier for anyone involved, is the route the bus driver is taking. I live fairly close to school, but she always drives to the furthest stop first and then makes her way back. Meaning, I'm one of the last people to get off about an hour after school ended. But when the doors finally open I'm blessed with relief as fresh air embraces me.

I don't actually know why I take the bus sometimes. It's louder, longer, and more exhausting than just taking the 20 minute walk. But honestly I just don't feel like walking sometimes, including today.

Something about today just doesn't sit right with me. Maybe it's the air, or maybe it's just the fact that I'm going back to the house someone just broke into a few days ago. It's not that I'm worried that someone could come back, but I'm just so stuck on how, whoever it was, got in. Nothing was broken, no open window, no unlocked door, no broken lock. That just doesn't make sense. *How did they get in?*

Either they figured out a way to lock and unlock the door from the outside, or they did just that with a key. But that's not possible so what could they have used to open the door? The trick with using a credit card just doesn't seem real, and something forcefuln like that would have left marks.

I don't understand.

I unlock the door, step inside, and immediately take off my shoes and put them in their designated spot. The air around me feels the same as it always has, yet the warning pressure in my gut tightened. As quietly as I possibly can I set my backpack down against the inner side of the door.

My heart is hammering now, the sweat in my hands building up as my knees turn into jelly. I take the umbrella that's hanging on the side of the shoe rack, and hold it like a baseball bat. If I have to swing, I will swing and run. Swing and run.

I'm probably just paranoid, I tell myself. But better to double check than die because someone stabbed you in the back. Better safe than dead.

Carefully I step along the hall, into the kitchen area. Where… nobody is. I lower the umbrella.

That was kind of anti-climatic but better than the opposite.

But I know what comes next. The unavoidable path into the garage and laundry room. If someone was here in the kitchen and heard me come in, they'd have enough time to just sneak away and hide in there.

Dreading what comes next, I pick up the umbrella again and force the door open to the hell beyond. I turn on every light possible and glance behind every corner and behind every possible hiding spot. And again nothing. Apparently the umbrella was not needed, thankfully.

My pulse has relatively regulated itself by the time I turned off all the lights and closed each door. I walk back to the front door and hang the umbrella back to its original spot on the shoe rack.

After remembering to grab my backpack, I turn around once more and make my way upstairs. Upstairs, the only open doors are mine and the one for the master bedroom. *I must have left it open when we were here yesterday.*

I drop my bag on my bed and slump into my chair. I could sit here forever if there weren't the consequences of missing out on school and essentially ruining my own life. But I can sit here for at least twenty minutes, and just rest my eyes. Not sleep, but rest. There's a clear difference.

So I convince myself to close my eyes and try to rest for 20 minutes or less.

I awake not shortly after by a muffled noise from down the hall.

My heartbeat quadripples in seconds and I don't dare to move too fast, to make too much noises. I know instantly that I was wrong about nobody being here, but they didn't hide in the garage, but upstairs. Genius. And I played right into their plan.

221

Logically, I shouldn't go look, because in every single horror movie where something similar happens, the guy who ends up checking what it is, dies. Quite frankly, not a fan of dying in at the moment, so no thank you.

On the other hand, I could find out who has my letters and if they plan to do anything with them.

I hate decisions. Especially the obvious ones, when you really don't want to choose the obvious choice. It's horrorful.

After successfully getting out of the chair without any major sounds, I tiptoe to the end of the hall, where the still opened door reveals people. People who definitely should not be here.

CHAPTER 26

Liam

Patricia and I haven't texted much in the last week. Mostly because of how busy I am with Matthew. But on rare occasions when I have time to spare, Patricia does not. Until today.

On the way to my house after school, she told me all about how two guys in her third period were caught vaping in the bathroom, which caused a huge scene and eventually earned them a referral. Unfortunately, it wasn't any of Josh's friends. I would have loved that.

After only a ten-minute drive we're both already cackling up about the conversation, yet we didn't even get to the good stuff yet. My dad just rolls his eyes every time one of us starts to wheeze.

Patricia enters the house with me while my dad still parks the car. She follows my example of taking off her shoes and putting them onto our rack. While we hurry up the stairs, I sort of tell my dad we'll be back down soon for lunch.

He replies with an unbothered "Aha."

We're upstairs in a rush and shut the door behind us. Patricia is still giggling about the car when I say, "I need to tell you something."

The giggling stops, along with apparently any breathing in this room.

"Is it bad? Please don't tell me anything bad. If I don't know about it, it won't bother me. So, please. Is it bad?"

I shake my head grinning, "No no, calm down. But you do know that that's not how problems work in general, yes?"

Patricia rolls her eyes, so I just continue.

"Well anyway. The thing I wanted to tell you is about Matthew."

"Oooh," Patricia exclaims. She sits on the edge of my bed, expectations looking up at me.

"He may have spent the past two nights here, and not even in the guest room if you know what I'm saying."

"Woa," her mouth hangs wide open for a second before she continues, "so you two finally did it?"

"Did what?" I ask confused.

"Oh come on, you know what I mean," is Patricia's only, and not-so-helpful, explanation.

"I do not." She looks very irritated now. As if it's the most obvious thing ever.

Spoilers, it is not.

"You know… Sex?"

Ohh.

"That's what you meant, got it. No we did not. He just slept here. We kissed and cuddled, like a lot, but that's about it."

"Hm." I don't like the tone in which Patricia expresses this. So judgy.

"What do you mean by that?" I raise an eyebrow, in a what–the–hell kind of way.

She shrugs, "Nothing, I just thought you guys would have done it already. Especially Matthew."

"Huh?!" I express my confusion as clearly as I possibly can, "Why's that?"

Patricia says, "Well, in case you haven't noticed, he is one of those hot popular kids who gets a new partner every week. Not that it won't work out with you two, but he does have a certain reputation."

I had never thought of that. *Does Matthew want to have sex? Is that the only reason he's together with me? To use the inexperienced shy guy to experiment and then move on?*

No. Matthew wouldn't do that. Just wouldn't. A reputation doesn't define a person's character, behavior, or intentions. Right?

But what if I don't want to do anything yet? At least, I haven't thought about it. I mean, it's not even been a week since we got together. Will he drop me if I tell him that I do not want to do anything like that yet?

I convince myself over and over that Matthew is not that kind of person. I know him, and I know for a fact that he wouldn't do anything close to that. But every time I convince myself, another argument pops

225

into my mind. Mainly how weird he acts sometimes. As if he has something he doesn't want me to find out.

He's pranking me. I figured it out. Matthew just pretended to not be Josh's friend anymore to make the whole story more believable. He and Josh probably have some sort of bet going that I'm undateable or something similar. It's all an act.

How could I ever be this stupid and believe him?!

My breath stops in my lungs and I collapse on the ground. I don't feel it though, the burning in my lungs or the panic rising through my blood. Patricia's by my side immediately but I manage to shake my head when she says she's going to call my parents.

I'm just a little panicky. I won't die.

How did I not see it coming?! It was all too good to be true anyway. I should have never let myself go through with this. Of course, it has to be false in the end. Of course.

I want to cry. I want to scream. Or both.

I want to break something. Anything. But more than that, I want to break Josh and all of his friends. Except Matthew. *How pathetic of me.*

He stabs me in the back with at least a dozen daggers, and I still can't be mad at him.

I think I'm crying because when I look up again, Patricia is coming back from somewhere with a bunch of tissues in her hand.

I grab them and hold them in front of my eyes. They're forced shut. I can't face the world right now. *Why would anyone do this to someone? How can someone be so cruel?*

Thinking of my history, I quickly know that I deserved this. Everything. Someone faking their interest in me for a bet, me believing him, me being unable to be mad at that person because of course it had worked.

Of course, it had.

How could I be so oblivious? I should have seen it coming. Should have known. Nobody like him would ever like me, much less purposefully start something like a relationship. It's pathetic. I'm pathetic.

About 40 minutes go by before I somewhat manage to gather myself. While trying to remain relatively quiet, I cried. I cried a lot. More than I have in months. Patricia was the most wonderful friend through these horrible 40 minutes.

She gave me one tissue after the other and didn't even try to tell me not to cry. She didn't call my parents either, though she tried multiple times, but luckily always asked me first, so I made it clear not to.

I hate that I did that to her. Well, kind of still doing it, just not as dramatic anymore. Patricia came here to have fun together but instead, she gets a fellowship in the psychiatric hospital for minors. That's probably not how that works, but whatever.

I'm still sort of heaving, trying my best to breathe normally but failing. Patricia looks at me with dead-serious eyes that could scare the life out of anyone.

"Do you now want to tell me what the hell is happening?"

I'm like a waterfall of words. Once I start speaking, it's like I can't control what or how much comes out of my mouth. So I tell her everything. About the police at Matthew's house, and how he was convinced nobody was there but then started acting strange after. And about all the things I became clear of within the last hour.

Patricia looks baffled by the time I finally finish.

She exhales slowly, then states, "For the record, I don't think Matthew is the kind of guy who would do that. Yes, he has a past, but so does everyone else. But if what you're saying is true, I will walk over there and TAKE HIS HUGE EGO AND SHOVE IT HIS OWN..."

She doesn't get to finish this vivid thought because I cut her off, "As lovely as that description was, that job is already reserved for me. No offense but destroying him is now my job... If anything I believe is even true. It's not like I have any evidence whatsoever."

I sight. Patricia nods and huffs in agreement.

"So the question is, how do we find evidence?" I ask out loud. I don't want it to be true, so finding no evidence would be a good thing. A great thing even.

"I mean, you could just ask him." I almost start laughing at that joke of a suggestion. As if he'd tell me the truth then. I shake my head and so we forget that idea immediately.

In situations like these, I wish I could read minds so that I'd know if Matthew was really doing this. He wouldn't have gotten this far. Or shapeshifting, to talk to him as someone else could also have saved me a lot of trouble, pain, and despair.

I get up and I know what I have to do.

Priority number one is talking to Matthew, but not asking him anything. I need to stop this before it gets any further. Although I don't want any of this. I wish I had never gotten so involved with him in the first place. *Fuck him for being so sweet.*

I never would have thought this day would come so soon, if ever. The day I break up with Matthew Gaines and kick him out of my life for good.

Almost a week has passed since the realization. A week of heavily avoiding Matthew and always being too busy to answer him. A week of trying to find the right time not to ignore him. A week of trying to find a good time to confront him.

Pro of taking many advanced classes, you can say you have a lot of work to do even if you don't. Nobody would question you because everyone knows Stanford requires sacrifices. Not even your boyfriend who has been trying to talk to you for the last six days.

I don't even know why I've been avoiding him for so long. I have a plan, I know what I want to say, and I know what I want out of the conversation. Yet I have not brought myself to go up to him.

Maybe it's a fear of loss, of my first boyfriend and my first everything. Or maybe I'm just unsure about every decision I make in life because I never have any evidence whatsoever. Though, most of the time I turn out to be right. I just really do not want this to be the reality of our relationship.

In the past six days, I have thought about any conversations and interactions the both of us had, trying to find a moment where he acted weird. And, as if that wasn't enough by itself, I also reflected on all the times I saw Matthew and Josh together.

Nothing that seemed abnormal at the time. I thought that maybe it was really obvious and I was just blinded by Matthew, but now I can't see any clear signs either.

It'd be really embarrassing if I made all of this up out of nowhere. But I know that something is wrong, something has to be. And most likely it is that he doesn't actually like me. Simple.

Which is why I need to end it. As soon as possible. Actually… today. It needs to end today.

Easier said than done.

CHAPTER 27

Matthew

I haven't spoken to them in all the days they've been here. I refused to, and still do. They just showed up out of nowhere, after not talking to me for years, and then expecting me to forgive them and just move on with life… I think the fuck not.

My parents have the biggest audacity of any human ever because both have no sense of shame whatsoever. They showed up, with no notice at all, breaking in, and then acting like they haven't abandoned me for the past *years*.

When I saw them in that room I completely froze up. My brain stopped working and I'm pretty sure I didn't have a pulse for a couple of moments. When they saw me standing in their doorway, my dad just waved and continued unpacking his suitcase. My mom greeted me with a "Hi, honey." Which was enough for me. Way too much.

My brain was activated by her voice and finally permitted the rest of my body to do its job. I practically ran into my room, slammed my door shut, and made sure it was locked, twice.

The man who pretends to be my dad, who also does a very bad job at that, didn't try to reach out to me, which makes it way easier to avoid him. The other person, who pretends to be my mother, tried once. On the second day. I, very clearly, communicated that I have less than no interest at all in talking to her. She hasn't tried since.

Luckily. I don't know what I would have done if she did. Murder? Possibly.

I want them gone. Back to whichever hole they crawled out of. How do they think it's okay to come back into my house and act like nothing ever happened? I have prayed every day that they would just be gone again when I come back from school. They're still here.

So many things are going wrong. Everything was perfect just a few days ago, but now, it's like everything I devoted my life to not happen, is happening.

On top of that, Liam is acting weird around me too. That is if we are ever even in a room together. It's like he is trying to avoid me. When I asked him what's up, he slammed a door to my face and told me he was busy with all his classes. Sure, that might be a reasonable excuse for anyone else, but I know Liam. He takes time for people even if he doesn't have any to spare.

Yet he does everything not to talk to me. I don't understand what I did wrong. What caused him to not want to be around me anymore?

The last time we hung out together, Monday morning before school, he was fine. He smiled, talked to me, and acted like he always does.

I just don't know what's going on. Everything is falling apart.

While more and more problems are coming up, one mystery has been solved at least. I found out who took the letters. My mother did, big surprise. And as far as I have heard of their conversations through the walls, the letters are shredded up into tiny little pieces that nobody would ever be able to puzzle back together.

Good. That's less work for me if I had gotten them back.

At least that also means one less thing to go crazy about. But it doesn't mean that I can lean back and relax now, the opposite. I need to find out what's up with Liam. That's my number one priority. And the more time I spend on that, the less I have to see my so-called parents.

Sometimes I wish I would just tell Liam what's going on. Especially now. I just want to talk to him, and only him.

School flies by in no time today, class after class with basically no work at all. It's Friday, so there's not much to expect anyway. French ends in two minutes, meaning in two minutes I will finally talk to Liam again. Hopefully, I will find out what's going on with him.

There are less than two minutes left of class, but Madame Vielleux is still deep inside her lecture about the different types of stores there are in France. I didn't listen to anything this whole time, and I don't think I'm the only one. Most people have already packed all their stuff and are actively eyeing the time on their phones.

233

That includes Liam, he looks ready to sprint out of here any second now. Wouldn't surprise me if it was just to get out of my range. But I am prepared. The bell rings and as I had suspected, Liam is one of the first people to vacate the classroom and hurry down the halls.

I didn't catch him fast enough, and more and more people keep getting in the way which makes keeping up with him even harder. *Can't you guys just walk faster?! Be so serious! Don't just stop. KEEP MOVING!*

Many thoughts race through my mind as I race after Liam. Surprisingly I can still see him when I exit the building.

"LIAM!" I yell across the sea of people, but I'm overtoned by the crowd. All I can do is hurry after him until we are away from the crowd, or until I get close enough that he can hear me. He slowed down a bit, which I can only tell because the distance isn't getting bigger but rather staying constant.

"LIAM!" I try again, but no reaction besides the people around me who look at me like I'm out of my mind. I might be soon if he doesn't acknowledge me at all. People become fewer over the next five minutes of what feels like a goose chase.

I try yelling after him multiple times, but even as the crowd thins, he keeps walking. Maybe he heard me but just really doesn't want to talk to me and therefore is running now. In which case, I would be the worst human being alive, but I need to talk to him.

I can't go back to my house, where my children-hating parents are, and have my boyfriend avoiding me for a reason I am unaware of. My mental capacities would end there.

So I do the only logical thing and run after him. Which seems to be more productive than walking because it looks like I'm getting closer this time. *Hmm, guess he isn't as fast as I thought he would be.*

I'm panting by the time I finally catch up to him. I grab him by the shoulder which finally brings him to a stop. Liam doesn't turn around though.

"Liam," I say, demanding him to look at me. He doesn't so I try again, "Liam, can you please look at me? I'm trying to talk with you."

Now he turns, face expressionless. "Well, I don't want to talk with you."

"Why?" I ask, my voice shaking. "Why don't you want to talk to me? Did I do something to make you upset?"

"Yea and you know exactly what's on." Everything feels like it stopped, the cars, the wind, time itself. *Has he figured out that I lied about my parents? Does he believe me to be a liar now? But how would he even know…?*

"I don't," I say, trying to sound convincing.

"Bullshit." His face is filled with disgust but also a flicker of pain. Behind everything else.

Doing everything in my power I try to keep my voice restrained and ask, "Why don't you tell me what it is that I'm magically supposed to know? It's not like you told me or gave me any signs at all," I take a deep breath before I plead, "Please just tell me what's bothering you..?"

Liam looks at me once more, his face still with the same expression, but he says nothing. He probably is even more disgusted now

235

because in his eyes it must be entirely obvious, yet I can't even guess. *Great. Awesome. Totally great that he doesn't want to tell me. I guess I'm really just that oblivious and maybe Liam deserves better.*

"I think we need to.." Liam starts, his voice barely audible over those god-damned cars.

"Take a break," he finishes.

Time stops entirely. My heart stops along with it, or rather it should have. The air in my lungs fades into nothingness and there are no more sounds around me. Not even the pumping of my heart. It's like I'm completely numb.

"Wh…Wha..," I stammer, having forgotten how to talk.

"I'm sorry I had to tell you this way," tears is rolling down his cheeks, "but I think it'll be better for us. Take this as a chance to reflect on what you want."

I can't believe what's happening, but at this point, I don't care anymore. The numbness in me turns into rage and I'm full-on screaming now. "SO YOU'RE GOING TO BREAK UP WITH ME, BUT WON'T TELL ME WHY?"

Liam to his credit keeps a cool face, no rage visible whatsoever. Only disgust and despair. He nods. "You know why."

I'm unable to look at him much longer, without the fear of saying something that I will definitely regret, so I turn and start walking. Faster and faster, until I can't feel his eyes on my back anymore.

The last thing I want is to return home and be fueled with even more reason to be angry at everything, everyone, and the whole world. With no goal in mind, I run. Faster and farther.

CHAPTER 28

Liam

It's done. It's over.

It's horrible.

Matthew and I are on a break. So not technically over, but it already feels unbearable. But I know it's what's best. At least I hope.

I'm exhausted, flushed red, and disgustingly full of tears, though I am barely halfway home. My knees, back, and basically everything else hurt because of how much I tried to avoid that conversation. Running isn't my strong suit.

Matthew ran all the way back, I assume. He ran down the same streets we came from. I hope he gets home safe, I don't want him to be too distracted to watch the road for approaching cars. It would suck if he got hit by a car before we could get a chance to make up. Especially because it would be my fault. That's an understatement. I would despise myself for it.

I meant what I said though. Including the part about not wanting him to find out this way. This was pretty close to the worst-case scenario. But what did I expect when I was too scared to speak to him?

In the actual worst-case scenario, Matthew would have first completely broken up with me by admitting that everything was just based on a bet, and then get hit by a car right in front of me. He would deserve the second part, but I know it would hurt me even more emotionally.

Unfortunately.

Despite the various stings in my whole body, I move forward. Physically, not mentally of course. I don't need people seeing me like this on a random street. I don't notice cars, or time, passing by.

With every step I take, I keep reminding myself that it is the right decision for now. For us.

I really hope I'm wrong about this, all of it. Patricia was probably right anyway. Matthew wouldn't be the kind of guy who would do anything just for a bet. Especially not kiss me in private when there's nobody there to prove it. Would he?

Wondering is pretty much unavoidable.

When I finally get home, my tears haven't dried much and I don't feel any better. My plan's solid. Go directly to the bathroom, take the hottest shower in the world, and go right into bed. That way I won't have to explain myself to my parents and can just blame it on mood swings.

Another perk of moving again is that mood swings originating in the relocation are a thing apparently and I can put as much blame on them as I want.

The plan is going to be easier than I thought because my dad went grocery shopping and my mom is at work. Meaning I have the house to myself.

I drop my bag in my room and go straight into the bathroom, turn the hot water to the maximum, and wait. After not even two minutes, I submerge into the water and let it take me in.

Several realizations hit me in the hour I spent under burning water. First, Matthew had no right to do that to me. None at all. Logically that implies that it was my right to tell him off. I feel a lot better about that now.

Secondly, Josh, Manuel, Connor, and every single one of them, will not *talk* to me about this. Nor will they do anything else. I'm done with even bothering with them. My plan is simple, the next time they come up to me with the most ignorant reason ever, I'll just leave before they can even finish a sentence. It may not be the best strategy, but after doing that a few times, they'll probably get too bored to even try again.

Lastly, thinking about either of those things won't help me. Not a tiny bit. Thus, I shouldn't be thinking about it, and I won't. For sure.

The comfort of my room has never been needed as much as when I stepped out of the shower. 40 minutes have passed, yet all I did was put on clothes and lie on the floor. I didn't even make it to my bed before the remaining spark of energy burned out.

239

Or at least it feels like it. Maybe I'm just imagining it all and am just too lazy to get up. Either way, that won't change.

Maybe it will, if I were to wake up from this reality and realize everything was a dream and Matthew didn't stab me in the back after all.

When we first moved into this house, I thought it fairly odd that every scrap of the upstairs floor was carpeted. It didn't make sense to me, but I think now I'm learning to appreciate it. The soft welcomeness of the floor.

Usually, when this happens I want to move and can't, but not now. Now lying here is perfect.

Everybody knows the saying 'Rather sooner than later', which is why I force my arm to get my phone out of my pocket and call Tess.

It's about 4:30 pm right now, 10:30 pm in Germany, so there should still be a good enough chance for them to be awake and answer my call.

I was right. The phone doesn't even *beep* three times before Tess opens the conversation.

"Heey," they say, their voice kind of sleepy. Immediately I feel bad because I probably woke them up.

"Hi, did I wake you?" I whisper in German.

Tess replies, voice more steady now, "Nah, not at all. I'm just tired though. I have a presentation for Ethics in the morning, but of course, my group isn't doing what they're supposed to. I could snap this stupid pencil in half."

"Oh. I'm sorry. I don't want to distract you, and you probably need your phone to call your classmates," I say. "I'll call you tomorrow."

I'm about to hang up when Tess asks, "That's fine if you want to go, but I already tried calling them a bunch of times, so I doubt one more call would change anything. As for distraction, I need to get my mind off of this for a while anyway. So what's up?"

I exhale into the carpet and let out a soft groan.

"That bad huh?" Tess already knows something is up now, so they for sure won't let it go. Might as well tell them now, that's the least I can do for distracting them anyway.

"So, a funny thing happened," I start, in a very non-amused tone. "I finally figured out that Matthew doesn't actually like me. My guess is that he became my boyfriend to win a bet or something. So today I told him we should take a break. And now I'm lying on the ground like a stranded fish at the beach."

"Excuse me what? HE DID WHAT? I'm going to need you to give me more details." Tess exclaims. After two minutes of slightly arguing back and forth, I tell her everything that's racing through my mind. Even the part where I question my own credibility.

When I'm done I'm just praying that Tess doesn't think I'm crazy.

"Wow, that's… wow. That's a lot. But not to be *that* person, you never said anything about any kind of evidence. Maybe you're just paranoid because someone finally shows serious romantic interest in you and you aren't used to people caring about you..?" Their tone is more questioning than anything else. They really called me out with this one.

I know Tess might be right, that I'm making all of this up for whatever reason. But I'm currently not willing to take the chance. If I get heartbroken, I would rather it happen sooner than later.

When I don't respond for several seconds, Tess continues, "Of course, I don't know much because I'm not there. And I'm not you. However, if you're right, I will fly over, to Georgia, find his address, drive to his house, and fake-date him just to drop his ass when he's deeply in love with me."

That makes me smile. Not the idea of Matthew getting emotionally manipulated to create the most damage possible, but knowing Tess would be willing to do this for me. Even if it's only theoretical.

Though, before this can go any further I say, "Tess, you are aware that hurting Matthew, however satisfying it would be, is not the solution to anything, yes? Besides, you're probably right, it's all in my head." Breathing in and out in a slow, deep rhythm helps to silence the noises in my head. At least long enough to start the next sentence, "If he didn't not like me before, he definitely does now. Like, let's say it was all in my head and he did like me for real, then I came out of nowhere and hurt him for no good reason. Of course, he would despise me now."

Even thinking about that makes my chest pinch, like all the air was pushed out. Before the pain swallows me whole, Tess argues, "Well, maybe. But even then, I don't think he would hate you. At least from what you told me about him."

I stay silent, trying to comprehend my options. Either he hated me enough before to 'prank' me with this; he hates me now because of me going psycho on him; or he doesn't hate me and didn't before. But what does he think about me in the last scenario? Can it be any worse?

While I've been making a whole fuss about my hypothetical drama I didn't even bother to ask Tess how they're doing. They might have been wanting to tell me something and all I do is prevent them from telling me.

"Oh shit. I'm sorry that I'm such a selfish brat. Any things you would like to vent about now?"

"It's fine, it's obvious you are going through something. But I'm okay. I have a few stories though if you want me to distract you?"

I grunt, "Mhm."

"Okay so, you remember Macy right? She was in your class in second grade. And you also know that she went to the same school as I did after primary, yes?" Tess usually just asks me if I keep up because they want to be polite. I don't object to anything, letting them know that I am fully aware of all of these things.

Macy was always a pain in the year I had spent in a German elementary school. Sure, now she might be a nice person or whatever, but back then she was very far from that. Macy was in the same kindergarten as I was, luckily in a different group, but even back then I heard all the stories about Macy's latest victims.

Her most common, and maybe most annoying, acts of cold-heartedness was squirting the contents of a toothpaste tube into someone's shoe. Down to every last drop. I don't know how she even did that, or who paid for the many tubes she wasted. Though, that wasn't

243

even the worst part. The worst part was that she never faced any consequences.

Most kids knew it was her behind the tyranny, but the adults seemed to be oblivious and instead always punished the entirety of the kindergarten.

"She's paralyzed now." Dead silence follows as if that's the most normal thing to happen in the last few days.

"Like," Tess continues, "As of yesterday. Her aunt got in a car crash with her as a passenger. As far as I know, the doctors said it's only temporary. But she still has to learn how to use a wheelchair and everything."

Wha-

WHAT? I wouldn't wish that on anybody. not even Macy.

I don't know how to respond, instead I just gape at my phone where Tess doesn't say anything that further.

"And Tina, you know Tina right?"

"Yes, your bestie. Besides me of course."

"Yeah, sure. Tina's bestie happens to be Macy for over a year now, so Tina always goes to help Macy when she's struggling in the hospital, which has allowed me to do so as well. So I'm confused why you said you didn't like Macy. She seems nice so far."

"Well, you are aware that I only knew her through half of primary school, yes? I can imagine, or at least hope, that she developed into a nicer human than she was back then."

"Oh, right. I forgot. Sorry," Tess says.

"So, anything else I should know about before I let you get back to sleep again?"

Tess takes a second and then shrugs my question off with a simple, "Nope. Good night!! I might text you tomorrow if I don't forget!"

"Okay, do that! Sleep well," I respond and hang up, being once again left alone in the silent comfort of my room.

CHAPTER 29

Matthew

My lungs haven't burned this much in what feels like years. It's like there's acid in there just eating away at the lungs themselves. Who knows, maybe that would be the more tolerable option. I don't think I understand what just happened.

He dumped me. Liam dumped me. But why? What did I do to make him that angry?

Liam didn't even explain. Instead, it's over, just like that. Technically he didn't exactly break up with me, but he did say we need a break. And realistically, of all the couples that ever take a break, none of them recover for longer than a year after that.

If he had at least told me what I did wrong, I could have tried to fix it, but now I can't do anything except sit back and wonder.

Assuming my lungs don't fail any time soon.

I stopped running about two minutes ago which means it'll be a while before I can be sure. After playing football for a few years, you would assume that I can run at full speed for more than 30 minutes, but nope. Kind of disappointing if you think about it.

There is no goal where I'm going, just farther and farther. Maybe I can outrun my problem, aka Liam.

Since home isn't an option, school is closed, and I officially have no friends left, I make my way to the only other place I can think of. Maybe it's the only place because my mind is still racing, or maybe it is the last and only option. It doesn't matter much now either way.

The small space behind the football field is empty even as there are still many students roaming around campus. This is the perfect spot to just be empty, be nobody at. Through the bushes in front of me, I can see the team, my team, warming up and getting ready for training.

I must have burst into tears a while ago because I am suddenly aware of the jolts of water running down my face. I should be down there with my team training for the next game, even if they're not my friends anymore. And Liam should be nearby, watching me, cheering me on, and being happy with me.

Though, the last thing I need is for them to see me in this… condition. It would just give them even more reason to make fun of me.

Right about now it abruptly hits me that this place, the semi-hidden free spot behind the football field, is *the* place. The place where Liam and I had our first actual conversation, that didn't happen because of school. My heart aches even remembering it. I wish it could just go back to how it was back then. Sure, we weren't together yet, but

247

that only meant he couldn't suddenly hate me and destroy my emotional well-being.

I wish I could control it, but my mind keeps drifting back to that conversation. We both skipped sixth period that day. I was here leaning against the tall birch tree towering about ten feet to my left. I told Liam I had a free period then, which at the time wasn't entirely wrong. I did have nothing to do during sixth period, but technically I was required to be inside.

Sixth period is my elective, which this year is tutoring. Usually, I tutor two kids, Marshall and Pax, but fortunately, both of them were sick which meant I was relieved of my duties for the day. Both kids are in the same math class during sixth period, so I was able to convince the teacher to let me go early. I did promise her though to stay inside the building. Looking back I do not regret disobeying that promise.

When Liam left this spot, after I had invited him to stay with me, it did hurt. But I could see, even then, why he wouldn't want to hang with me. Meaning, I know I offended him before that but I didn't think it would be such a big deal after I apologized.

The faint roaring of the team pulls me back into reality, no matter how much effort I put into not existing in said reality. I don't know how long it's been since I've settled here. The tears have mostly dried, but the pain in my chest only deepened.

Knowing the tears have dried is enough for me to stand up, and step out into the now almost empty parking slots. I need to get away from here.

I need to get somewhere, any place where there's no trace of Liam. No memory of him attached. This is just even more reason not to go back to my house. *Great.*

So again I run. Fast as before. Aimless as before.

CHAPTER 30

Liam

1. It had to be done.

2. Matthew wouldn't stop following me.

3. At least he understands me now.

Those three things are the main arguments my brain keeps building around, using every literary element known to mankind to persuade me to believe myself. And I probably do believe them, why else would my brain keep repeating it if I didn't believe in it at all?

Luckily when I arrived home about 20 minutes ago, I was alone. That meant nobody could see or hear my cry in the bathroom, over problems that I caused. Maybe I'm just being dramatic because it's not like we broke up. We're on a break, so that I can see who Matthew really is, or so that he can drop the act. Whichever comes first. I'd think that if we had broken up, this whole act of pain would be justified but something in my head tells me it's not appropriate right now, that I'm just faking it for attention.

By this point in my life, I already know I'm either already crazy or on the way there. I don't know what else I could do than lean against my bathroom door and cry the soul out of my body. It's pathetic if you think about it.

I chose to enact the break. I chose to not trust him enough for it to work. I chose to ghost him for the past week. Yet I feel like absolute crap.

Not fair universe!

The arguments in my head don't seem to quiet down so I just start singing in my mind, a tiny melody in the back of my head to focus on. A melody to hide behind, away from the loud and dangerous arguments taking over.

No, it's never been quiet up there, but it's rarely ever this loud. There's always something going on, which I used to hate with a burning passion because I just wanted a moment of peace, but recently I didn't mind much. 'Recently' being the times I had with Matthew.

Here we go again.

It's like a spiral staircase that never ends. A cycle of pain and torture. I think of anything, somehow connect it to Matthew, feel hurt, and think about him more, making me even more hurt, and then start to pull myself out of it again.

The cycle keeps me trapped for the weekend. My parents don't notice because I rarely talk to them when I'm alone, making my job much easier. Patricia doesn't text me to check on me. Finally, to conclude my ever-shrinking social circle, I have been ignoring Tess' messages and calls for the past two days. I'm pretty sure my phone died a couple of hours ago because it's been silent for more than twenty minutes.

When Monday rolls around, school is the only inspiration for me to get out of bed. Ironic really. But I won't let Matthew, or any other guy for that matter, keep me from going to school. Surely one absence won't be noticeable, but one absence leads to multiple, which then leads to grades declining, failing classes, and eventually not graduating.

I want to go to college. More specifically, I have no other plan for my future than going to college.

On the ride to school, that's all I can think about. How much better would life be if I could just skip ahead and start the first year at Stanford. Leaving this life behind again feels like the perfect solution to all my problems. Realistically impossible but it feels true.

There I might even find a new boyfriend. Someone who doesn't play with my feelings.

Why are the expectations so low, yet barely any guys meet them? That is a little concerning for the world's civilization, but whatever.

During class is the only time Matthew and the cycle leave my mind, until seventh period that is. Class has helped to keep my mind occupied and not stuck in one place, which feels incredibly refreshing even if it's stressful most of the time.

But by the time I walk into seventh period, I feel like I'm going to collapse any moment now. But the final blow, which's supposed to knock all the air out of my lungs, never comes. I scan the room three times before I can silently confirm that Matthew is not here today.

Madamma Veilleux has kept a mini-review going for the first twenty minutes of class but then hands out our assignment that's due by the beginning of class tomorrow. That gives me the perfect excuse to avoid the thought of Matthew until the end of the period, finishing the sheet before class is over.

This morning while I was getting ready for school I realized that I hadn't charged my phone the night before, and surprisingly did bother enough to start charging it before I left. It hits me at the end of class that that means I will have to text Tess back and explain myself. I'm not ready to tell them about the break, but I need to tell them something. Anything believable.

Avoiding Patricia wasn't hard today. To be honest, I'm not so sure I'm even avoiding her. Maybe she even texted me during school today, which would be less than optimal timing but better than nothing.

My dad picks me up after class and asks me the usual questions, to which I reply with my usual answers, not bothering to go much more into detail about anything. When I arrive at home the first thing I do is go upstairs and unplug my phone.

74 new messages, most from Tess, and 113 unread messages from yesterday. *Lovely*.

I go through all the messages Tess has sent me in the past 24 hours, often skipping a few because they're just random letters, and draw my conclusion that Tess is now mad at me for not responding.

I send one quick message and set my phone back on the table.

253

Hey, sorry! My battery died and then I forgot to take my phone to school this morning. Don't be mad, thanks.

Before going back to bed, I change out of my school clothes and into my home shirt and sweatpants, check my phone a last time for anything important, and let the cycle inhale me again.

CHAPTER 31

Matthew

I didn't go to school on Monday. Or on Tuesday, Wednesday, or Thursday. I didn't so much as get out of bed. Not further than the bathroom anyway. My mom brought me food every so often, but I rarely ate any of it. Fortunately, neither of my parents had the sense to ask me to get out of bed. Or ask anything else of me.

Neither of them asked me if I was okay, not that I wanted them to. But it might have been nice to hear, even if they have no right to know. I emailed the school on Sunday evening through my mom's made-up email address to let them know that I wasn't feeling well, as I always do but usually only when I'm physically sick. I purposefully didn't say anything too specific because I'm a terrible liar, and sticking to some of the truth doesn't feel like lying too much.

This week I didn't have nearly as much energy as necessary to go to school, but I know I have to get at least a little more because I'll

255

have to go back on Monday. Though today, my guess is Friday night or Saturday morning, I won't worry about that. Not that I could if I tried. My mind is numb. Along with the rest of my body. After my almost marathon on Friday, I realized that it doesn't do me any good to think of Liam, so I didn't think of anything at all.

Matter of fact, I didn't do anything at all. Not thinking, not any homework, not any housekeeping, not talking. Only sleeping, occasionally drinking something, and going to the bathroom and back. I'm sure my room and I are very gross right now. The blinds are down, a few plates of mostly untouched food that's starting to go bad, and even more half-filled water glasses all around the room.

Scratch that. Those aren't the only things I did, I also cried. So much. I didn't know it was humanly possible to produce that many tears in such a short time. When I first talked to Liam, I knew he was special but I didn't think it would hurt me this much to see him go.

I wake up sometime during the day, the footsteps of my parents sounding far through the house interiors. Not bothering about the time, I close my eyes again in hopes of falling back asleep. I jump every time they make a noise. I'm used to living alone, not sharing the space.

The last time I went to the bathroom was a while ago according to the pinching in my lower stomach, but I really don't want to move right now. Eventually, I convince myself to stand up and walk to the bathroom. Closing the door behind me I look in the mirror. I was right, I do look disgusting and probably smell like it too. My hair is as greasy as a frying pan, the circles under my eyes are as big as onions, and I'm pretty sure I have a ketchup stain from days ago on my shirt, right above my heart. Kind of looks like the blood Liam practically drained it off. I take one look to my left, at the shower head hanging from the wall, and decide I don't have it in me.

After I'm done and back in bed, ready to return to the painless realm of dreams, I hear a knock on my door. Once. Then twice. Without any response, much less permission, my door opens. As expected my mom stands in the doorway with a plate in hand.

Wordlessly she takes one of the older plates and replaces it with the new one. As usual, I just watch her, though this time she doesn't immediately leave as if in fear of catching whatever sickness I have. She's standing in the doorway again, hesitating to leave. Then she turns around and looks at me.

"I wasn't sure if you're up for it, but I guess it's your choice," she breathes, "You have a visitor."

That's it. That's the end of my life. My heart stops pumping anything through any part of my body. Through whatever energy I have built up inside me, I almost jump out of bed. I would ask Mother who it is first, but it's not like she knows anyone in my life.

Liam can't see me in this state, that much is for sure. My mother only stares at me while I hurry to my closet, pick out some presentable clothes, and run inside the bathroom.

"Tell them I'll be right down." is all I reply. Not waiting for confirmation I lock the door behind me and put on a record time of changing clothes, roughly brushing my teeth, putting on a lot of deodorant, and going through my hair a couple of times.

Not even two minutes later, when I emerge again through the bathroom door, I still feel less than confident in trying to appear convincingly clean and healthy. About 30 glances in the mirror from all angles didn't change that, but I don't have the time to go back either. It's only forward now.

With each step I take I get more unsure about what Liam wants from me now. *Has he had enough of this break? Does he finally want to explain what the hell has been going on? Does he want to get back together?*

Honestly, I'm not sure what I would do in the last scenario. *How am I supposed to trust him if he randomly pulls something like this without any kind of explanation or apology?*

I don't see anyone at the bottom of the stairs which encourages me enough to finally stop hesitating. Each step grows heavier than the one before, being weighed down by the possibility of the conversation that needs to be held.

Surprise is an understatement when I see who's waiting for me right in front of the front door. Relief and a breeze of disappointment wash over me when it's not Liam standing before me, but Patricia.

Patricia, who I thought hated me- who I am pretty sure hates me, is looking into my eyes without any sort of kindness, no smile on her face. The blue in her eyes seems to slowly darken until it looks more like an endless black void. I greet her with a simple nod, not bothering with too much hospitality. The outfit she chose today does not support the idea of her kindness either. Her arms are fully covered with long black sleeves, stopping right before her wrist. To match that vibe, she's wearing black jeans that are ripped up almost completely. I doubt they sell them that way but I don't question it any further.

Awkwardly, if only to break the silent stares, I ask, "So… What's up?"

Patricia clears her throat and says, "What happened?"

I'm unsure how to reply, unsure of what exactly the question is referring to. She must see the confusion on my face and clarifies, "Why is it that one day we're all happy best buddies and the next nobody talks to anyone?" Her voice is louder than before.

Oh. So Liam didn't tell her.

Just great.

"Let's go upstairs," I suggest, "oh and shoes off," a reminder mostly out of habit. Not that it matters now anyway.

Patricia follows me to my room. I haven't had much of a chance to look around the house since my parents returned, but I almost immediately notice the now lively dining table in the kitchen. The sight of the two used coffee cups facing each other sparks another pinch of pain through my chest, knowing my parents willingly left me here. The coldness following the pain that emerges in my chest is like a confirmation and reminder that I won't forgive them for that. Ever.

I hesitate to open my bedroom door, knowing what kind of disgusting hell lies behind it, and decide to warn Patricia, "Uhm so, before we go on. Just please don't judge. It's been… uh… tough."

"Uh-huh. And are you going to tell me what has been so *tough*?" She uses her fingers to mimic air quotes.

259

I open the door, step inside, and illuminate the troll's cave, also known as the room I just crawled out of. Patricia a step behind me stammers, "I-."

"Yeah sorry, I know it's not great."

"Not great?" Patricia asks doubtfully, "This is way beyond that. This is almost as bad as my cousin's room. For the record, he's nine and lives at a junkyard."

"Ouch. Well, I guess that's fair enough. But to be fair, I bet your nine-year-old cousin isn't going through the same thing I am."

"Right," Patricia agrees, "and what would that be?"

"Liam hasn't told you?" I ask skeptically.

Patricia just stares at me, before practically screaming, "Would I be standing here, literally asking you, if Liam told me?"

Right, I guess that does make sense.

"You should sit." Based on my advice Patricia does exactly that. She sits at my desk, the same desk we first worked on together as a trio on that French project, and looks at me expectantly.

"I'm just going to rip the bandage off," I warn before I say, "Liam broke up with me and I don't know why." It's the first time I've said it out loud.

"Okay well," I correct myself, "he didn't technically break up with me, but he did put us on a break. And everyone knows once a couple is on a break, there's no turning back."

Patricia looks speechless. No words of encouragement, not any sort of reaction. The only sort of confirmation that she even heard me is the calm question she asks about a minute later.

"I'm sorry?"

"Yeah. I don't know either. As you can see, I've been rather busy with lying in bed and being sad. The only reason I'm not in there now is because I thought you were Liam."

"I'm sorry to disappoint. But I have to say I do not forgive you, however sad and depressed you are."

Confused again, I ask, "What do you mean *forgive me*?"

"Both you and Liam, because it was both of you who ditched me into the bushes. If you may recall, we were a trio of friends before you two became a thing. Yet as soon as you two separate, nobody even bothers to tell me?! I haven't heard a word from either of you in over a week, not even a text god dammit!" Patricia is physically pulsing with rage now, which is fair because she does have a good point, but I may also be a little scared now.

Swallowing I say, "You're right. I'm so-"

I don't get to finish because Patricia isn't done yet either.

She stands up, walks closer, and looks me dead in the eye when she says, "Of course I'm right! Look," she says before continuing, "I'm planning to talk to Liam to give him a very similar speech, and if you want I'll try to find out what happened."

I nod, glad she doesn't hate me so much that she's still willing to do something like this.

"But to be totally honest," Patricia continues, "when I last saw him he had this massive breakdown in his room. I'm talking crying, not talking, being huddled up in a ball, and everything. He refused to get his parents or to tell me what happened. My theory is that this whole breakup thing has something to do with that."

I swallow, not knowing how I can even respond to that.

Realistically that doesn't help me much. It only makes it even more apparent that Liam is upset about something, 'upset' being an understatement. That doesn't provide me with any specifics, as in, I still don't know if Liam is angry, sad, frightened, or all of the above, nor do I know the cause or how to fix it.

"I… I'm sorry and I also do not know how I can ever repay you for even trying to find out."

"Yeah yeah, but I do want a big proper apology after this whole couple-drama is over."

I laugh and agree, wanting to go in for a hug but restraining myself after remembering I haven't showered in ages. I can do big apologies.

That's when it all clicks into place, the solution part at least. I'll just have to show Liam how much I want to be with him, no break and all. He'll see how much I care and forget about whatever is eating at him so much, and then everything will be perfect again.

Foolproof plan. What could go wrong?

CHAPTER 32

Liam

I was surprised to not run into Matthew at all, surprised he wasn't in school the whole week. However, that did make my life a lot easier for now. It gave me space to think, not to be constantly pressured by his presence. That may be an exaggeration but it's true, to some degree.

Patricia didn't respond to my message. She probably knows it was a lie because even though my phone was dead I didn't respond to anything further, and neither did she. I may have just buried a good friendship into the ground, but I'm sure I can fix that. Eventually. I only need enough time to fix both, my relationship with Matthew and my friendship with Patricia.

That's assuming there's anything to fix with Matthew., because if I was right, then I'd rather eat a cactus than speak to him right now. Speaking of, since Matthew wasn't in school I had no sort of opportunity to get any information on his true intentions. Maybe the pause idea wasn't the smartest decision after all. What a shocker.

Maybe he didn't come to school because he's out there in the world, finding himself an actual boyfriend, or even a girlfriend if everything was a lie. I'd assume he's doing just that with Josh, but unfortunately, I have felt and heard his presence. More than enough.

A small part of me thinks he might have stayed home just to avoid me, or because he's angry and sad and whatever else. But the rational part of me knows that's both impossible and kind of selfish of me to think that. A little entitled even, therefore it is better not to listen to that tiny part of me.

That's the only thing I was able to think about the entire week, to the point where I can almost tell you exactly what a heart attack feels like. Every day I walk into seventh period, dreading the fact that Matthew could show up again. Just like that, no warning whatsoever.

On the other hand, I want to know how he is doing. Maybe I did hurt him more than I think so I need to know if he's okay. I just want to know what he is up to. *Next week,* I think to myself, *Next week I will see how he is unless he doesn't come to school either.*

That thought jolts an alarm through me, bringing me back to reality. Laying in the darkness of my room, I close my eyes again, not wanting to be swallowed up again, but ready just in case. I try focusing on some of the other stuff in my life to distract from this. First I think of positives… or at least I try, right now there's not much. Then I think of school, about classes, about the essay for Creative Writing that I haven't so much as started. Okay, maybe that wasn't the best thing to think of because now I'll be stressing about that as well. *Thanks so much, me.*

But I'd rather worry about an essay, than about Matthew because at least I have some control over the essay.

Does wanting control make me a controlling boyfriend? Is that why he doesn't want to be with me? Potentially.

After a while of tossing and turning, trying to fall back asleep, I give up. I sit up, check my phone, and go to the bathroom. Putting on clothes, brushing my teeth, eating breakfast, and going back to my room feels weird. Not in the something-is-off kind of way, but in the it-is-oddly-quiet kind of way. I haven't gotten any texts. Not even emails.

Wow. I know I fucked things up with two people, but now everyone's siding with them and completely ghosting me?

Lying in bed, I realize how annoying I must sound to anyone who could hear my mind. That needs to change. If it's at the point where I can't bear to hear my thoughts, then something needs to change.

Not now though. However much inspiration and need I may have, I would rather stay where I am, watching TV shows on my laptop. But on the other hand, I should get up and do something. Such as texting Patricia to try and save what I can. Damage control.

I force myself to sit upright, grab my phone, type a simple Hey, and hit send. It's dry but how else do you start a conversation with someone who you ghosted for the past week?

I don't wait for a response before I continue typing and sending, one message after the other.

265

I'm sorry I ignored you

I wasn't feeling well

We should talk

There is something you should know

Which will also be the explanation for why you haven't heard from me

Not an excuse though, so Im sorry again

That should do, I hope. While waiting I just kind of sit there, tapping my phone every 20 seconds to see if I had missed the notification. It's technically impossible at the rate I'm checking, but whatever. I don't dare to go into the chat itself, to try to learn if Patricia read my messages, because I know Patricia isn't the type of person to leave me on read.

After almost exactly 12 minutes my phone lights up with a notification from Patricia.

You bet your ass we will talk. I'll come to your house in 15 min so you better be there.

I swallow once before I send a thumbs-up emoji back.

Patricia will come here, and to make matters worse, she doesn't sound very happy in that text.

Patricia is standing in front of my front door exactly 15 minutes later, as she said she would. It's like the air decided to thin out around us, too scared of the tension. And I hate that already. Yet we haven't even started talking.

"Hi," I say. Or at least I'm trying.

"Mm. I see," is all Patricia says. *What's that even supposed to mean?*

"Let's go upstairs before we start this conversation," I suggest because I know damn well my dad would be listening and reporting back to my mom if I don't avoid him.

Patricia nods and follows me up the stairs. Halfway there she mutters, "I'm getting an odd feeling of deja vu right now."

Confused, I turn around, "Huh?"

She shakes her head and motions for me to go on. One could say I'm lucky that Patricia is even willing to look at me so I won't waste this opportunity.

We hurry into my bedroom and as soon as I close the door behind me I start pleading.

"Please forgive me. I'm so sorry for just ghosting you like that. You don't deserve that!"

"Aha, and?" Patricia's question catches me off guard.

"And that will never happen again…" I add. *And? What do you mean by 'and'?*

"Okay sure, I'll take that. You are temporarily forgiven, but I do expect better than that for when this whole thing is cleared up."

Fair enough. I nod and exhale deeply.

"So… has Matthew told you?"

Patricia nods, telling me far more than I need.

"Okay, so you can imagine how that emotionally impacted me..?" I ask, testing the waters.

"Sure, but to be fair," Patricia continues with crossed arms, "he only told me yesterday, so I had a whole week of not knowing what the fuck happened. Which by the way, I still barely do. Care to explain?"

"What is there to explain? Matthew doesn't like me, so I made it easier for the both of us. At least for now, 'cause I will still have to break up with him for real."

Do I want to do that?

No.

Should I do it anyway, because I'm probably right about my theories?

Yes.

"If we weren't friends again, I would slap you so hard right now. You don't *need* to break up with him. Why in the boiling hell would you have to do that?"

I swallow, not knowing how to respond. So I start from the last time I saw Patricia because I'm hoping it makes more sense that way. I tell her about how I am sure that Matthew doesn't actually like me. I tell her about all the theories and possibilities I made up, and confess to the one I believe in the most.

All the while Patricia just stands there, in the middle of my room. The only sign of any reaction in her is the skeptical look she gives me through my rambling. When I'm done, I don't look at her or for her reaction. I close my eyes and collapse into my bed.

It feels off, venting this much to someone who isn't Tess, while Tess doesn't even know about this whole thing. Naturally, I would have called them a while ago, but at first, they didn't pick up, so I assumed they were busy. I tried again the next day, but again no response and no follow-up text either. And then I finally took the hint and figured that Tess just didn't want to talk to me right now. Which is totally and completely *fine*.

When Patricia finally says something, it's really not what I expected. My guess would have been that she points out that I am being very delusional and unfair to everyone around me, and that I should seek professional help. Which may still be true.

"You know, Matthew also told me he doesn't have a clue why you would pause this thing you had. He told me that he thought it went well actually. At least, he implied it."

"He knows what he's doing then. Master in manipulating the friends of the subject."

"Oh shut up. Respectfully, you need to get your shit together and stop rolling around in your self-pity."

"How am I being sad about Matthew considered self-pity?"

"You said it yourself, you made up all these "worst-case scenarios" because it doesn't make sense to you that someone like Matthew would be interested in someone like you."

"Ouch. Great thanks," I groan into the mattress.

"I have a point, I promise. Your thinking just proves that you generally don't think much of yourself, which to be fair, most of us do. But you went up at least ten stages of that, which resulted in the various scenarios in which you are the victim."

She's right and we both know it.

269

Though, finding time to work on the planning is tougher than I thought it would be. Due to the lack of energy in the week before, I had missed way too many assignments and didn't bother to do any of them.

So now not only do I have all of my teachers kicking me in the ass to catch up on work, but also all the actual work. Mr. Lange and Mr. Flenning, for history and language arts, are the worst.

When I came back on Monday, Mr. Lange pulled me aside, away from the podcast analysis going on inside the classroom, and *reminded* me about his late work policy. Which is essentially that I have 48 hours to complete all missing assignments before he starts taking points off. Fair enough if you're missing a day or two with a maximum of two assignments, but when you've been out of school for a whole week… let's just say my hand was in a chronic cramp from filling in worksheets and typing out an essay the same day.

Coach has been a handful as well, giving me an hour-long lecture about why missing practice for a whole week is unacceptable. I just nodded and forcefully agreed to everything he said because he wouldn't understand, nor would he care for any of the excuses I could tell him. The lecture ended with me promising him that it won't happen again. If I'm honest though, it may very well happen again because I'm not very interested in football anymore. Besides, right now Liam and the plan have priority. Who knows, maybe I'll just quit the team. My grades are good enough to get into community college and continue my education there. Quitting would also be worth it just to see Josh's and the other guys' faces when they lose the best player on their team. If gossip in school is to be believed at least.

And now, after completing most late assignments semi-successfully, I can finally continue working on anything else. But for most of the time that has been the plan. So far, for the limited time I had, I'm making a good amount of progress. I'm pretty much done, except for finding good locations and trying to find the right words. I figured I'd write Liam something since he loves reading so much but turns out that's harder than expected.

I started with one little text and quickly figured that it was too short to pull it off, but I couldn't make it any longer either. Then I concluded that I would make many short texts, some poems, and some stories, and spread them out for Liam to find. Just like a little scavenger hunt, except that he doesn't have to search for them because they will appear to him during his usual routine.

Patricia hasn't talked to me since the weekend, so I'm assuming she hasn't been able to get a reason out of Liam yet. I didn't even get a text from her, which is kind of worrying me… just a tiny bit. But I'm sure once Patricia knows something she will tell me.

Talking about people who I haven't talked to in a while, my parents still haven't said a word to me and I'm sure as hell not going to be the first. Seeing them in the house feels kind of like having two roommates I can not stand at all. Just worse. We pass by each other in the kitchen or on the way to our rooms, but we never say anything. We also have our sections of the house with an invisible curtain drawing a boundary neither of us crosses.

However, I do not have the focus to worry too much about anything right now because Mr. Flenning is currently talking about the importance of being on time. He's been repeating the same thing for the last 40 minutes because he believes some people in the class aren't getting it. To his defense, he's right but repeating it over and over won't do much to change that. Sometimes I think he wants to take every chance he can to talk about anything besides the actual coursework and usually I don't mind.

But usually, he isn't as loud during his personal speeches, so I can clock out mentally and concentrate on something else until he is done. Gracefully class is over in less than two minutes and I have lunch next, during which I won't go to lunch. Instead, I will spend the whole period in study hall and work on the plan.

As soon as the bell dismisses us I'm out of the classroom without looking back.

Later, I arrive home with an unwelcome surprise. Both of my parents are seated at the dinner table and turn their heads to me as I step through the door. It's creepy how in sync their heads moved, but what's even creepier is that they're both together in one room… with me. And they're not moving to escape as fast as usual, in fact, they don't make any effort to get up at all.

Staring at them I take another step, not risking moving too fast.

After carefully taking my shoes off, my parents still expectantly looking at me, I make a run for it. I don't get far before my mom shouts, "Matthew wait! We want to talk to you!"

I stop on the first step of the stairs, turn toward the kitchen, and yell back "Oh suddenly, after so many years, you finally want to talk? Talk to a professional before you talk to me!"

The anger I was holding all these years is on the verge of emerging but I stomp upstairs before that happens. If I were to let myself talk to them with that limitless rage, we would be "talking" forever. There's so much I want to tell them.

I'm so mad at you. Words can not possibly describe how much I hate both of you. How could you just leave me like that?! Without any notice or explanation either. NOT EVEN a goodbye. Just a notebook with stupid instructions which, BY THE WAY, I TOSSED OUT.

Every day I thought about you returning, at first with hope, later with fear. Everything that I did from the moment you left until now was to protect my own life and future, WHICH IS SUPPOSED TO BE YOUR JOB, and I won't let you ruin what I have gained.

There is no space for you in my life anymore. My life is better the way it is because I didn't have parents, so you should leave. I might as well call myself an orphan because if you were so willing to leave so fast, you probably didn't care for me at all. Which is why both of you DISGUST ME.

Mom, the letters were a nice effort but they could never in a million years make up for what you did. I never read any of them, just stored them away, but it was a nice touch to the whole 'abandoned your own child' thing. But you know, at times I thought that maybe Dad forced you to go with him because you were afraid or whatever. Then I considered the way you always seemed to be the one in charge when you were still here and I came up with a new theory.

Would you like to hear it? No? I don't care.

With every day that I grew older, I thought how maybe you're the one who forced Dad away. It would explain a lot of things, like why he never bothered to have any sort of relationship with me even when he was still here.

It was at my 14th birthday party that I stopped wanting to know what really happened. Well, not exactly stopped wanting to know, but stopped worrying too much about it. I still want an explanation at least. It was just then that I stopped making up excuses for either one of you.

Because no matter the reason, we all ended up in this scenario.

Now, Dad, where should I even start? Maybe with the fact that you always were too occupied to talk to me anyway so maybe you didn't realize that you left me behind until it was too late to get me. Not that I think you would have bothered to get me anyway. Or maybe we should start by addressing the fact I barely know you? Sure you showed up in the house while I grew up, but that's about all I knew. I was told you were my dad and that you're too busy, but at approximately five years old I understood that you saw me as nothing more than a talking houseplant.

Mentally I knew I didn't have a real dad, which made it even easier to get over you leaving me.

I guess the purpose of this whole speech is to prove to you that I'm much better off without you and that we should not talk again.

Or something like that. I had a lot of time to think about a lot of things to say…

Having a plan for what to say is one thing, but actually saying it is a whole other deal. Especially when the two of them just sit there and ask to talk to you as if you're about to have a normal family meeting. The whole speech thing would be a whole lot easier if they would finally say something to make me angry, or at least scream at me first.

Turning my attention away from the thoughts about my parents, I walk the next step and the next. When my mom calls for me again, I don't look back.

CHAPTER 34

Liam

Not talking to Matthew in so long has had a toll on me, more than I would ever admit out loud. The only thing on my mind is him and the time we should have had. With that always comes an empty sting in my chest. It's like a two-in-one package which consequently means that I now have a chronic hole in my chest.

That probably sounds like the stereotypical diary entry from a 12-year-old teenage girl who was just rejected by her crush, like how it is in the movies before she finds an even better one and gets her happy end.

The line between movie and reality will never be clearer though. I'm not a straight girl who just got rejected by one guy and therefore have so many more options. Matthew is one of the few openly gay guys at my school, and from those the only one who was interested in me. Meaning he's one of approximately seven good choices in my whole lifetime.

Besides, he is the nicest guy ever and openly portrays his good intentions. Throwing him away like that will forever be the biggest regret of my lifetime. And if he doesn't want me anymore then I'm convinced nobody ever will. If I can't even keep a guy who was as open and as happy to be with me as Matthew, then I can't keep anyone.

Maybe it's what I deserve for being the spoiled brat I am, but I'm also sure that Matthew didn't deserve to be treated this way. Thus it may be better if we don't get back together, for his sake at least. But quite frankly, I don't give a shit right now because I know that me, and Patricia too, did not go through all this trouble just for me to back out at the last second.

As every "wise" person ever says, "You have to fight for what you want."

So I'm gonna fight as much as necessary unless there's actual fighting involved because then I'll be forced out much sooner.

For this very moment, however, I have other priorities. I'm sitting in my room, my dim desk light illuminating just enough, staring at the open document on my laptop. It's almost April and I still have not started the assignment for Mr. Lane's class. I have barely a month left before final exams, before the assignment has to be done before it has to be perfect.

Yet I have no clue what I should write about. The prompt was to write about the best thing that happened in our lives and how that affected us. Sure, there've been a lot of great things in my life, but none that stand out for this assignment.

I've thought about the time I went back to Germany in seventh grade and finally got to see Tess after so long. That was a really great time, but also the most recent time we met in real life, which makes me depressed to think about that. So no.

I've thought about the overall fact that I got to see so much of the world even though I am so young but then realized that, so far, moving away from my hometown didn't have many perks. Mostly just loneliness and more loneliness.

Then, as I was desperate, I thought about just the event of moving to the States. Surely Mr. Lane would eat that up. But again, moving here has brought me two things, Patricia and Matthew, one of which I'm on very thin ice with. Unless the ice has already cracked.

So that's also not an option because then I'd think more about Matthew than about what I want to write. Or even worse, my writing would get influenced by him.

So now I'm just stuck. I've thought about so many possible topics and so far my last trip to Germany is the top runner, but it still doesn't feel right. This assignment has to be perfect. I plan on using it for a writing portfolio for the Stanford Application next year. So far the portfolio only has two other pieces, a nonfiction attempt at poetry and a short fantasy story about seven enchanted daggers. Neither of these is perfect yet either, meaning I'll have to work on those in the summer. Because everything I do ties back to Stanford in one way or another and I HAVE to get in. I don't know what I would do if I didn't.

I spin in my chair a few times until I'm dizzy enough to accept that I won't come up with anything anytime soon. The books are glooming at me from the shelf as if urging me to close my laptop and start reading. Not that I'd be reading one from the shelf though, I still have two novels on my bedside table not even three meters away from me.

Finally giving in I shut my laptop, turn off the desk light, and flop myself on the bed. I reach for one of the books at random and turn on the reading light that's screwed to my headboard. Without one last thought about Matthew or Stanford or the essay, I drift into the different world in my hands.

CHAPTER 35

Matthew

It's been suspiciously long and Patricia still has not reached out. Not that I don't trust her, but maybe she doesn't trust me enough anymore to tell me anything. Great.

However, it would calm my nerves if she could just tell me something. Whether Liam has a good reason to break up with me for real soon, would be great info. Or whether or not Liam could ever forgive me for whatever I did. Or even better, is he planning on telling me what the heck happened?

It doesn't matter much now anyway. I have officially worked my ass off and it will pay off. I finished planning out every single detail of my master plan. Soon all questions shall be answered, or should be at least, theoretically.

The only two components missing are Patricia because I need her to deliver part of the plan, and Liam himself. Assuming he'll want to.

After fourth period, on my way back from lunch, I usually see Patricia walking into lunch so I plan to intercept her and quickly ask for help. Again. When the bell rings I head to the hallway, where Patricia usually comes out of, and just lean awkwardly against the wall. Many familiar faces walk by, who I'm trying to avoid as much as I can. All but one.

When I finally catch Patricia in my sight I walk towards her, locking my eyes with hers. She sees me and waves as a greeting. I don't wave back but instead stop right in front of her and say, "Hi, can we talk really quick?" as fast and unsuspicious as I can. Patricia nods so we each take a step away from the traffic coming in and out of the cafeteria.

"What's up?" Patricia asks me.

"Well, you haven't talked to me in a while so I was wondering if you had any updates on, you know what. And actually, there's another thing… So you know how I want to win Liam back? I kind of need your help..." I start describing all the details right then and there before I can help myself. In front of so many people who could potentially overhear what I'm planning.

Patricia stares. By the time I'm done, we're the only ones left in the hallway and lucky that whoever is on hall duty hasn't admonished us yet.

I'm almost out of breath but Patricia still only stares, her brown hair hovering above her shoulder fitting excellently with her emotionless face.

"Of course I'll help," Patricia says and it's like a mountain has been lifted off my heart, "And just so we're clear, I did talk to Liam and he told me what caused all of this. However, I can't tell you, I'm sorry."

This must be one of the top three times I have felt the stupidest in my entire life. So Patricia knows what's going on but didn't tell me because she chose Liam over me, even though I specifically asked her to find out. I knew she would choose him. I knew it.

Patricia must see the frustration on my face because she continues with a much more cheering voice, "But I can tell you one thing. This epic gesture you have planned is going to fix it. I know it."

The muscles in my neck and face relax all at once.

"You think?"

"Absolutely! He'll love it."

I swallow. "I really hope so. Thanks, that helped."

I pull Patricia's part out of my bag and nod in thanks, hoping she can see the security of it in my eyes. She accepts and we part ways back to lunch. I hope everything goes perfectly.

CHAPTER 36

Liam

Another weekend has passed without any sign from anyone, not from Patricia, not from Matthew, not even from the universe. Sure, I talked to Patricia during school at least, but neither one of us has any idea what's going to happen next. I know I need to talk to Matthew, but I also know that I can't face him. Not mentally.

I also know that my essay hasn't moved one bit. Nor any other homework assignment from last week. Not that I didn't do them, but that teachers collectively decided to cut short on assignments and it's making me kind of uncomfortable. I've had so much free time on the weekend that I finished a whole book. IN TWO DAYS.

That is almost a new personal record, were it not for the 250K fanfiction I read in one night in seventh grade. To be fair, it was a gay Cinderella retelling while I was just on the verge of discovery.

On top of that, I'm also almost suffering a heart attack because at night when I'm trying my best to sleep, I keep jumping up thinking I forgot to do my assignments. It's driving me crazy. As if I took all of these academically challenging classes for nothing.

Once Monday morning rolls around I have slept more than in the past month and am still not ready to go to school. I guess it's not a matter of sleep, but a matter of motivation. Although the extra hours of sleep do help.

I'm in and out of first period AP Calc because Mr. Brunting's only instruction was to finish an assignment online which I completed in less than 30 minutes. With today being the first of April, exams are only about a month away, and most of my teachers right now, including Mr. Brunting, are giving us the most useless review games to work on even though they haven't finished teaching all the content.

The stress is like weights on my every nerve and tensing muscles that get worse with every day.

I don't realize the time passing in second and third period until Mrs. Usher releases us and I start walking to Creative Writing. I want to stop by my locker to drop off the AP Macro textbook that they force us to carry around all day. That is pretty much the only purpose of the locker but it is still worth the 50 bucks I paid when I enrolled.

At first, I couldn't even get my locker to open because I didn't understand how to turn that stupid wheel to open the even stupider lock. If I'm honest I still don't quite get how they work but I learned not to question it.

After the second attempt of twisting the lock, it mercifully opens. I stop with the book in hand. My locker is usually empty if it's not for the exact book I'm holding in my hands right now, but now I'm looking at a single piece of paper.

It's folded into an origami swan. This might be kind of mysterious, in a good way, if it weren't for the fact that only three people in this school know where my locker is. Patricia, Matthew, and one of the many people who saw me at this locker before AND know who I am. There can't be more than one person, so that makes three total.

So unless that total stranger decided to give out origami pieces and Patricia doesn't want to verbally talk to me anymore, it has to be from Matthew. I put the book into the locker and take out the paper. Before doing anything else I snap a picture of it and send it to Tess. They would be furious if I let them miss out on any of this.

Especially something that involves folded-up, "anonymous" messages.

The warning bell rings and before I can think better of it I throw the locker door closed and pocket the swan to look at it later.

I make it to Mr. Lane's classroom just in time.

As I sit down I hear Mr. Lane start talking to the class, reminding them to sit down and listen to him.

"Now that I have everyone's attention," Mr. Lane officially starts class, "I want to remind everyone about your project that is due at the end of this month. As you should know by now, the essay will count as your final exam and a separate test grade."

As much as it hurts me to say this, I've known all of that for long enough but trying to put it into practice is a whole other thing. The

289

prompt itself should be simple enough but something in me makes it way more complicated than it has to be. The same part of me that's comforting my lack of work by arguing that the essay has to be perfect. Future-Stanford-Student kind of perfect.

Mr. Lane repeats most of the instructions and important factors to keep in mind for the 700th time this semester before sending us off to work. As I look around everyone is pulling out a laptop and beginning to type their essay or look at handwritten notes. I'm sure some of the overachievers are already done and are just editing at this point. Ugh.

After I open my laptop I pull out the now slightly malformed swan from my pocket and stare at it. Its left wing was bent in my pocket, making the swan seem as if it just came back from a rough fight at a bar. Or a fight at school, with the inner depths of my pocket.

I just stare at it for a few moments longer before being forced to stop by my phone vibrating on my desk. I pick it up and read Tess's response to the photo.

Dude... is that a swan? What did I miss?

I respond with the only thing I can think of.

It's from Matthew, I think

Tess answers by sending three skull emojis.

I found it in my locker just now

I'm scared to open it

Matthew hasn't talked to me in over a week- what if this is his way of saying bye?!

I have to get myself together if I don't want to collapse emotionally right here and now. That would be the most embarrassing thing to happen to me since moving here and I do not want that under any circumstances. One of the few perks of moving is being unknown in the new place.

The gift of anonymity. Nobody here knows about any of the very embarrassing stuff that happened before moving. Not even Patricia or Matthew. While they know more than the rest, which is a broad idea of my life before, they don't know all the details. And they never will. At least I hope.

Tess replies.

He wouldn't do that

Open it already, I want to know what is in there too

Their urgency to open it is making me even more nervous than before, but without thinking much longer I decide to go for it.

It's written in pencil but the handwriting is undoubtedly Matthew's, confirming my suspicions. My eyes scan the words before registering what it says.

Hey, please just go alone no matter how weird this is.

Your clue is:

I'm watching a football game from underneath.

Where am I?

Huh. That's the last thing I would have expected. I guess it's supposed to be some kind of scavenger hunt. As outdated as this might be, Matthew is bold, I gotta give him that. Sending me on a scavenger hunt before trying to talk to me. Interesting strategy.

291

But on the other hand, MATTHEW DOESN'T DESPISE ME AND WANTS TO COMMUNICATE WITH ME. Even if the method is questionable.

A smile spreads across my face as relief settles over me. This is good news, definitely the best news this week. By the end of the scavenger hunt, I will have to apologize to Matthew, maybe even during if I get the chance.

I feel guilty about how I handled things, and am still handling them in a way, and I don't want to hurt Matthew. He doesn't know that though. I need to hope that him knowing that will somehow fix things. Or at least begin to fix something. Baby steps.

That boost of dopamine in my body is enough reason for the decision that I will skip lunch and if necessary study hall today and go wherever the message wants me to go.

Speaking of, I have no idea where that is. Well, I have some ideas. It must be near the football field so that's at least an area to search in.

I scan the message again, completely disregarding the work I should be doing. Reading it over and over again fails to make my brain think about the actual riddle. I keep circling back to the fact that Matthew doesn't hate me.

It takes at least a full ten minutes of smiling ridiculously for my mental self to come back and focus. My first thought is the football field, but how can somebody watch the game from beneath the field? So that's not it.

Then I decide to take the message apart, maybe I'm missing something here.

Where do people normally watch a game from? A TV at home? Probably not the answer to this one. The bleachers? More likely.

Let's say the answer is the bleachers, can you even go beneath them? Is that allowed? Or even physically possible?

I guess I'll find out soon enough.

During the remainder of class, I try to think of any other possible locations the message could lead me to, but none of the things I came up with are plausible enough.

After catching them up on the message and all my thoughts, Tess agrees that the bleachers have to be it. Unless I'm missing something major. There's just no other way.

The bell rings and I'm out of the back door in an instant, taking a left instead of the usual right turn towards the cafeteria. My goal is the nearest exit door to the field and then the field itself, kind of. The only two problems will be to remain unseens from whoever is using the field at the time, and finding an actual way to get below those gods-damned things.

CHAPTER 37

Matthew

There are so many things that could be going wrong and it's inevitable to think of every single possibility throughout fourth period. I skip both lunch and study hall and take the time to find the perfect position to hide my second clue.

Liam should have found the first one by now and maybe even figured out where the next one is supposed to be. I have to hope that my message is easy to understand for anyone, specifically Liam, who doesn't have access to my brain. When I came up with the riddles I thought most were pretty understandable and all were relatively easy to figure out, but maybe that was just because I wrote them. I should have asked Patricia, or anyone really to try to solve them first, as a test run.

But asking Patricia to do more than helping me fan out the clues seems sort of… I don't know. It doesn't feel right. I want to do this on my own. As much as I can at least.

Nervously pacing up and down underneath the bleachers, yes I purposefully chose this spot, hasn't provided any opportunity to drop off the next clue.

There's no reason why I picked the bleachers for the first clue or any clue. The only thing I can think of is that nobody ever comes down here, at least not in this season. Meaning that nobody could accidentally stumble upon my clue and ruin the whole thing without even knowing it.

A cold wind is blasting in my ears which is not particularly helping with finding a good spot, but rather threatens to give me an ear infection soon.

I tried placing the next clue on the ground, very obvious to see but it unfortunately just flew away into the sky, so that stopped being an option. I should have honestly known that would happen.

The next pathetic thing I tried was to place the paper under a rock, to keep it from being blown away, but naturally, none of the rocks nearby were good enough. I know how ridiculous that sounds, but all the rocks I found nearby were either too small and unable to keep the paper from flying away, or too big to the point that they would cover the whole paper. And those that I could physically place on the paper, half covering and half leaving it open, were wet and/ or dirty. Dirt would ruin the paper and I would have to redo it. Nope.

So much effort goes into all of these clues, I can't risk remaking them. I spent so much time folding them, writing in my most neat handwriting, and sketching all the cute little drawings on the side, trying to make them perfect. And now they are. So there is no way I could pull off another one of those, even if I tried.

So that option also leaves me disappointed. But after 30 minutes of pacing back and forth, I finally have an answer. I stop pacing and take off my backpack, which I probably should have done a while ago since I didn't go anywhere else. It's taken me embarrassingly long to think of, but I don't need rocks. I just need something to steady the paper, but without attracting too much attention to the thing itself.

Cramming in my backpack doesn't take too long before I decide to go with my pencil box and close up my bag. It's unrecognizable to strangers, making it more likely for them to miss it. For Liam, he must recognize it after seeing it so many times at my house, and when he does he'll know that's the sign for the next clue. Not that I think anyone will come down here, but it's better to be careful.

I place the pencil box and the paper in the far corner of the last bleacher, turn around, and leave. I say one last prayer to whomever will listen that everything goes smoothly, before returning inside the building.

CHAPTER 38

Liam

Fifth period arrives faster than I thought it would. Thank god! As much as I wanted to immediately storm off to the football field, Patricia texted me to meet her in the cafeteria and as the good friend that I aspire to be, I turned around halfway and walked back to meet up with Patricia.

Luckily the halls aren't as crowded as they usually are when I go to lunch. It takes me only half the usual time to arrive in the cafeteria, which is unfortunately as crowded as ever. It's not hard to spot Patricia as soon as I get closer to the mass, because she's sitting with some of her friends at our usual table.

Patricia's friends, not very many but sure as hell more than I ever had, are friendly but they don't really talk to me. Mainly because I don't talk to them either. I know some of their names by eavesdropping on their conversations. Just because they're kind, doesn't mean I like them. The good news is, I don't hate them either. Most of the time it's annoying when they randomly drop in and completely steal Patricia from our conversation, as possessive as it may sound.

All four heads turn to me as I approach the table. Way to not make things awkward! Great!

I wave awkwardly but only direct my attention towards her. She waves back, stands up, and excitedly walks towards me. With a big smile on her face, she comes close enough to whisper into my ear.

"Did you get it?" she asks expectantly. Without needing to think about what she means I back away and smile at her. Saying enough with my eyes to confirm her questions.

"I was going to go there now," I hint, "if you want to come?"

"Is that even a question? Of course, I'm coming!" Patricia almost screams to overtune the crowd in the background.

She takes her tray off the table she had been sitting at moments before and throws it away, then heads directly to the door. I follow her, hectically trying to catch up. It's still early enough for the teachers on lunch duty to let us through without any questions, assuming we're going back to class.

When we're almost alone in the hallway, on the way to the closest exit to the football field, I ask, "So you knew this was happening?"

Patricia shrugs, "I knew Matthew was planning something and that he wanted to start today. Never any specifics though… So what is it?"

Without another word, I pull out the roughed-up paper swan and present it. She reads the message before asking, "Oh wow. He did origami and pulled off great handwriting! Why couldn't he be this organized when we had that project? But anyhow, where do you think he wants you to go next?"

"Honestly, the only idea I had is beneath the bleachers, but I don't even know if it's physically possible to go there."

Patricia turns to me with a grin. "Oh, it's possible, very possible."

The smile on me grows bigger with the hope of what's expecting me, apparently below the bleachers.

To my relief, the field is unused when we get there. I let Patricia take the lead for this one because she has way better knowledge of the school and probably way more experience sneaking into areas that we're not permitted in. But in this case, I don't know if there's any regulation against us going down there, so I'm not going to question it.

Patricia leads me around the whole field before slipping through a hole in the fence blocking the area behind the stadium. She leads me back to the bleachers, this time behind the fence. It is easier than I anticipated to slip behind the scenes.

We are standing under the biggest of the three bleachers of our school and sure enough, something stands out instantly. There's an object, maybe a bottle or something, in the far corner, almost too far to be visible.

Maybe it's nothing and this is the wrong bleacher, or the wrong spot entirely. But I go for it anyway. With every step, the object gets clearer and I was wrong, it's not a water bottle. It's a pencil case, and not just any.

My heart races unnecessarily when I pick it up and retrieve the paper from underneath. This one is not folded like a swan, but a shark, or some other fish. I keep the pencil case in my arms as I jog back to Patricia, excitedly shoving the paper into her hands.

"Open it," I demand.

"It's yours, you open it," Patricia exclaims and shoves the paper back into my hand. She's right, but I'm so freaking nervous. Not only about the message or the meaning of this scavenger hunt but also about accidentally destroying these papers. As weird as it may be, I want to keep them and probably cry the next few times I look at them because I know no other guy will ever put as much effort into anything for me.

Carefully I unfold the shark and scan over the next message.

After school today, when the halls are empty and it's just you. In the room that holds hundreds of thousands of lives.

I snap a picture and send it to Tess before I pass the note along to Patricia and look at her expectantly. This time, however, I don't have to think even for a minute about where this next location would be. It's pretty obvious to me because I hear that phrase all the time.

Living a thousand lives while others only live one, that's called reading. The phrase was so beautiful when I first heard it and I still stand by that. It's poetic and most of all, it feels true. Reading about someone else's life, preferably someone made up, is a relatively fast way to live a different life.

So he either means, my room which would be too creepy to consider, or he means the library. After school at the library it is.

"I like this little sketch of a dragon on the side," Patricia points to the paper, "At least I think it's a dragon."

I haven't noticed it before but there it is. Its wings hover above the A of "After" and its tail majestically curves around the foot of the word. It looks way cooler than anything I could ever draw. Weird how I missed that.

"I think he means the library because all the books tell many different stories about many different lives." I think out loud to get a reaction about my thoughts. Maybe I'm focusing too much on that one assumption and missing the actual point.

Patricia doesn't say anything and just shrugs, which, for right now, is agreeing enough. I'll see after school if it's right anyway. I take the paper back and put it into the same pocket of my bag as the first one.

I turn around and start walking, not waiting for Patricia because I know she's on my heels already.

"Wait up," she yells but by the sound, I can tell that I was right.

"Do you want me to come with? I can text my mom to pick me up later, or I can come home with you, if that's okay of course. Unless Matthew already has something planned. Ahhhh I'm so sorry, oh my god. I'm gonna shut up now."

301

"Jesus, you are even more nervous than I am," I say jokingly. "If you want to risk staying you can wait up and we can go to my house after," I suggest.

"What about Matthew's plans?"

"He won't ask me to go anywhere after this. I'll take like 10 minutes trying to figure out where the next clue is hidden and that'll be it."

"Okay but how do you know?" she asks with an arched eyebrow.

"The thing you said… You know, the thing where Matthew told you that whatever he had planned is supposed to *start* today." I put emphasis on "start" to hint at what I mean.

"I still don't get it," Patricia says, turning around and walking backwards beside me.

"Ugh," I sight as overdramatically as humanly possible, "If it's supposed to start today, don't you think that means it's going over multiple days? So I doubt that he'll keep me chasing him after school hours. Besides, if I know one thing about him it's that he's considerate, and he knows that I have a lot of work to do after school."

Just saying it out loud makes me sad all over again. I need to play this game in the best way I possibly can. For now, I should give him his pencil case back though, at least in French later.

"Oh, yeah that makes sense. You got all of that from one sentence?"

I nod, looking into her eyes.

"Damn. Maybe I should watch what I say in front of you."

I laugh her off and instead ask, "Where are we going now?"

"Back to lunch?" Patricia asks.

"Oh come on. I'm full of adrenaline, I don't want to go back to the loudest place within 20 kilometers. Show me something cool."

Today is the best day in ages and I'm not going to let a bunch of the most annoying kids on the planet ruin that. Those kids couldn't ruin my mood if they tried, but why be around unnecessary risks?

"Besides," I add with the biggest smile I can muster, "It's not like the people on lunch duty are going to let us in without any explanation. So might as well stay out."

Smiling back at me, with the warmth I admire so much about her, she gives in.

"Follow me."

No need to tell me twice. I start to jog but give Patricia a chance to catch up before turning into a sprint. I'm not sure where we're sprinting to but I'm living for the feeling. The feeling of the wind in my face, even behind my eyes, and the feeling of finally having energy.

The feeling doesn't last long because about five minutes later I stop, heavily trying to catch my breath. My lungs are burning and there's sweat all over my forehead. I'm not an athlete, I can't deal with this that often. By the looks of it, you would probably think I can't deal with this even once.

I breathe in and out. Slowly. In and Out.

The aching in my lungs persists even when I have my breathing back under control. Patricia, who has been watching me dry-heave, looks like she barely stood up. Not a single hard breath or drop of sweat anywhere. *How the hell did that not do anything to her at all?*

"Do you want to keep moving or should we sit somewhere Grandpa?" She asks sarcastically.

"Ughhh" I groan, not appreciating the comparison to a senior citizen.

"Fine, fine," I say once the burning eases.

Patricia walks ahead, not sprinting this time, and I force my legs to follow. We're lucky that nobody is outside, especially not back on the field. We'd have to lie our way past any teacher or other faculty member, which would be no delight at all. Both Patricia and I aren't terrible liars, so it would be possible, but the morality of it all… rather questionable.

Patricia brings us around the building, and through the parking spots on the other side. It's so quiet. No angry parents yelling at each other, no teenagers fighting each other, and no impatient cop blowing his lungs into a tiny whistle, trying to get cars to move.

I follow Patricia's example and maneuver through the cars, around another corner of the school's main building until she finally stops. I look around and see absolute nothingness. Apart from an empty wall, a few bushes, and the trees behind us, there's nothing worth spotting.

"We're here," Patricia declares and looks at me as if I know what she's talking about.

The sun is high above the school and unfortunately directly blinding me. Maybe I'm just oblivious when I say, "There's nothing here though."

She shakes her head and points at the wall. I squint against the sun and realize Patricia is pointing at one of the bushes covering a part of the wall we've been staring at. When my face isn't suddenly overrun by a clear sense of understanding, Patricia moves and pushes the bush aside. At least the branches cover the remainder of the wall.

It's like in a movie when the hero goes into strategic hiding in a secret safe house. Except this isn't a safe house, or so I hope. What's beneath the branches looks like a cellar door, right into the ground.

"This is exactly what I meant when I told you to show me something cool!" I say with the remaining adrenaline in my body.

Patricia yanks on the handle and with a shrieking sound the cellar door opens, exposing a pitch of darkness inside. If this were a horror movie we would totally die within the next two scenes and I'm not a fan of that idea.

I cautiously step closer and examine the darkness beyond. Patricia steps inside without a second thought and descends deeper into the ground.

"You coming?" She yells back.

Naturally, I'm not going to be caught alone outside of school, so I guess going into the dark and creepy and unknown cellar in the middle of nowhere isn't such a bad idea. I hurry after her, trying hard not to trip on the oldest stairs in the school.

I don't know what I expected, but a fully decorated and furnished underground living space was not it. Maybe not a "living space" because I don't see a bed or a bathroom, but at least a fully furnished living room.

It looks like a stereotypical man cave like the ones straight guys always want. There's a table tennis table in the center of the cave, illuminated by a single light bulb right above. There are four armchairs against the wall, two on each side along the plate.

Holy shit. There's even a microwave and a mini fridge on a counter at the farthest wall.

Patricia slumps down on one of the chairs as if this were the most normal place to hang out in school.

"Uhm? What even..?" I try, but I don't know what to ask specifically. What question would I even start with?

"Wait," Patricia sits up, "You haven't been here before?"

"Uhhh.. no? You have?"

She shrugs, "I come here a lot, especially after school. I thought Matthew would have told you by now, even before the whole 'pause drama'." She uses her fingers to make quotations in the air.

"Well, whatever this is, he hasn't mentioned it. Wasn't that clear when I looked so confused out there?"

"I assumed you didn't know that I knew, since we technically aren't supposed to tell people, and that you're just pretending. But I guess you're not."

I just stare at her awkwardly, waiting for some sort of explanation.

"Fine, fine, stop burning holes in my body. We call it 'The Grotto'. The football team set it up after some sophomores discovered this empty room a few years ago. It's like a tradition for the football team to be in charge here and keep it tidy. The general rule is that only the football team and the people they choose can know about this place. So technically I'm not allowed to show you, but since you're in a relationship with the captain, as dry as it may be right now, it should be allowed."

I stare at her.

"And teachers let you guys have this space?" I ask suspiciously, not believing what I'm hearing.

Patricia snorts, "No?! Why do you think only a limited number of people are supposed to know about this? As far as I know, the whole faculty forgot this place exists."

"Wait, back up," I spin around myself once, "If only the team and their chosen ones can know about this place, how do you know it exists?"

Patricia looks at me with sorrow in her eyes.

She groans, visibly digging herself further into the chair, "Do we have to talk about that?"

"No," I grin, "But it would be very much appreciated?"

"Okay fine, but don't you dare judge!"

I place myself in the chair next to hers and shrug still with the same grin that will probably grow even wider with the story that is about to be told.

"It was in middle school that I dated a guy, for two weeks only though, who then in high school joined the football team. Essentially I kindly asked him about it after I had heard rumors. With that I mean that

I may have threatened to spread all the secrets he told me while we were dating and he gave in."

My jaw hangs open when she's done confessing to literal blackmailing.

"So you blackmailed him?" I ask disbelievingly, trying to confirm if I heard that correctly.

"Well, when you say it like that…"

"Wow." That is all I can manage because of how flabbergasted I am.

"It's his fault too. Who tells someone that many deep secrets in the first two weeks of dating?! Nobody, exactly. If he's gonna feed me that much gunpowder he could've predicted that I would shoot at some point."

My jaw is on the floor. There's no way that is true, it can't be.

"I don't believe you," I say outright. Maybe Patricia is just trying to make a joke in a very American way that I don't understand, or maybe she's just exaggerating a little.

"And why not?" Patricia asks curiously. She doesn't say anything that would confirm or deny my suspicions.

"Well," I start, "Because when I met you, you were quiet and nice. Talkative but not in a loud and rude way. I get that now the barrier or whatever is down, but I still can't imagine you would blackmail someone. Like, you never even get late to class and never get in trouble with any teachers, so that wouldn't make sense."

Patricia's smiling now, but not the warm smile from before. Now her face looks like she's at the highlight after getting high or possibly drunk, even though she isn't. I hope.

"Li, no offense, but you're the stupidest man alive if you think that the person I am at school is the same person I am outside of it. I thought you of all people would get that, but instead, you're just judging me."

That is a fair point. And she's right… again.

"Fine, okay. I'm not judging. Not you at least. Maybe that guy who you blackmailed but I would never judge you of all people. It's just surprising, is all."

Before either of us say anything further, the bell rings to end lunch. We both leave the Grotto, carefully pulling the branches back before Patricia leaves for math and I have to wander to history. Although my mind won't be able to comprehend any of the boring facts that will be thrown at it within the next hour.

CHAPTER 39

Matthew

During language arts, Mrs. Lange didn't let me breathe for a second. She insisted on eye contact at all times and when I so much as faced my desk, she warned me to keep paying attention. It was brutal.

Okay, maybe that was a bit hyperbolic (a new word I learned thanks to Mrs. Lange's torture period) but it sure felt like the worst class all week. Either today is the day she finally accepted that she hates some students and decided to act accordingly, or today I'm more distracted than usual.

I know which of those options is the truth, but I don't want to accept it yet. So I do the only thing that I can accept, staying mad a while longer until I forget about it. Hopefully, that's sooner rather than later.

But to be fair, Mrs. Lange doesn't have all the context, not that she would particularly care but at least she would know that this is a one, maybe two-day, thing. Nothing changed during the past few hours, as much as I tried to concentrate on something else. Mostly school, but when that didn't work I gave up and tried thinking about the stress Coach would put on me if I decided to quit. However, that didn't do much to distract me either. I can't escape my own mind.

I wonder if Liam received and understood my first message. I wonder if he went to get the second message. I worry if he found and understood that riddle. I wonder if he will show up today after school and if he would be willing to talk to me.

After Mrs. Lange finally let us go, I quickly realized that I was right. I am more distracted than usual, to the point where I bump into not one, not two, but three people in the hallway.

In Physics my seat is in the back of the class, Patricia two rows in front of me. I'm sure she spent lunch with Liam but didn't say anything to me at all. Maybe Liam hasn't told her, but I doubt it. From what I know they tell each other everything with only extreme limits.

At least Patricia seemed completely confident in my plan working out. And she's right. I should trust the process.

I can't hear any of the instructions, or any other voices for that matter, over my heartbeat pulsing through my mind. Otherwise, I feel numb. It feels like I'm stuck in my body, standing behind my eyes and watching as my body moves without me.

Mr. Gaidarov, probably the best physics teacher in the school, doesn't seem too bothered by the obsessive head rubbing and heavy breathing. Hopefully, he hasn't even noticed yet, but a few kids already turned around a couple of times and gave me weird looks. I must look pretty bad after seeing the concern on their faces. As little as there was,

311

because most of it was just pure annoyance and teenage anger. That's relatable too.

The rest of the day will be the most annoying experience ever if this doesn't stop. It might settle down a little, but in seventh period, it's going to be so much worse.

CHAPTER 40

Liam

Seventh period comes in the blink of an eye. I don't know how I should act around him now. Am I supposed to talk to Matthew? Greet him? Give him back his pencil case? Or should I ignore him until after school? Maybe just a wave?

Just when I'm done pulling out my binder, Matthew walks through the door looking oddly shaken up. His whole face is paler than usual and his hair is a mess, completely out of shape. Not sure how it's even possible, but his hair still looks so fucking good. When I look at him it's like a rush of serotonin flows through my veins, I want to be with him and his messed up hair, and his smile, and the way he cares for people, I want to be with all of him.

Before I can overthink this any longer I smile and wave to him in greeting. Nice and brief. He looks genuinely surprised and waves back before he takes his spot in the front of the class. Patricia comes in shortly after him and takes her seat next to me, after assumingly bugging Madame Veilleux to allow her to switch seats.

"Hey, how are you holding up?"

"Fine, just nervous I guess. How about you?" I respond.

"Don't take this the wrong way, but I'm so excited to see this whole thing play out."

I turn to her with a raised eyebrow. She angles her head, her cherry earrings dangling with the movement.

"What?" she asks.

"Never mind, it's nothing," I say and turn back to Matthew.

Then I add, "Did you notice how Matthew looks kind of off today?"

"Of course he would feel a little off, given how he made the biggest plan of the century for a special boy he likes," Patricia whispers.

My heart sinks into my stomach but I suddenly feel funny. Still nervous, yes, but also cozy of sorts. It's weird. It's nice to hear that Matthew thinks I'm his special guy and that I'm worth doing this whole thing for, even after I treated him so unfairly. 'Nice' is a very strong understatement, it's the best feeling ever.

This class will be pure torture, with Matthew in the room but no way for me to apologise to him right now and with the end of school being so far yet so close. I wish I could time travel, just to skip over this. But with Patricia next to me, and the class being French, it will still be twice as fun as history.

Madame Veilleux walks in with a stack of papers in her hands and begins talking in French, slow enough for us to understand. It makes her sound a bit awkward compared to when my mother speaks with me.

"The end of the year is coming closer guys. That's why I will hand you a form to fill out about your French path next year. Whether you will be going into AP French or French Four, or not continuing French at all, is your choice. This form is not binding yet, I just want you to think about what you want to do. Today we're just going to go over some questions, comments, or concerns you guys have before making a decision."

On and on she goes, explaining the difference between French four and AP French, emphasizing that an AP course is challenging and that most colleges like to see commitment on your transcript and how that relates to the benefits of continuing French. My eyes are closed pretty fast and I don't bother to listen any longer until Patricia taps me on the shoulder.

"Did you decide already or why do you feel the need to close your eyes?"

"Actually yes. I decided within the first month of moving here because I was stressing so much about school and additionally had so much unexpected free time." The good old times.

Patricia crosses her arms and asks, "So which is it?"

"AP," I say, closing my eyes again. A few awkward minutes later, I'm suddenly reminded of the kindness policy of the United States and ask, "How about you? Have you decided yet?"

315

"No," she whispers, "But if you're taking AP, I think I'll do the same. Would at least save me the trouble of finding another elective to get into."

"Right. Well," I start, "I would be very glad if you do decide to take it but please find a proper reason."

The muffling sound of Patricia turning toward me makes me open my eyes again and I'm a little surprised by the slightly angered Patricia I see looking at me. Arched eyebrows, single-lined mouth, and the change in her aura signalize me that I said the wrong thing.

"Elaborate," she demands in a quiet enough voice for only me to hear.

"Hm?" I ask careful of the fear of being ripped in half.

"I just mean, you know… If you want to do a class then have a good, or at least proper, reason for it. Me being in a class is not a proper reason."

Patricia looks taken aback but then says, "You are a good reason though, because it would be way more fun to have a friend in the class."

I chuckle as quietly as possible, "True. Just think about it a bit more though."

With that we both turn away, Patricia directing her attention back at Madame Veilleux and me back to the relaxation behind closed eyes.

When the bell rings, dismissing us for the rest of the day, Patricia and I take our time packing up. Well, I'm taking my time, Patricia is just standing there and waiting for me, because I wanted to make sure to give Matthew enough time to set up in the library. At least I choose to believe that there is something to set up.

Walking wasn't much different either. I'm taking all the time in the world for each step after the other. Patricia has rolled her eyes at me multiple times and about 20 different versions of "Can you hurry up already?" and "You're walking slower than my grandma, and SHE IS USING A CANE."

Even though people have been passing by me with no end, I do not rush. Part of it also is that I might have a heart attack if I walk any faster because I'm certain my pulse is already at 180.

My knees are shaking with every step I take, but Patricia is a pretty loud reminder to keep going and also not collapse on the floor. By the time we reach the library, we're almost alone in the halls, except for a few kids who forgot something in their locker or are going to some after-school meeting.

With an encouraging nod from Patricia, I step into the library where only a handful of students are sitting quietly at scattered desks to complete their homework. Eagerly I test my neck in every direction in an attempt to find Matthew waiting for me. Almost immediately I spot him in the very back corner, in the non-fiction section, aka the most boring section in here, but also the least open for view.

I smile and start walking over there, at least four times faster than on the way here. I'm sweating extensively but I hope it's not too noticeable. Either way, it doesn't help to make me any less nervous.

What could he have planned now? An invitation to a date night at his house? A hand-made painting of us? A poem he wrote? If he wrote me a poem I would simply just pass away. In a good way. In a great way.

317

Anything at all is already more than I could ever ask for.

I doge tables and shelves while keeping my eyes on the bit of Matthews's head I can still see, before turning around one last shelf.

And there he is. The most beautiful and most caring person ever standing with his arms behind his back and looking at me.

"You came," he says with a hint of surprise in his voice.

"You thought I wouldn't?"

Matthew hesitates a little before softly shaking his head.

"I have something for you."

"Me too," I say and take out his pencil case from my bag. "Sorry if you needed this during the day, I just wasn't sure if you would have wanted to talk to me before all of this."

Matthew smiles and zips it up in his bag.

While he does, I take the opportunity to start, "I want to apologize. It was far from fair that I just paused everything we had as if it was a TV show. I-," he cuts me off before I can continue.

"Not right now," he decides, with a smile on his face that could light up the whole city, "Now is happy times, not sad apologetic times. Which is why you should have this."

Surely enough he extends his hand from behind his back. In it is another origami figure made from a bright orange color, it's a frog. Seeing the little frog on his hands reminds me of how underappreciated frogs are. They're so cool if you think about it.

This one has a tongue and eyes drawn onto it with coloring pencils. It's really adorable. Hubert is adorable. That's right, its name is

Hubert from now on. I take it from his hand and admire it before looking back at Matthew.

With a hint of a giggle in my voice, I say, "Thank you, I love this. I really do."

All I want to do at this very moment is kiss him and hug him and thank him even more. Every inch of muscle in my body surges to just lean into his arms and stay there until the next day.

"Can I hug you?" Matthew asks silently. *Thank the universe!*

I don't even nod before almost literally throwing myself at him. He laughs in surprise and wraps his arms around me. The familiar heat embraces me and I let it sink in, really sink in. I take a deep breath filled with the also familiar scent of Matthew's deodorant. Never in a thousand years would I have expected to miss someone as much as I missed Matthew, especially if we're in the same classroom every single day.

I don't want to let go.

When he lets go I don't feel sad, I feel hopeful. Hopeful, to be able to do this again soon enough. This and much much more.

I'm the happiest I've been in weeks and it's all thanks to Matthew, Patricia, and Tess. In the moment, just looking at Matthew makes me want to burst into tears because of how everything turned out. Or… how it will turn out.

When I moved here I was convinced love wasn't in the cards for me. Not even friends, plural. But ever since that project, everything changed. For the better.

But for now, I pull myself together and laugh it off.

319

"What now?" I ask cheerfully.

Matthew points at Hubert still in my hand and says, "You should open it."

"Another riddle?" I ask pretending to be a little frustrated, but in truth, I love the riddles.

He nods and encourages me to open up Hubert, but, as ridiculous as it sounds, I don't want to hurt him or ruin him by accidentally ripping up one of his pages. I hand him back to Matthew and say, "You open Hubert for me, I'm afraid of breaking him. I want to have him in my life afterward."

Matthew laughs and asks, "Hubert?"

I grin and nod in confirmation.

Unlike my shaking and clumsy hands, Matthew goes slow and steady as he undoes every single fold before handing a normal piece of paper back to me.

It reads,

Friday at 5 pm, meet me at our spot. Where it all began and where it will end (in a good way).

My heart melts as I think back to the times Matthew and I talked for the first time. Even though it didn't end well for me, I still secretly enjoyed the few moments with him. Back then I probably wouldn't even have admitted that to myself so I'm still far from telling anyone else.

"Will you give me a chance to explain then?" I ask curiously.

He nods and says, "Yes, please. I want to know what happened, but I hope we can fix it together."

I close my eyes, relaxing every muscle in my body while listening to the people around us. We're almost the only ones in the whole library, especially this far back, but there are a few damped rustles from farther to the entrance. When I came in I only saw two kids and the librarian, who I still don't know the name of even though I totally should.

"Yeah," I whisper, "I'm sure we can."

With that I jump into one last quick hug before I turn around and exit the library, leaving Matthew behind.

Patricia is leaning against the wall opposite the library entrance. She's listening to music but graciously pops out one earphone as she sees me approaching.

"So? How did it go? Never mind, I can tell it went well based on that stupid grin. New question, what happened? I want details."

We start walking while I tell her everything. From the near-death experience of a heart attack experience to the conversation with Matthew to Hubert. I haven't dared to put him in any of my pockets for fear of accidentally breaking him, so he's been sitting in my hand all the way.

Carefully I open my fist and show him to Patricia.

"Hubert is such a cute name too!" she squeaks. Very appropriate reaction if I'm honest.

"Careful," I warn, "Don't crush him."

She turns to me now, a certain anger in her eyes. "Why on earth would I crush him?"

I know it's a question but it sure as hell sounds like she's demanding an answer. On this careful territory, I am wise enough to know to choose my next words very carefully.

"Accidents can happen to anyone," I shrug and hope my distraction works.

Patricia doesn't say anything but just turns and looks at Hubert, then she asks, "So he wants you to come back to your Spot?" She creates quotation marks in the air with her fingers.

"Yep, isn't that thoughtful?" I ask.

If I could see myself now from the perspective of me a year ago, I would hate myself even more. Dazed from the affection of another boy, dreaming about all the romantic and fun and beautiful moments we could have together. I would have told myself to stop hoping and to just let go before it gets any worse. Now I'm willing to take the risk. If that's not character development then I don't know what is.

Patricia slumps down on my bed like it's her own. That might have bothered me a year ago but now I realize that I would have been sad if none of my friends ever did it. I never expected it to be a possibility either since Tess and I always knew that if we saw each other again it would be when I'm in Germany, not the other way around. Never the other way around.

But now I have a local friend, a real friend, in person. I like this way better.

"Li, I have two things to say before anything else," Patricia says confidently, not moving a centimeter from the same position she threw herself in.

"Shoot," I try some slang I picked up over time now. It feels very weird.

"Okay so, starting with a suggestion."

An intrigued, "Hm?" is my only response as I continue to walk back and forth in front of my bookshelf, trying to find the perfect place for Hubert. At first, I thought about placing him next to some orange spines, to fit the color of the paper he's made off. But either the spine is too dark, or the story in the book is something I don't want to expose Hubert to yet.

"We should have some sort of movie night," Patricia's words rip me out of my mind and I turn around.

"Aha, and where would we do that?" I ask half seriously.

"Well…," Patricia drags the word a little too long before I realize what she means.

"I was hoping we could do it here..? It will only be like you, me, and Matthew if he wants to come. Like a triple sleepover."

"I don't know," I hesitate even though I know it's pointless when talking to Patricia.

"Pretty pretty pleeeaaase," she howls from the bed, "Your parents are way more likely to let us stay over. One because they're generally great, and two because they've already met all of us."

I sight, "Fine, I'll ask but I won't make any promises." I can see Patricia's grin from here even though she still hasn't moved one bit. A movie night would be fun, especially with two out of three of my favorite people ever.

323

Snuggling up with Matthew while laughing about the movie and maybe even falling asleep with him again, is the best scenario ever. But before that, he'll have to hear me out and not decide that I'm too crazy to date. Although I'm not too nervous about that, for now, I am worried that things might not go back to the way they were before the whole thing. Back in the good times of our relationship.

Again Patricia's voice rips me out of my thought, this time for the better though.

"And secondly, I have something to tell you that you can't tell anyone else. Mainly because I'm not even sure if what I think is right. But if it is, we need to do something, like seriously."

I place Hubert on a random corner, deciding to set him up later, to give Patricia my full attention.

"What is it?" I ask verily.

"It's about Matthew, more specifically, it's about his parents."

"Okay? Get to the point please," I say urgingly because I want to avoid all the different worst-case scenarios to find an entrance to my mind.

"Well, you know how at the beginning of the semester they were gone?"

"Yeah, Matthew said they're on a business trip."

"I don't think that's true, at least not entirely. When we were at his house for like the second or third time, I saw a business card on a counter and so I took a picture of it. Not that I didn't believe him then, I was just curious about what exactly his parents do to leave their child alone for multiple weeks. Anyhow, later that night I looked up the company and then the employee directory but I couldn't find any connections to Matthew's parents. Except, I did notice one thing. Neither of his parents seemed to have any online presence at all. No socials, no addresses in the books, and not a single result when searching them up. I didn't tell you until now because I thought it wasn't important and I was just overreacting. But when his parents came back, he didn't seem to be happy about it. He actually started avoiding everything, homework, both of us, practice, and especially going home. About two days after I heard his parents were back, I saw him go the wrong way after school and when I asked him about it the next day he said he needed to have 'a walk in nature'," Patricia explains, using her air quotes to emphasize her point. And I have to admit, that does sound kind of weird.

But Matthew would have told me if something was up, right? I hope so.

"So wait, if you're saying they weren't on a business trip, where do you think they were?" I try my best not to break apart and repeat the whole sentence after almost tripping over those few words. Such simple words yet I can't pronounce them properly.

"That's what I'm trying to figure out and that's why I need your help too."

Hm. That is weird but I'm sure there's a logical explanation, there always is. Because what's the alternative? Matthew's parents are some sort of criminals who left their child unsupervised and neglected for multiple months?

"Fine, but don't you dare force me into something that will ruin whatever it is Matthew and I have right now. As soon as that's compromised, I'm out."

Patricia nods, "I know I know, and I won't. But if something is going on we need to do something about it."

"That sounds a little dramatic but I guess that's fair enough." I swallow down the nausea building up in my throat.

I turn back to Hubert and pick him back up again. The next spot I think about putting him, is with the high fantasy books because he could be interpreted as some high fantasy creature frog, but as soon as I think the whole thing through that doesn't seem like the right place either. Hubert is special, he's unique, and he needs a place to stay that's just as unique as him.

"Anyhow," I say, still facing my shelf, "Let's talk about something happier. How are classes going so far? Did anything ridiculous happen that I need to know about again?"

"Not really, unfortunately. And I thought you said to speak of something happy, my classes are not that," Patricia groans.

"Noted," I say, "This is random but you know my friend Tess right? I mean, I told you about them existing and all, yes?"

I turn around and see Patricia nodding into a pillow, so I continue, "Well, I told them about everything as it was happening, like the whole Matthew situation, but they haven't responded at all. Do you think that's weird?"

I noticed it a while ago when they suddenly left me on read, out of nowhere, and only replied when I texted about something non-Matthew related. At first, I thought it was a coincidence and that their internet wasn't working properly or just their phone, but eventually, it started to be a pattern—a pattern I do not like.

Matter of fact, I think this is the first time I said it out loud.

CHAPTER 41

Matthew

I'm more than relieved when Liam leaves the library and I have his confirmation that he'll come to the final stage of this plan. Now it'll just be waiting and relaxing until Friday, no more worrying and no more planning. Most importantly, no more things that could go wrong.

I pack up my things in the library and wait a few more minutes before I leave to avoid an awkward moment if I were to run into Liam accidentally.

At home, things haven't changed much. All the planning I've been doing has given me an excuse to spend even more time in my room. Amazing.

When I open the front door my mom waves at me from the kitchen counter. I just stare back and take off my shoes. When I head upstairs I hear my mom shout, "Matthew, please talk to me. Let me explain."

That makes me stop. I take a moment to listen for any other footsteps or some sort of heavy breathing to indicate my dad's presence. When I don't hear anything at all, I turn around and head to the kitchen where mom is still standing at the same counter.

"Is dad home?" I ask her.

She shakes her head and goes, "Which is why I think now is the best time to finally tell you what happened. Your father doesn't want me to tell you."

"Oh," I sight, "So you dare go against him for once? Why should I believe anything you're going to tell me? For all I know this could just be another lie to try and make up for what you did."

I didn't realize I raised my voice that much but from the look on my mom's face, it sure did.

"You don't need to believe me, matter of fact you shouldn't. Otherwise, as your mother, I'd be very concerned for your future. I just want you to listen, before your father comes back."

I cross my arms, standing at the other end of the counter, and wait for her to start.

"We left because of the company your father works for. Or worked for, that's in the past now. They made him do some very gruesome things, most of which were probably not legal. As stupid as it might sound, your father had no choice but to do as they told him to."

"Why?" I demand.

"Because they threatened him. With us, they threatened to hurt you and me. Which is why he wanted to leave, and why he didn't want to

329

Thinking about it, this whole week has been great so far in every aspect. My parents haven't been in the worst moods at home, my grades are way better than when I started, and none of Josh's friends have given me any shit. Although that luckily hasn't happened in a while, maybe they grew bored of me. Thank the universe.

I've been walking through school smiling all day, most of it at least, because my mouth started to cramp. But mentally I have been shining and smiling and shitting freaking rainbows.

In seventh period today, it's obvious that I can't wait any longer. Two of my favorite people are in the same room, while all of us are aware of the anticipation hanging in the air. Patricia has been shooting me thousands of side glances since class started, while I can only look at one thing. Matthew again waved to us before class, and again nothing more. Not even turned to look at me once. Mature as I am, I don't let that bother me.

I focus my eyes away from him and back on Patricia. She has her light brown hair tucked behind her ear, a beautiful floral earring dangling from it. Patricia's doing what we're supposed to but is pretty much the only one in the room anyway. Madame Veilleux isn't in class today and the sub looks like she's just about done with her job. Fair.

I tap her on the shoulder and she looks up from her worksheet, already grinning.

"Are you done drooling over the boy who's literally your boyfriend?" she whispers just loud enough for me to hear. Which, to no one's surprise, was almost talking at normal volume because everyone else around us is going crazy anyway.

No. Never.

"Hmm, for now, yes," I say, "But let's not talk about him for once. Anything new that I should know about?"

Patricia turns to me and I can see the pupils in her light blue eyes widening just as I finish. There's something.

"What is it?" I ask excitedly.

"Well," Patricia starts, "There may be this guy. But it's nothing because I don't even know his name. We just see each other daily between third and fourth, I think he's new because he's only been going there for three weeks now. We always make eye contact though."

"But it's nothing *yet*," I squeak, "That's so exciting. Oh my god! You have to ask him out so that we can go on double dates and stuff. That'd be so fun!"

"I don't even know him," she counters.

"Tell me what you know about him." I take out my phone, open social media, switch, and wait for some information to use.

"Okay well, I know he's a junior because he came out of some classroom that I know for a fact only does junior English classes. I also know that he's on the debate team, and I know that his lunch is in fourth period. That's about it."

I smile, "That'll be enough anyway. Give me one moment."

Scrolling through the very limited list of the people I follow, I quickly find the page of our school's debate team and scroll through two posts before finding a team picture. I hold up the phone and ask, "Which one is he?"

333

Patricia takes the photo and points at a guy standing in the back. Curly brown hair with a downward smile. Not as bad as I thought it would be.

I take the phone back and go to followers of the debate team's page. It doesn't take me long to find another account with a guy in the profile picture with that same downward smile. The account name reads *alex.her56*.

"Okay, so, his name is Alex. According to this, he moved here from Colorado, wherever that is, earlier this month. He has a dog named Jefferson, a sister who he calls Milly, and he has a lot of superhero figures in his room."

Patricia's gaping at me, "You found out all of that in less than five minutes. That's kind of creepy, to be honest, but helpful. Show me."

I don't hesitate to take a screenshot of the page and send it to Patricia. While she's busy going through her crush's profile, I sneakily take her worksheet and start copying answers. Not that I don't know how to do the stuff on my own, I'm just lazy.

The rest of class is more like what I thought would happen, time slowed indefinitely like there is no end to class or the rest of the day. After eventual dismissal from school, I get home and sit on my bed for hours.

Two full hours and twenty-three minutes to be exact. For the first hour, I sat upright and stared at a point on the wall in front of me. My mind kept telling me to get up and move but my body didn't want to give in. Even though my mind kept telling me to move, and with the thousands of other sounds up there, it felt quieter than usual. As if that point on the wall had some damping powers. For the rest of the time I lay on my side, always staring at that same spot. I feel defeated that I didn't do anything because I always have things to get done. Yet my stupid body didn't want to move at all. The whole time it had felt like all of my muscles were a thousand times heavier than they're supposed to be.

Whatever it is, it happens sometimes. Certainly not often but when it does, it's always in the worst possible moment. It's weird. I hate it.

The only motivation I had to force myself through that barrier of heaviness was the thought about Matthew's message. I see Hubert sitting on my shelf, silently judging me, and that does the trick. I stand up and forcibly take a step, then another, towards the bathroom.

I need to be at school in half an hour so there is no pressure at all.

Thank god it's the weekend because with the lack of energy in me right now, as I do my best to make myself look presentable, I know that I won't survive another day in school.

I don't know what is wrong with me, I should be happy and excited that I'll get to see Matthew again and that I'll get a chance to finally explain myself, but instead, I'm feeling *Bleh.*

It'll get better though in the next few minutes, when my mind is fully awake again. It has to. There's just no way I will let myself ruin this. No way in hell.

I change my black hoodie to a light blue one, comb through my hair, brush my teeth, and do everything I possibly can. By the end of it

335

all, I have fifteen minutes to get to school, but luckily managed to look less like someone who just crawled out of bed and more like someone who spent all afternoon planning what to wear, and then decided to go with the simplest version of it all for a sense of casualty. Good that I didn't actually have to worry too much about that.

My dad's downstairs sitting at his computer when I ask, "Can you drive me to school?"

"No," he deadpans.

"Please, I have to meet someone there," I try with my very last effort.

He pauses and looks at me, "I'm not your chauffeur."

Great. I'm about to go wallow in bed, crying because I won't be able to see Matthew after all, when he sights, "Fine, but you'll have to walk home."

"Mhm," I reply.

During the whole drive we're silent, because not daring to say anything at all is safer than saying the wrong thing and ending the conversation in an argument again. He drops me off at the front entrance and drives off without another word.

I check my phone and it's already 17:01. I send Matthew a text, the first one in weeks, saying that I just got here and will be there in five minutes. Five minutes might not even be enough time to walk around the whole school, plus almost the whole football field. With that in mind, I try to walk even faster than I normally do without awkwardly running.

It would be very embarrassing if I were walking to the wrong location right now. He could have meant a thousand different spots, so maybe I wouldn't be there in five minutes, but not at all.

Pretty sure my energy is back because now my heart is pounding like never before and with every step I feel closer to just breaking down and crying, right here on a random sidewalk.

It might be five pm but there are still a hell lot of cars here and the occasional person. I suspected some teachers would be staying late and maybe about 20 students for some team practice or club, but this is way more than I thought. Nobody questions me as I go through the parking lot in the direction of the football field, mercifully nobody playing on it.

Trees cover me the rest of the way which gives me enough security to jog a little to be faster, but when I see lights shining through the bushes in front of me, I start sprinting. Around the bushes is the most beautiful thing I've ever seen.

A red-white picnic blanket is spread across the grass with a wooden basket holding it in place. The scene looks like it has been cut out straight from a movie and pasted into the real world. There are candles on each corner, fake ones but they're still really cute. And above it all sits Matthew.

When he sees me gaping at the scene, he stands up smiling and motions for my hand. I put mine in his, my heart missing a beat again, and he guides me onto the blanket next to him.

337

My jaw is practically on the floor, my heart doesn't know how to act, and my brain wants me to collapse within the next minute and wake up again to make sure this isn't a dream. But when I look into Matthew's shimmering brown eyes, I know it's real. His hair and smile harmonize perfectly to make him look like a Greek god coming down from the upper world.

His hand on mine is steady and warm, letting a calm wave rush over me. I'm smiling so hard I might pass out from using too much energy at once. Everything is perfect. The location is in nature, quiet, and cut off from the outside world. The setup is everything I could have ever asked for and so much more, literally the most romantic thing anyone could ever do. The perfect boy, who puts so much effort into planning and setting up a whole scavenger hunt and picnic just for me, is sitting right next to me and looks at me like I'm the most beautiful thing he's ever seen. He makes me feel worthy, amazing, and most of all loved.

"Hey," he says, his voice so steady that it has a calming effect on my nerves.

"Hi," is all I can manage while trying not to burst into laughter and/or tears.

"How are you?"

I laugh again, surely sounding like some 14-year-old straight girl discovering fanfiction for the first time, "I'm shocked, in a good way. This is the most amazing thing anyone has ever done for me," I say with a happy tear rolling down my cheek.

His smile grows as he replies, "I'm glad you like it. Here," he opens the basket and pulls out a bowl filled with strawberries, "Have some."

He got us strawberries?! Nope, I'm sure, this is a dream. Just cannot be real.

I take one from the bowl and jokingly say, "Very cheesy of you."

"The cheesiest," he says with confidence.

I giggle after biting into the best strawberry of my life.

When I'm done eating and giggling at once, he's still watching me with a warm smile. I just want to wrap my arms around him and never stand up from this very spot ever again.

"So," I start, my smile fading from my lips, "I owe you an apology."

He nods, waiting for me to continue.

"Well, I guess I was afraid, like a lot, because you're Mr. Goldenboy and I'm nowhere near that so I came up with all these scenarios in which you were just messing with me for fun. Which is why I paused us, I wanted to see if you're serious about this."

Matthew's smile is gone completely and he inhales sharply before he says, "*Mr. Goldenboy*? Really? And why the hell would you think something like that about me? Did I do something that made you not trust me anymore?"

I swallow. This is going to be so much harder than I thought.

"That's the worst part. There was nothing besides you being perfect. And you don't understand how sorry I am for freaking out like

339

that, I know I should have trusted you more. I'm really, really, really sorry."

Matthew sighs while I look on the ground, not wanting to see the anger and pain that would be on his face at this exact moment.

"It might have not been entirely fair to either of us, but hey," his hand brushes my chin and lifts it up so that I'm looking directly into his eyes, "At least now we know we need to talk more."

I don't know what did the trick, his hand on my chin, his eyes, his smile, or a combination of all, but tears start streaming down my face. Once it starts I'm unable to stop it. But I can feel that these are good tears, not tears of pain but tears because I'm in the happiest moment of my life. My heart is beating so fast that I fear it might jump out of my chest at any moment.

Before I can even comprehend what's going on, Matthew has his hand on my back and pulls me into him. His radiating warmth has the weirdest effect, it's comforting and it makes me want to stop crying, but at the same time it makes me want to cry even more because it feels safe.

"Thank you," I heave against his shoulder. In response, he starts rubbing circles on my back and that's how I know everything will be okay. At least with us.

CHAPTER 43

Matthew

Things couldn't have turned out better than they did. My plan worked and I think Liam really likes it. I'm not sure how much time we spent lying on the ground, Liam crying on my shoulder, and arm, and chest, and neck. As much as I do not want to see Liam cry, ever, this was a good cry, the kind where he's happy and relieved. And so am I, very much.

"So, you think I'm perfect?" I ask tauntingly when his tears have dried.

He laughs and says, "You're never going to let me hear the end of that, are you?"

I shake my head and smile down at him. His deep, foresty green eyes are already looking up at me.

"Well yeah," he confesses, "You're really smart, really attractive, captain of the freaking varsity football team, and managed to pull all of this off just to be with me. I can't believe you would see that differently."

"I'm not perfect. Speaking off, I actually think I will quit football. Or at least the team, not the sport."

I haven't said it out loud before this moment, but from what it looks like Liam overcame so much stuff because of me, so it's my turn to face my fears.

He sits up and looks down at me, his face neutral.

"What do you mean? Why?"

I rest my head on the ground, close my eyes, and say, "It's hard to explain, but uhm," I breathe in and out, "I never really wanted to play football. I know I'm good at it and all, but I never really wanted to play professionally. Most of the time I just did it because it would be the only thing getting me into a good school and because of how people around me acted. Besides, there's less than a month left of school, and I missed so many games and so much practice that I doubt Coach will let me back in just like that. Plus," I sit up again, almost forgetting what I wanted to say because of how the sunlight shines through his dark brown hair, "Next year will be our last year of highschool and I don't want to waste it by spending all my time on the field with people I can barely stand."

Liam smiles at me, dimples showing on both sides of his cheeks.

"I'm happy for you. If that's really what you want, go for it."

It means the world to me that Liam is supporting me in this, without a single sign of judgment in him.

"Speaking of things I want," I say and pull Liam in. This time not because of tears, but because of love. With closed eyes, my lips meet his and it sends a spark through my whole body. Our lips move as if they have been starving for ages, at least mine have.

I break the kiss to breathe, my hand still on the back of his neck, and before I can think better of it, I whisper, "I love you."

Liam pulls away, his eyes huge and his smile even wider than before. Didn't think that was possible but here we are. He seems happy to hear that, or at least not repelled. Seeing him this happy inflates something in my chest and I just want to hug him, and kiss him, and hug him again.

"I love you too," he laughs and I wish I could hear that exact sound every night right before I fall asleep.

He loves me. Holy shit. He loves me.

"So does that mean we can unpause our relationship now?" I ask him.

His eyes have a sparkle in them, making me want to jump right into the green of it and never emerge again. He replies, "I'll have to ask my boyfriend first but I think that would be okay."

I grin and say, "More than okay."

He nods and takes out the strawberries again from the basket. We each take one, clinking them to each other in celebration.

"This is so fucking great," I say truthfully, "And the best part hasn't even arrived yet."

Liam with a half eaten strawberry in hand gapes at me, "There's more? Boy, you're crazy."

I can't help myself but giggle and say, "Crazy for you."

Liam covers his open mouth with one hand when he says, "Damn. I could get used to this."

343

Confidently I say, "Good."

There's still a lot of daylight shining through the trees, but I have no idea what time it is. The last part of my plan is supposed to meet us at the front of the school at 6:30. I take my phone out of the basket and check the time. My heart stops when it reads 6:39.

"As much as I don't want this to end, we're late so help me clean up quickly," I say as the only warning before I jump up and start collecting the fake candles and the bowls and store them in the basket. With Liam's help it doesn't even take us a full minute to fold up the blanket and store it away.

His hand in one hand and the basket in the other, I drag him right across the field, not bothering to go around it, and towards the front of the school.

"Can I ask what we're late for?"

"Nope," I say and grin back at him. This final stage of my plan was the hardest to plan, to coordinate, to pull off. But luckily I got help everywhere I asked, even Liam's parents. Having to meet with them while sneaking around Liam was almost as hard as convincing them to let me go through with this. But all of the struggle will pay off very soon. Especially for Liam.

My hand is sweaty around his, but I don't let go.

We rush to the school entrance, through the almost empty parking lot, and I can already see it as we're approaching. Erick's and Iressa's car is waiting in one of the visitor's parking spot.

"What are my parents doing here?"

I don't answer but pull him farther and farther. As we approach the back door of the car opens and someone steps out. The final part of my plan steps out of the car. Meaning it worked. The hard work is about to pay off.

Liam behind me sees them too and stops dead in his tracks.

"You did not," he says.

"I so did," I confirm, "You're welcome." I smile at him and wave at the one person that Liam might love just as much as me.

CHAPTER 44

Liam

I'm going to cry again. Or pass out. Or both. I don't believe who is walking towards us right now. But when I'm sure I'm not hallucinating and that this is real, I let go of Matthew's hand and start running. Running so fast I practically throw us both on the ground when I go directly into a hug.

Tess is here. I'm hugging them. They're here. Their arms around me have a familiar feeling which I welcome with every passing second.

"Oh my god," I say in German, "What are you doing here?"

Tess pulls away and says, "Someone told me you needed to be cheered up a little, so here I am." They grin and flip their long pink hair over their shoulder.

"He got you to come here?" I ask fully in doubt.

They nod. He's already behind me when I turn around, which makes it way easier to again practically throw myself at him to kiss him.

"How?" I ask switching back to English.

"It's a long story," he says, "But it worked."

"Thank you," I reply with all the sincerity in my whole heart. I do want to hear that story later though.

I'm pretty sure tears are currently soaking the rest of my face, but I don't care. Matthew really did this. He got my favorite person to fly across continents just to make me feel better. They are here, in person, in reality, and not in a dream. Tess is standing right in front of me and I'm not dreaming. I can't believe it, probably won't for a while.

Matthew really is the best fucking person on this planet and now I'm even more sure then before, I love him. And he loves me. We love each other. AND TESS IS HERE!!

We're going to have so much fun as a squad. Tess can meet Patricia and we can all go somewhere fun to do something even funnier or just to hang out.

I turn back to Tess and hug them again, ruining her jacket as well as Matthew's sweater with my tears.

"I can't breathe," they squeak, their accent a lot thicker than mine. I laugh and let go.

"So what now?" I look around to search for either one of them to tell me, because it's starting to get dark outside and I don't think any of us want to be on school grounds when it does, simply because that would be depressing.

"Now, we're going home. Get in!", my mom yells from the car.

347

All three of us hurry to the car, but before I get in I run to hug my mom. Maman was in on it too. She must have been, but how did I not notice anything?

"Merci maman," I say.

"De rien Cherie," is all she says before getting back in the car.

CHAPTER 45

Matthew

All the way to his house Liam has been sleeping with his head on my shoulder. I've never been happier.

No more stress about football, because the conversation with him really helped me decide to quit the team. Coach will hear from me on Monday, in person because I want to pay him the respect I have even if he won't be my coach much longer.

No more wondering what happened with my parents as I choose to believe what my mom is telling me, whether that's true is another story which I will not worry about anymore. I don't want to think about that anymore but as much as I try, it doesn't leave my mind. I thought about trying to make up with them, somehow create a friendly relationship, but I'm sure now that I can never forgive what they did, even if they had a good reason.

No more being lonely because I have the most amazing boyfriend, two amazing adults who care about me just like actual parents would, and two real friends that I can always talk to.

By the time we reach his house, I'm still smiling like a child who was just permitted to open his presents a few days before Christmas. Liam's parents are more than okay with me staying for a few nights, which I fully plan to take advantage of. On the other hand, my parents don't know where I am, maybe that's a little payback. One of many to come.

However, there will be a lot more fun with people I actually enjoy being around. There will be a lot more cuddling and romantic dates and many more firsts with him, and I could not put into words how excited I am. There will be a lot more self care too, only doing something that I really want to for example.

Never have I ever been happier.

CHAPTER 46

Liam

We get home about 20 minutes later because of bad traffic, but I didn't really mind because I was as good as asleep. We help Tess settle into the guest room, with the three of us the whole process was done within minutes. Tess tells us they're super tired from traveling, which is very understandable and we leave them in the guestroom to sleep.

Matthew and I go into my room and just when I was about to thank him again with a kiss, he wanders off to my shelf. Right where Hubert is placed in his own little corner, overseeing the rest of the room.

"I love that you put him on here," he says in awe.

"His name is Hubert and he will forever have a home on my shelf," I confirm.

Matthew laughs, "Why Hubert?"

"It just felt like the perfect name," I shrug.

He takes off his sweater and jeans, puts them neatly folded in a spot on my floor between the bed and the wall, and he collapses into my bed.

He is so perfect. And he looks so gorgeous. I want to lay right next to him and let him hold me until both of us are asleep.

I don't do that though, not just yet. Sitting down at my desk I open my laptop with the English essay in mind. I finally have an idea what I can write about for my semester project.

What is the best thing that happened in your life and how did it affect you?

Even with the most beautiful boy in the world being in my bed, I open a blank document and start typing. Matthew is the greatest distraction of this assignment, but also the greatest inspiration to keep going. All night if I must.

Epilogue

The best "thing" in my life isn't a thing at all. It's a person, well, multiple people.

My best friend Tess has been with me every day since primary school, even if she wasn't physically there. Phone calls, texts, and face times were a substitute for the physical friendship we could barely have. Only on special occasions would I get to see them, sometimes Christmas or sometimes on my grandma's birthday, but never just because we wanted to see each other. Even without that privilege, our friendship stayed true and that's something irreplaceable.

My newly made best friend Patricia only came into my life a few months ago, but has already improved it so much. I'm never one to immediately fit in everywhere I go, not even after a while of being in the same spot or around the same group of people. Fitting in and finding friends is way harder and more complex than movies make it appear to be. Usually by the time you come in, there's already a lot of friendships built that you can't just disrupt by adding yourself. Besides, being the stereotypical "new kid" who is an introvert is not as aesthetic as some people make it be. Everyone's constantly judging you, maybe even wondering where you came from and making up false scenarios to spread around class. That's not easy to ignore, the stares, some full of questions,

353

others full of pure dislike. All of that makes it particularly hard to make any friends at all, but Patricia was the exception. She came into my life with the same introverted energy, and nothing of the judgemental side. I'm so thankful for that, I can't describe it with words.

My parents haven't always seen eye to eye with me, but they sure loved me every step of the way, even if I didn't see it sometimes. Every decision they made they always had the best for me in mind. Not always was it the best for me in the moment, but the thought counts.

My boyfriend has been the best person to ever exist on the face of earth ever since the day I met him, though that was under weird circumstances. One time he invited me into his home to work on a project for school, but then invited me back for more hangouts. That alone made my heart jump around and do all kinds of tricks and flips. Another time he made me breakfast while I was sleeping on his couch, which warmed my heart more than he could have even imagined. To highlight everything, when I was unsure about his intentions he created a whole scavenger hunt with a romantic picnic at the end of it to prove he was telling the truth. But not only that, he flew my best friend Tess into the country for a few days as a surprise for me. That was the best gift anyone has ever given me, and probably will ever give me, and I don't know what I did to deserve all of that. My boyfriend has proven many times over and over again that he is the definition of the perfect boyfriend. Sure, everyone has flaws, but his suit him very well. He recently learned to sort out what his priorities really were, what he wanted to do with his time and not what other people told him to. I'm so proud of him, of us.

All of these people improved my life in so many ways, they define me. They made me who I am and what I aspire to be. So I don't think the question should be about the best thing that happened, because that limits it too much to an event or similar, but should generally be a broader question, because sometimes events don't have as much impact on you as the people in them.

THE END

Jonas Noelting

Acknowledgements

I'm so grateful for every single person in my life who contributed to this project. It has been in the making for a while now, so seeing it finally come to a final product is really really really exciting. All these people contributed to making this come true.

Never will I forget the feeling of starting this book. Never will I forget the feeling of finishing that first chapter, or hitting the first ten thousand word count. I will never forget the feeling of typing that very last sentence. I'll never forget that feeling of getting all that overwhelming amount of positive feedback from all my beta readers and close friends. I'm so grateful to all of the people that made all of that happen.

The first two people who I would like to thank have always been on my side, no matter what. My parents supported the book idea since I randomly came into their bedroom one night at almost 10pm and declared, "I'm writing a book!" Even if they doubted it would ever come to a finishing point, which they did because at some points so did I, they did not show it.

I want to thank the people who gave me inspiration for characters, but noone shall be named for legal reasons (I'm kidding… maybe).

I want to thank my wonderful Beta Readers who have scooped out a lot of mistakes in this progress. So, a special thanks to Josh

Morales, Matthew Cohen, Marie Wang, and Mac Preston. Your feedback was more motivating than you can ever imagine!

Now some independent thank yous to people who really deserve one, mainly because it's my book so I can mention whoever I like hehe.

Valerie Robert for all the random late night writing sessions and book yapping, I will never forget those. Emma Kunesh for the constantly passionate conversation between us, you helped me with so much decisions for this project just as much as with life itself. The exclusive members of the BreakfastBench: Toni Jafojo, Molly Zhang, and Vidhi Golchha for pushing me in the right direction when I needed it most.

I want to thank all the people who, along the way, gave me advice that completely changed, or at least altered, the course of this story.

I will never forget a single one of you.

Author Biography

Jonas Noelting is an 18 year old high school senior, soon to be studying Modern Languages in the UK, at the University of Nottingham. He was 15 when he started writing The International Love Story but the three year journey was one of the most passionate projects he has ever done.Even throughout his future studies he wants to keep writing as a big part of his life.

When he isn't reading, doing homework, or playing animal crossing, he can be found watching TV shows with his dog, Ebu, and his cat, Kisa. He loves hanging out with his friends during his free time, or just being on FaceTime with them when they're overseas.

Lastly, a fun fact about him is that, if he was to be reborn as any animal, he would want to be penguin.

www.ingramcontent.com/pod-product-compliance
Lightning Source LLC
Chambersburg PA
CBHW061502120726
48001CB00004B/1177